DEMELZA
& the
SPECTRE DETECTORS
Holly Rivers

A MESSAGE FROM CHICKEN HOUSE

Demelza and Holly Rivers are a perfect team – sometimes I forget which is the brilliant author and which the crazily inventive, sparky and brave heroine! If you're after spooks, inventions, surprises and a stonking sense of humour then you're in the right place – Demelza and Holly have all of those in bags. There are also plenty of twists and turns . . . I promise, it's dead surprising!

BARRY CUNNINGHAM
Publisher
Chicken House

DEMELZA

& the
SPECTRE DETECTORS

Holly Rivers

Chicken
House

2 Palmer Street, Frome, Somerset BA11 1DS
www.chickenhousebooks.com

Text © Holly Rivers 2020
Cover illustration © Alex T. Smith 2020

First published in Great Britain in 2020
Chicken House
2 Palmer Street
Frome, Somerset BA11 1DS
United Kingdom
www.chickenhousebooks.com

Cover and interior design by Helen Crawford-White
Cover illustration by Alex T. Smith
Typeset by Dorchester Typesetting Group Ltd
Printed and bound in Great Britain by CPI Group (UK) Ltd, Croydon CR0 4YY

The paper used in this Chicken House book is made from
wood grown in sustainable forests.

1 3 5 7 9 10 8 6 4 2

British Library Cataloguing in Publication data available.

PB ISBN 978-1-912626-03-8
eISBN 978-1-912626-82-3

For Grandma, Mamgu
and magnificent grandmothers everywhere.

CHAPTER 1

Screwdrivers and Soldering Irons

'Lights out, Demelza!' called Grandma Maeve from the bottom of the attic stairs. 'And no sneakin' out of bed to work on your inventions again tonight, d'ya hear me?'

Under her patchwork quilt, with soldering iron in hand and fully dressed in her lab coat, Demelza grinned. 'Yes, Grandma!' she called back. 'I promise!'

'And that means no stayin' up late reading them big science books of yours either, you understand?'

'*Yes*, Grandma! See you in the morning!'

Demelza switched off her bedside lamp, and through the darkness listened to the creak of the landing floorboards below as Grandma Maeve hobbled back to her own bedroom. There was the rustle of curtains being drawn followed by the thud of slippers being kicked off, and

1

before long the purring of the old woman's snores was echoing through Bladderwrack Cottage.

Demelza pushed back her quilt and reached for the torch she kept hidden beneath her mattress. *I'm sorry, Grandma*, she thought to herself, clicking it on. *But nothing's going to stand between me and my inventions. Especially something as unnecessary as sleep!*

Wasting no time, Demelza hopped out of bed and replaced her normal glasses with a pair of Inspection-Spex, from which a series of magnifying lenses hung down over her eyes like jam jars. Her thinking cap came next. Having once read that all inventors owned one, Demelza never sat down to invent without her bottle-green deerstalker, which she felt gave her the look of a true professional. (She'd quite fancied growing a moustache similar to that of her hero, Professor Humbert Heinsteene, to complete the look, but being an eleven-year-old schoolgirl, it had so far proved trickier than she'd hoped.)

Night-time was Demelza's favourite time to invent, when everyone else was asleep and she could let her imagination run free under the cover of silent darkness. As she tiptoed across the attic, her torch cast a dim yellow light over the walls. The shelves were lined with antique microscopes, spindles of copper wire and tools of all shapes and sizes. Bottles of chemicals were alphabetically arranged from aluminium to zinc, and jars of nuts and bolts glimmered brightly like colonies of metallic beetles. Under the window a telescope pointed towards the stars, in anticipation of any exciting astronomical activity.

'Right,' said Demelza, sitting down at her desk and flicking on her little lamp. 'First things first.' She opened up one of her desk drawers and pulled out a lunchbox of cheddar and peanut butter sandwiches – cut into perfect isosceles triangles, of course. The ideal brain food for the long night ahead!

From the shelf above she pulled down a notebook which was labelled *Demelza Clock: Inventor*. She flicked through the pages of notes before stopping at a sheet of calculations scrawled in jet-black ink. At their centre was a technical drawing of a large robotic hand, its jointed fingers outstretched like a bunch of metal bananas. Beneath it was written:

Are you fed up of writing lines in detention? Sick and tired of wasting time doing homework? If yes, then you need Dr Demelza Clock's

REMARKABLE ROBOTIC HAND
FOR HOMEWORK HATERS.

This revolutionary device can be programmed to write out any assignment set by your teacher, and ensures perfectly forged handwriting, every time.

Its remote-controlled technology also means that you needn't lift a finger to retrieve your pencil case, refill your ink or sharpen your pencils. Simply use the control pad on the device's wrist to eject the hand and navigate it through the air.

Demelza grinned as she reread her words, her left knee jerking up and down the way it always did when a good plan was coming together. She'd come up with the idea for the invention after her headmistress, Ms Cardinal, had given her detention for smuggling her pet mouse Archimedes into class the previous week. 'Rodents have no place in a school,' Ms Cardinal had hissed, holding the trembling creature by his tail. 'They belong in a cage, or better still, decapitated in a trap! You will write out 1,000 lines of "Stricton Academy is a school, not a zoo" by the end of the day!'

For the next hour Demelza worked solidly, sparks flying as she sawed through tubes of copper piping and welded together metal sheets. She'd been interested in inventing for as long as she could remember. Her first contraption had been the Magnificent Belly Button Cleaning Machine she'd made from an electric whisk when she was just four years old. The wonderful feeling she got from seeing a design coming to life was only equalled by that of solving a tricky scientific equation.

It was gone midnight by the time Demelza put down her tools. The robotic hand was almost complete – a miscellany of clock cogs, engine parts and kitchen utensils, all held together with blobs of solder and bits of sticky tape. Under the moonlight it glimmered like a strange alien creature, and a bolt of excitement coursed through Demelza's body. It felt as if each and every one of her freckles were tingling.

'Right, I just need to tighten the kinetic valve,' she said, coiling a strand of auburn hair around her finger in thought, 'then recharge the battery pack. After that, I think I'll nearly be ready to—'

'DEMELZA CLOCK! WHAT'S GOING ON UP THERE?'

A sudden shout from downstairs jolted Demelza from her thoughts and she jumped back from her desk, sending her wrench torpedoing through the air. 'Nose-diving neutrons!' she gasped. 'Grandma Maeve's woken up!'

The staircase began to creak and there was an approaching *tap-tap* of footsteps on wood. Panicked, Demelza frantically tried to waft away the smell of molten solder before flinging an old dust sheet over her desk. Grandma Maeve wasn't strict, but she was a stickler for bedtimes, and a sleep-deprived Grandma was not the kind of Grandma that would make you boiled egg and soldiers for breakfast.

Without a moment to lose, Demelza leapt back into bed, pulled her patchwork quilt over her shoulders and began to let out some loud and zealous pretend snores.

The attic door flung open.

'Demelza Clock, I know you ain't sleepin'!' Grandma Maeve's voice was cracked and brittle, but its volume was on par with that of a foghorn. 'Those fake snores don't fool me!'

Demelza slowly opened her eyes. Grandma Maeve was standing in the doorway, her wrinkled face illuminated by a lantern. A shock of grey hair hung to her waist, and even though her skin was thin and papery, her eyes were as bright as cogs.

'Oh, Grandma, it's *you*,' stuttered Demelza, rubbing her eyes with the theatrics of a well-rehearsed actress. 'I-I thought I was dreaming.'

'Nice try, young lady!' snapped Grandma Maeve,

hobbling over to the bed. 'But since when did you sleep wearing this, *hmm*?' She whipped away Demelza's thinking cap, which was still perched atop her head, and waved it in the air. 'You've been inventing again when you should've been sleeping, haven't you?'

'N-no,' Demelza gulped, desperately trying to come up with a convincing excuse. 'I was busy doing some . . . erm . . . homework, Grandma.'

'Ha! *You?* Doing homework? I'll believe that when I see it! How many letters have I had from Ms Cardinal this term, hmmm? How many detentions has she given you for daydreamin' in class?'

Demelza groaned as she pictured the cantankerous old headmistress. 'Urghh, but the things we learn at school are so boring, Grandma! Why can't Ms Cardinal teach us something useful? Like how to build a spaceship . . . or breed our own fungus?'

There was a second of tense silence before Grandma Maeve's frown curved upwards into a forgiving smirk. 'You cheeky little grub,' she said, pinching her granddaughter's cheek. A shiny crimson scar ran along the length of her hand. 'It's lucky that I love you so much, ain't it? I don't know how many other grandmas would put up with living under the same roof as such a mad professor.'

'*Inventor*, Grandma,' said Demelza with a tut. 'I'm an inventor!'

Grandma Maeve sighed. 'I'm serious though, Demelza, it ain't good for you to spend so much time up here alone inventing. Why don't you invite a friend from school over one day? Spend some time out in the garden?'

'Because I don't have any friends from school, Grandma,' replied Demelza curtly. 'No one in my class can hold a decent conversation on electromagnetic induction or atomic energy. The most advanced debate they've ever had was about which coloured crayon tastes the nicest!'

'Well, why don't you ask that nice lad who lives at the bottom of the hill over for dinner one night this week, eh? I thought you'd become quite chummy with him. What's his name again?'

'Percy?'

'Yeah, that's the one. He ain't lived here all that long and he could probably do with bein' brought out of his shell, especially with his ma not bein' around and all. I could make your favourite chicken pie?'

'I've already told you, Grandma, he's not allowed to go to other people's houses. It's to do with all the allergies he has. He's not even allowed to go to school and he has to take special medicine instead of food.'

'Shame,' said Grandma Maeve. 'He could do with a bit of fattenin' up. He's far too pale and skinny, poor thing.'

'The way his dad mollycoddles him, you'd think that he had the bubonic plague!'

'Well, I'm sure his pa knows best.' Grandma Maeve tucked Demelza in and stroked her head. 'Right, off to the Land of Nod with you, young lady. You want a story to help you drift off? How about the one where I wrestle the three-legged sloth in Patagonia?' She clawed her wrinkled hands as if grappling with an imaginary creature in front of her.

'Grandma, come on.' Demelza scowled. 'How many times do I have to tell you? I'm too old for silly stories.'

'All right, all right, just asking . . .' Grandma Maeve bent down and gave her granddaughter a whiskery kiss on the forehead. She smelt of lavender, cough drops and something musky that Demelza could never quite place. 'Goodnight, my darlin'. Love you more than teapots.'

'Love you more than circuit boards,' answered Demelza, snuggling down. She looked to the framed photo of Humbert Heinsteene on her bedside table and sighed. 'Sorry, Professor, but scientific progress will just have to wait until tomorrow.'

CHAPTER 2

Noises in the Night

Psst, psst, psst ... Psst, psst, psst ...

Demelza awoke suddenly, lurching up in bed. She didn't know what, but something had pulled her from sleep, a strange whispering noise coming from somewhere in the attic.

She fumbled for her glasses and, with sleepy eyes, gazed around the dark room. Under the moonlight she could make out the glint of her telescope's lens and the flash of Archimedes's wheel spinning round as he took a midnight jog, but there was nothing out of the ordinary.

How strange, she thought, lying back down. *Must just have been those owls up in the roof. Either that or the wind coming through the windows. I did tell Grandma that double glazing would be far more efficient than parcel tape.*

Demelza closed her eyes tight and pulled her quilt over

her head, burrowing down like a red-haired mole.

But, soon enough, the strange susurration came again.

Psst, psst, psst . . . Psst, psst, psst . . .

Demelza's eyes sprung open and she jumped up once more. She was certain that she'd heard something this time. The whispering was coming from all directions now – the floor, the walls, the lintel – as if the cottage was speaking to her in some mysterious ancient tongue.

Pulling her covers around her shoulders, she got out of bed and flitted to the window. She ducked under the heavy curtains and, as she peered into the night, her brain began to whirl into overdrive. Maybe the noise signalled that a portal to another dimension was being opened? Maybe it was the beginning phases of a multiple vortex tornado? Or, even better, perhaps it was the call of a family of genetically modified vampire bats?

Demelza gazed into the distance, hoping for evidence of some strange scientific happening, but outside there was nothing to be seen apart from the moon hanging over the village like a shiny new coin, and the autumn trees swaying gently in the breeze.

Note to self, Demelza thought as she hopped back into bed and plumped up her pillows. *No more vintage cheddar after 8 p.m. It does strange things to your brain!*

11

It was only when she was awoken for the third time that Demelza realized perhaps her cheese-based supper wasn't to blame. A new set of sounds was now echoing through the attic, louder than the last.

Whoosh... Whoosh... Whooooooooosh.

Whoosh... Whoosh... Whooooooooosh.

Demelza began to sweat. It felt as if an invisible flock of birds was flapping around inside her room, as if their wings were beating back and forth against her skull. She peeked over her covers and all around her the air felt thick and heavy. Someone or *something* was in the room with her. She couldn't see it, but she could definitely feel it. An energy, a force.

She gulped and called through the blackness, 'Wh-who's there? Grandma Maeve, is that you?'

Nobody answered.

'G-Grandma?' she tried again. Her voice was wavering now, panic plucking at her vocal chords. 'Come on, stop fooling around!'

Still no reply.

With her heart beating like a locomotive, Demelza pulled herself on to her knees, each one of her senses as sharp as a knife edge. She fumbled for the torch under the mattress once more, and with a sudden jolt brandished it in front of her like a cutlass.

Click!

A beam of pale yellow light flashed across the room and Demelza moved the torch erratically from side to side, trying to illuminate every shadowy corner.

Nothing.

Whatever was there was either very small or very good at hiding.

'I know you're in here!' she cried out, pulling herself on to her haunches. Slowly, she peered over the edge of her bed, and with every molecule of courage she could muster, let the torch light up the shadowy space beneath. 'Show yourself! Come out or I'll . . . I'll–'

Demelza's words were robbed from her lips.

Her body had started to shake. First her toes, then her knees and then her hands, until every inch of her being was trembling ferociously as if she were at the receiving end of an electric shock. Trying to control it she flopped back on to her bed, but her limbs continued to twitch and fizz as if they had a life of their own.

'Leaping light years!' she screamed, the torch dropping from her fingers. 'Grandma! Help me! Something's happening! Help!'

But Demelza's cries were of no use. All around her the

whooshing sound continued to rise, getting nearer and nearer, stronger and stronger. She put her hands over her ears, trying to block out the hideous tirade. She was petrified – more scared than when she'd accidentally been locked in the garden shed while looking for samples of mould, more frightened than when she'd set the sitting room curtains on fire with her Bunsen burner! What was happening?

She felt herself fading, and with the last ounce of her energy, all that Demelza could do was draw her knees towards her and close her eyes tight. *Please don't let me die*, she whispered. *Please don't let me die, please don't let me die . . .*

Chapter 3
The Fortune-Telling Toaster

Demelza awoke to the din of her alarm clock. For a second she couldn't make out where she was. Her mind felt fuzzy, as if she'd been hibernating for centuries, and her pyjamas clung to her skin, damp with cold sweat. She pulled on her spectacles, blinking the attic room into focus.

Why did she feel so strange? Had something happened last night? She couldn't remember falling asleep and now every muscle of her body was groaning with a dull ache. Had she fallen down the stairs while sleep-inventing again? Or was she coming down with German measles? (To be honest, she wouldn't really mind having a spotty bottom for a few days if it meant having some time off school.)

It was only when she let her head flop back down on to her pillow and gazed up at the dark wooden beams above that something suddenly clicked in Demelza's brain.

Psst, psst, psst . . . Psst, psst, psst . . .

As if in double time, everything from the previous night suddenly came rushing back, memories exploding across Demelza's mind's eye like fireworks. The unexplainable whispering, the unearthly sounds, her trembling body . . .

Demelza sat bolt upright.

Grandma Maeve! Was she OK? Whatever she'd heard last night might have got into her grandmother's room too! She had to check that she was all right.

Within the blink of an eye Demelza had leapt out of bed, and without even stopping to give Archimedes his morning tummy tickle, she pulled on her dressing gown and flew through her bedroom door.

'Grandma! Grandma, where are you?' she shouted, lowering herself down the higgledy-piggledy stairs from the attic. She flew across the landing, ducking under the collection of overhanging cuckoo clocks and avoiding the cabinets of china nick-nacks and the taxidermy animal heads that protruded from the walls. As she leapt down the main staircase, the old wooden floorboards groaning beneath her feet, the sound of the grandfather clock chiming eight greeted her at the bottom.

She bounded into the kitchen.

'Oh, Demelza, it's you,' said Grandma Maeve. 'I thought it were a fairy elephant comin' down them stairs!' She was huddled over the rusty gas stove, copper saucepans of various sizes bubbling away over the flames. The shelves above were lined with jars of potted meat, tins of soup and containers of herbs, spices, grains and pulses. Shiver, their long-haired dachshund, was nuzzling at her feet.

'Grandma, are you OK?' Demelza panted, letting her hands rest on her knees. 'It didn't get you, did it? You're not hurt or anything?'

'Hurt?' replied Grandma Maeve, drizzling some amber-coloured honey into the largest pot before giving it a stir. 'Why on earth would I be hurt?' She shuffled her feet as if tap-dancing, her slippers scuffling against the limestone flags. 'See! Fit as a fiddle, me!'

Demelza's brow furrowed. 'But . . . but last night . . . didn't it wake you up?'

'What *are* you talkin' about, Demelza?' replied Grandma Maeve. 'Didn't *what* wake me up?'

Demelza's voice rose. 'The thing that was making the horrible noises! The whispering, the whooshing, the wailing? You must have heard—'

Grandma Maeve dropped the ladle she was holding on to the counter and a deafening clatter echoed around the kitchen. Shiver jumped from his spot and dashed to the safety of the pantry.

'N-n-noises?' stuttered Grandma Maeve, quickly averting her gaze to the floor. Her tiny frame had suddenly stiffened. 'No, I didn't hear no noises. Probably just the wind outside, my darlin'. Them old windows rattlin'. You know how ancient this cottage is, don't you?'

Demelza tutted. 'I know all that, Grandma. But these noises were different. They . . . they . . . weren't normal.' She sat down at the oak breakfast table and poured herself a cup of tea from the chipped china teapot. Beams of autumn sunlight fell upon the cotton tablecloth, wild flowers blooming from a jug at its centre in shades of red and ochre and green.

'Well, it's probably just your imagination,' said Grandma Maeve, fiddling with the hem of her cardigan. 'Too much stimulation from all them big books. I told you inventin' ain't good before bed.'

Demelza frowned. There was something strange about Grandma Maeve's tone of voice, something nervy, curt. 'Well, let's just check the news at least,' Demelza suggested, reaching towards the radio on the dresser. 'Maybe something happened in the village? Or what if there's been some kind of apocalyptic worldwide disaster? We could be the only survivors!'

Demelza switched on the radio, but as she turned the dial from station to station there was no mention of anything out of the ordinary – one news reporter talked of the birth of a baby panda at Little Penhallow zoo, while another gave the results of the local tiddlywinks team's home win.

Grandma Maeve brought the saucepan over from the stove and slopped some porridge into her granddaughter's bowl. 'As I said, just your imagination. Now, eat up and I'll see you after school. I'm goin' down to me greenhouse. There's an egg boilin' in the pot for you, give it three minutes if you want a runny yolk.'

Demelza looked over to her grandmother's empty bowl. 'But Grandma, you haven't had anything to eat yet. And you always say that breakfast is the most important meal of the–'

'Not hungry!' interrupted Grandma Maeve, pulling on her wellington boots at the back door. 'And besides, I've got marrows to harvest, plants to water, the hens to feed. And those pumpkins you got me to plant for Halloween won't pick themselves . . .'

Demelza noticed that Grandma's cheeks had flushed pink, but before she could say anything, the back door slammed shut and the old woman was hurrying down the garden path.

'*Fine,*' Demelza grumbled to herself, slumping over her bowl of porridge. 'If Grandma Maeve doesn't believe me, then I'll just have to *prove* that something's going on.'

Demelza pondered for a moment, ideas shooting through her brain like stars across a galaxy. She let globule after globule of porridge fall from her spoon, slopping back into the bowl with a satisfying splat. Shiver padded over and began to nudge her feet with his nose, letting out a small whine which either meant *walkies* or *food* or both.

'Frolicking filaments! I've got it!' Demelza exclaimed suddenly, pushing back her chair with a screech and jolting to her feet. 'My Fantastical Fortune-Telling Toaster! That should give me some answers! Why didn't I think of it before?'

She bounded over to the unorthodox-looking toaster that was perched atop the refrigerator in the corner and plugged it in. Coils of wire spiralled out of it from every angle and it was covered in buttons, knobs and switches. Demelza had recently constructed it after having trouble deciding what to do with her time one rainy Sunday morning. Now, when a question was asked of it, an answer would be given through the colour of the bread that popped out. If the slice was golden brown then the answer to the question was YES, but a piece of burnt toast meant that the answer was NO. Its results hadn't exactly been accurate every time (recently it had declared that, YES, Grandma Maeve was indeed a flesh-eating zombie giraffe from outer space), but Demelza thought that it was reliable enough.

She put a thick slice of wholemeal into one of the slots and pulled down the lever. 'Was there an intruder in this cottage last night?' she asked it.

She waited patiently as a series of timers and dials began to whirl, beep and flash before her eyes. There was a loud *ding*, a high-pitched *ping*, then—

POP!

The slice of toast shot out of the machine like a rocket and Demelza plucked it out of the air. It was a lovely shade of pale brown. 'Yes!' said Demelza. 'As I thought.'

She loaded in another slice of bread. 'Should I invent something to help me investigate further?' she asked next.

POP!

Once again, the toast appeared golden.

'Well, that settles it!' she exclaimed, reaching down to Shiver, who was now sniffing around for dropped crumbs. 'As soon as I'm home from school today, I'm going to invent a booby trap. Whatever came into my room last night is going to be caught.'

CHAPTER 4
The Greys

With her unbrushed auburn hair trailing behind her, Demelza cycled down the winding hill from Bladderwrack Cottage towards school, the reds and golds of autumn leaves crunching under the wheels of her bicycle. It had once belonged to Grandpa Bill – Grandma Maeve's late husband – but with a lick of red paint and a shiny new bell, Demelza had made it as good as new. As always, she was wearing her thinking cap, and her satchel was stuffed with a selection of her most useful inventions – she liked to be prepared for any eventuality and after all, who knew when a Self-Playing Harmonica, an X-Ray Periscope or a Glow-Worm Powered Headlamp might come in handy?

As she rode, Demelza took in the scenery of Little Penhallow and smiled. Everywhere she looked, pumpkins adorned front porches and windows, their triangular eyes and crooked smiles waiting to be lit up on Halloween night. It was just under two weeks away. *What costume should I wear this year?* she wondered. Last years' decision to dress up as Ms Cardinal hadn't gone down very well at school, and had resulted in a whole week in detention. Maybe a Transylvanian vampire would be a safer option this time? Or a warty-nosed witch?

But first, Demelza had the mystery of the night-time noises to concentrate on, and as the newly tiled roof of Percy's house came into view she had an idea. Maybe he could help her come up with the design for her booby trap. She'd previously read all about the different types in a volume of her encyclopaedia – there was the Leg-Hold Trap, the Cage, the Glue Trap, and her personal favourite, the Pit. But which one should she construct to capture an as-yet-unidentified intruder?

Arriving at Percy's house, Demelza leant her bicycle against the large front gate. Even though it was only a stone's throw away from Bladderwrack Cottage, it couldn't have been more different. Because of his allergies, Percy very rarely stepped outside, so it was just as well that the house consisted of ten bedrooms, six bathrooms, two lounges, a games parlour and a conservatory. Demelza didn't understand it. Yes, Percy might be sickly, but surely keeping him locked up like a prisoner couldn't be good for his health either. Maybe Mr Grey was just being paranoid? After all, it can't have been easy for him, bringing up Percy on his own.

Demelza crept across the immaculately pruned front lawn, where a couple of burly gardeners were busy clearing leaves and trimming hedges under the watchful eye of Tiger, the Greys' ginger cat. Demelza nodded to the gardeners as she passed, and thought that maybe they could come and help Grandma Maeve with her weeding before the winter frost set in. Even though her grandmother liked to insist that she still had 'the energy of a whippersnapper', Demelza knew that she'd secretly appreciate a helping hand.

At the front door, Demelza pressed the bell and the chimes of 'Greensleeves' echoed through the house.

'Who is it?' came Mr Grey's booming voice from within. 'If you're selling something, I've already told you that we have more than enough tea towels, thank you very much!'

'It's Demelza, Mr Grey. Demelza Clock.'

The door flung open to reveal a short, portly man, whose little grey moustache nestled under his nose like the gills of a mushroom. 'Ah, Demelza!' he said, flashing a welcoming grin. 'I'm so sorry about that. How nice to see you! Everything all right?'

Demelza nodded. 'I was wondering if I could come and say hello to Percy before school? I won't keep him long, I promise.'

Mr Grey smiled. 'Well, of course you can. It does do Percival good to mix with other children on occasion. And I know he enjoys your company. But you remember the rules, yes? NO opening curtains more than three centimetres; NO sharing food; and most importantly, NO skin to skin contact. Percival is a very poorly boy with—'

'With a very weak constitution,' interrupted Demelza. '*Yes*, Mr Grey, I know.'

'Of course you do.' Mr Grey coughed and reached into his pocket. He brought out a glass medicine bottle and shook a tiny white tablet into Demelza's hand. 'Why don't you take Percival's power pills up to him, eh? As much as he'd like a bacon sandwich for his breakfast, his poor tummy just won't abide it. His allergies, you see.'

Demelza took the tablet and frowned. A tablet for breakfast? How awful! If she couldn't have a nice fresh egg or a bowl of porridge of a morning, she probably wouldn't bother getting out of bed.

Mr Grey stepped back and let Demelza inside. 'Now,

you know where Percival's bedroom is, yes? But don't be too long. His private tutor, Fräulein von Winkle, will be arriving in twenty minutes.' He turned into the house and shouted upstairs. 'Percival, you have a visitor!'

'So, let me get this straight,' said Percy. 'You think that there might have been some kind of flesh-eating monster in your room last night?' He was tucked up in bed wearing more layers than an Arctic explorer, his pale white face peeking out from under a hooded dressing gown. A well-thumbed copy of *The Nautical Adventures of Captain Thalasso: Volume 3* was open on his bedside table – perhaps the closest that Percy was ever going to get to adventure.

'I don't *think*,' replied Demelza, who'd wasted no time in filling him in on the strange midnight noises, recalling every detail with over-dramatic vigour. 'I *know* there was!'

'Oh, come off it, Demelza,' said Percy, rolling his eyes as he pushed a lock of his bright white hair from his face. 'I know you've got a really vivid imagination, but that's just ridiculous.' He thought for a second. 'And besides, if there really *was* a flesh-eating monster in your room last night, then why didn't it gobble you up alive, eh?'

'Because . . . because . . .' Demelza stopped short, struggling to find an answer. '*Ufff!* Well, maybe the monster

26

idea was a *bit* far-fetched. But there's something strange going on and I'm determined to get to the bottom of it.'

'Using one of your weird inventions, no doubt?' replied Percy with a chuckle.

'Of course!' said Demelza, her knee beginning to jerk. 'When I get home from school this afternoon I'm going to make a booby trap to seize the culprit! When Grandma's gone to bed I'm going to wait up and see what it catches.'

Percy slumped back into his pillows and sighed heavily. 'It must be nice to have a hobby like inventing. I get so bored up here on my own doing next to nothing. There's only so many comics a person can read in a day.'

'Well, that's what I came here to ask you about,' said Demelza, leaning in. 'Why don't you come over to mine later, and we can work on the trap together? Do you think you can convince your dad?'

Percy let out a dismissive laugh. 'You are joking, aren't you? My dad panics when I go to the toilet on my own. He'd have a heart attack if he found me out of bed in the middle of the night, hunting for trespassers.'

'Oh, come on, Percy, it'll be fun! You're always wishing that your life was more exciting, that you were more like Captain Thalasso.'

'Demelza, I'm not even allowed in my own garden!

Dad's hired some men to do the front lawn, and I'm forbidden to go anywhere near them, let alone give them a hand. Apparently rakes and trowels are a "hotbed for germs".' He gazed down at the hero on the front of his comic book and sighed sadly. 'Look, there's nothing I'd like more than to run around after dark and solve mysteries but it's not going to happen.'

Demelza crossed her arms gloomily. 'I still don't understand why your dad's so overprotective. Are you really that ill? You seem all right to me.'

'I feel absolutely fine most of the time,' replied Percy. 'But you know what dads are like – such worriers!'

Demelza felt a lump the size of a toffee forming in her throat. She didn't really know what dads were like at all. All that she could remember of her own was the smell of his wax jacket, the warmth of his cuddles, his head of curly black hair. She could barely remember her mum either — they'd both died in a car accident just before her fourth birthday. Bladderwrack Cottage had been her home ever since, and Grandma Maeve her guardian.

Feeling the sting of tears in her eyes, Demelza hoisted her satchel over her shoulder and quickly made for the door. 'Well, I'd better get going, then. I'll pop by again tomorrow and let you know how I get on with the booby trap, if you want?'

'Yes, please!' Percy replied with a smile. 'Now, quick, escape from here while you still can. Fräulein von Winkle is scarier than any nocturnal flesh-eating monster, and you don't want to get on the wrong side of her.'

CHAPTER 5
Stricton Academy

Having successfully escaped Percy's house, Demelza set off through the village, and soon enough arrived at the looming grey building that was Stricton Academy. It was a gargantuan Victorian structure, with spiky turrets jutting upwards from its roof and sinister-looking gargoyles keeping watch over the concrete playground below. There were no plants or flowers, the only greenery being the weeds that poked up through the cracks in the ground. The school motto, 'Your Best Will Never Be Good Enough', crested the front gates in curling iron letters, and served as a constant reminder of the school's strict regime.

Demelza's stomach lurched with dread as she made her way through the gates. What ridiculous act of 'disobedience' would get her banished to the detention room today?

Wearing socks in the wrong shade of grey? Blinking too loudly? At least she wasn't a boarder – imagine having to go to bed here every night! She'd prefer to sleep in one of the pigsties down at Happy Trotter Farm.

As the morning bell rang, she pushed through the throng of brown-uniformed pupils and made her way along the school's labyrinthine corridors. Cabinets of sports trophies and framed certificates lined the walls, and portraits of the staff of yesteryear kept watch, as if they were still on duty.

Demelza was just approaching her classroom when some familiar voices echoed down the corridor from behind.

'Well, look who it is – Stricton Academy's resident weirdo!'

'How are you today, De-*smell*-za?'

Demelza spun around to find a pair of identical twin girls sauntering towards her from the boarders' wing, like some grotesque two-headed monster. Both were clutching files covered in golden merit stars, one neatly labelled *Penelope Ottoline Smythe*, and the other, *Persephone Cordelia Smythe*. They were so similar that if it wasn't for a small mole on Penelope's cheek, you might have thought that you were seeing double. Behind them stood Miranda Choudhury – their personal bodyguard and the brawn to

31

their brains – whose muscular frame was more akin to that of an Olympic wrestler than a schoolgirl. As usual, she loitered silently, fists clenched.

Oh, for fossil's sake, groaned Demelza to herself. *An early morning run-in with the smug-bottomed Smythes. Just what I need . . .*

'Got any of your marvellous inventions to show class today, Demelza?' continued Persephone, sauntering closer. 'You know how much we all enjoyed the last presentation you did on your Pigeon-Powered Lawnmower. NOT!'

She let out a spiteful giggle before Penelope chimed in, pulling her shoulders back and projecting her voice for all to hear. 'And I see that you haven't polished your shoes again. That's the second time this week, isn't it? I wonder what Ms Cardinal will have to say about that, hmm?'

Demelza dropped her satchel and squared up to the girl. 'Well, I'm sure *you* won't hesitate to tell her. I know how much you enjoy being a nasty little snitch!'

Miranda's dark eyes widened, and Demelza was sure that she could see a hint of a smile forming on her lips.

'I think you'll find the correct term is *corridor monitor*, Demelza,' said Penelope. 'Maybe if you weren't such an oddball, then you might be entrusted with an important title too. I don't think that *class freak* really counts.'

Penelope sniggered and Demelza felt her fists curl inside her pockets. 'You'll pay for that!' she hissed, and was just about to pounce when Ms Cardinal appeared from inside the classroom.

'Hands out, ready for inspection!' she snapped, clicking her bony fingers in the air. 'Chop chop, we haven't got all day. Wasted time is a wasted opportunity to learn!'

Every child in the corridor immediately jerked to attention, silence falling as Ms Cardinal began the rigorous process of scanning each and every set of palms.

Demelza watched the headmistress at work with dread. She'd only taken on the headship the previous year, but had quickly stepped into the authoritarian shoes of her predecessors, and was sterner than any army sergeant. She was extremely tall and extremely thin, the high collar of her grey dress buttoned tightly around her neck. Apart from a few purple veins on her cheeks, her skin was pallid, like the flesh of an uncooked oyster, her nose as pointy as a crow's beak. But perhaps the most striking thing about her was the dark eye patch that hung over her right eye. Rumour had it that she'd lost it while working as a prison guard at a high-security penitentiary, but the only pupil brave enough to have ever asked about it had never set foot in Stricton Academy again.

'Very good, Penelope, very good, Persephone,' said Ms Cardinal, as she looked down at the twins' dainty, manicured hands. 'Cut and scrubbed fingernails, that's what I like to see in an institute of learning. Exemplary.'

'Thank you, Ms Cardinal,' chorused the twins, reverting to the sickly, saccharine tones which they reserved exclusively for teachers. 'Our mummy says that cleanliness is next to godliness.'

Demelza barely suppressed a retch. How did the pair always manage to worm their way into Ms Cardinal's good books, when they were two of the most hideous organisms on Planet Earth? Maybe one day when she was a famous scientist, she'd be able to put them under her microscope and see what kind of repulsive mutant molecules made up their DNA.

'And how about *your* hands, Miss Clock?' taunted Ms Cardinal, coming to stand over Demelza and glaring down with her one good eye. 'Any engine oil under your fingernails today? Any soldering iron-induced burns?'

A wave of stifled laughter rippled down the corridor and Demelza sighed. She knew that her hands would never meet her teacher's exacting standards, especially after last night's inventing session. She reluctantly held them out and Ms Cardinal let out a snort of disgust.

'Disgraceful! If I've told you once I've told you a million times, inventing is not a suitable pastime for a young lady!' She spat out the word *inventing* with revulsion, as if it were an activity on par with eating scabs.

'But Ms Cardinal!' Demelza protested, her blood beginning to boil like liquid in a test tube. 'Lots and lots of things have been invented by *young ladies*. Dr Giuliana Argenta, for one, obtained more than one hundred and twenty-five patents for her creations and—'

'Do NOT answer back, girl! Your wretched grandmother might put up with such unorthodox practices, but I certainly will not!'

Grandma Maeve, wretched? Demelza felt a wave of anger building up inside her, as fiery and explosive as nitroglycerine. She couldn't hold it down. 'Don't you speak about my grandma like that!' she shouted. 'She's not wretched! She's wonderful! You've never even met her!'

'Of course I've met—' Ms Cardinal quickly stopped herself. 'I mean . . . of course she must be wretched, having raised such a beastly child.' She coughed loudly and shifted her gaze. 'As punishment for being so impudent, Miss Clock, you shall spend the morning helping Mrs Armstrong remove chewing gum from inside the gymnasium lockers. Do you understand?'

Demelza's body was poker-stiff with rage, but she bit her tongue – it was pointless trying to argue with someone whose ideas were stuck somewhere in the 1800s. And besides, there was *one* benefit to her punishment: at least now she could spend the morning dreaming up designs for her booby trap. The plans for Operation: Night Noise could officially get underway.

CHAPTER 6

The Incredible
Intruder Incarcerator

At four o'clock the school bell rang and Demelza was out of the classroom in a flash. As she burst through the front gates of the school she felt her shoulders soften – it had been such a long day and she couldn't wait to get up to her attic room and make a start on her trap. She'd decided on a simple cage design, with a trigger causing the door to lock shut once the intruder was inside. A bowl of baked beans would be left as bait – after all, who or what wouldn't be lured in by such a delicious delicacy?

But first, it was time for some sweets!

Demelza hopped on her bike and raced down the high street to the small shop at the very end, where the words *Emmanuel Barnabas: Confectioner* arched over the door in faded golden letters. The window was all ready for

Halloween – decorated with delicate sugar cobwebs which veiled a display of jelly eyeballs, liquorice rats and some white chocolate skulls that looked frighteningly real. As Demelza pushed the door open, the tinkling of a bell sounded somewhere in the back room, and a brown-skinned man with a mop of thick hair toddled out to the shop floor. He wore a bow tie which was the same shade of red as the polka dots on his pocket square.

'Demelza, my favourite sproglet! How nice to see you,' he said, walking over to the huge selection of jars behind the counter. The buttons of his checked waistcoat were shiny and gold, as were a couple of his teeth. 'And what takes your fancy today? Lemon drops? Chocolate buttons? Or –' he picked up a chocolate bar wrapped in shiny orange paper from the counter in front of him – 'one of the new Toffee-Apple Tongue Tinglers I have in for Halloween?'

Demelza gazed up at the shelves and licked her lips. Grandma Maeve had been bringing her to the shop since she was a little girl, but the novelty of ogling at the selection of sugary treats still hadn't worn off. There were jars of coconut macaroons, pots of gumdrops and boxes of delicate sugar mice which glistened in shades of pale pink and yellow. A freshly cut Battenberg and an iced lemon drizzle cake sat on doilies under glass cloches.

'I'll take a bag of the jelly beans and two sherbet fountains,' Demelza decided eventually. 'And maybe one of your walnut whips for my Grandma Maeve.'

Mr Barnabas smiled. 'And how is that lovely grandma of yours? Keeping well, I take it?' He reached for the jar of jelly beans and untwisted the lid. As he poured, the shiny multicoloured sweeties fell into his weighing scales with a satisfying clatter.

'She's fine, thank you,' Demelza replied. 'She's harvesting her crop of pumpkins today. I can bring you some for your Halloween window display if you'd like?'

'Well, that'd be wonderful! Just what I need to go alongside the chocolate bats that Mrs Barnabas is making.' He reached for the sherbet fountains and the walnut whip and passed them to Demelza with a wink. 'There you go. On the house. My little treat.'

'Thanks, Mr Barnabas,' Demelza replied, turning towards the door. 'I'll drop in tomorrow morning with those pumpkins.'

'Splendid! And please, do send my regards to your grandmother.'

The bell jingled again as Demelza left the shop, and with a mouthful of jelly beans she hopped back on her bicycle and made for home.

Bladderwrack Cottage was a run-down, ramshackle old place whose red bricks were half-masked by sweeping ivy. A wonky weathervane sprouted from the roof which, even in the strongest of gales, permanently pointed east. Along the garden path, crocuses exploded in marbled blues and purples, anchored by tangles of papery leaves.

As Demelza fumbled for the front door keys in her satchel she recalled the morning she'd first arrived at the cottage after Mum and Dad had died. She hadn't yet turned four years old, and was 'not much taller than a toadstool', according to Grandma Maeve. The cottage had been warm and welcoming, the smell of toasted teacakes and coffee thick in the air as she'd been scooped into Grandma's open arms. Upstairs, the little attic bed had been made up with the same patchwork quilt that she still snuggled under now and it wasn't long before she'd acquired her first micro-scope. As much as Demelza loved the life she had with Grandma Maeve, she couldn't help wondering what her world might have been like if things had been different, if her parents hadn't gone out on that perilous, icy night . . .

Shaking herself from her trance, Demelza unlocked the front door and let herself in. Shiver came bounding into the hallway, his stumpy little legs skidding across the tiles.

'Hello, Grandma!' Demelza called, throwing her satchel on the hallway floor and hooking her blazer on to the coat stand. 'Grandma, it's me! Where are you?'

The wooden walking stick that Grandma Maeve used when she left the cottage was leaning against the sideboard, so Demelza knew that she was in. Inside the small front room, Demelza found her asleep in her armchair, a half-drunk cup of tea on the table in front of her. All around, shelves were lined with cookery books, trinkets and mismatched pieces of china. The last few embers of a fire glowed jewel-like in the grate.

'Excellent,' Demelza muttered to herself, steepling her fingers as she watched her grandmother snooze. 'The perfect time to undertake my *booby trap apparatus heist*!' She'd decided to keep her plan a secret from Grandma Maeve for the time being – she didn't want to be caught inventing instead of doing homework again, and besides, what a brilliant surprise it would be if she could prove that there *was* something strange going on in the cottage.

As stealthy as a stoat, Demelza snuck into the kitchen. She knew from experience it would be full of useful things for her contraption. She went through drawer after drawer, cupboard after cupboard, pulling out anything that she thought might be useful. Nothing filled her with more wonder than picturing a new project coming together, and her heart raced as she found more and more things that could potentially be cut, glued or soldered.

After much deliberation she finally decided on a handful of clothes pegs, a dessert fork, a small weighing scale, some fridge magnets, a can opener and three sheets of grease-proof paper. The half-empty bucket of paraffin Grandma used for lighting lamps during power cuts was also added to the loot, as well as the plunger from under the sink. Shiver watched closely and Demelza took a chunk of ham from the fridge and threw it into his slobbering, pink mouth. 'There you go, boy, a little treat,' she whispered, giving him a scratch behind his ears. 'Now keep quiet and don't wake up Grandma Maeve.'

Up in the attic, and with her thinking cap on, Demelza worked tirelessly for most of the evening. As the booby trap came together she began to feel more and more convinced that she was going to be able to solve the mystery of the night-time noises. She hadn't been so excited since finding a copy of *Rocket Propulsion for Beginners* by Serge A. Head in the local library the previous week.

'*Voila!*' she said eventually, brushing her gluey hands together before stepping back from her desk. Fitted with a complex series of pulleys, levers and wire barbs, the trap resembled a medieval torture device that had somehow been transported into a futuristic galaxy. 'I shall call it the Incredible Intruder Incarcerator. Now all I have to do is wait until dark . . .'

She threw a dust sheet over her work and, having tossed a handful of lettuce leaves into Archimedes's cage, followed the delicious smell of dinner wafting up from downstairs.

Later that evening, and having gulped down second and third portions of pork chops and potatoes, Demelza went into the sitting room to say goodnight to Grandma Maeve. Inside, the curtains had been drawn and the old woman was reclining in her armchair once more, a glass of ginger wine in one hand and a bag of chocolate brazil nuts in the other. A roaring log fire filled the air with a sweet-smelling smoke.

Normally, Demelza would have cosied down under a blanket and hoped that Grandma Maeve would make her a mug of hot chocolate, but tonight she kept her distance. Grandma could smell mischief from a mile off, and Demelza knew that she definitely reeked of it.

'Right, Grandma, I'm going up,' she said with one of her well-practised pretend yawns. 'I'm feeling ever so tired. I think I'm going to get an early night.'

'All right, m'dear,' said the old woman, swigging the last

dregs of her wine before kissing her granddaughter on the forehead. 'But straight to sleep. None of that late night inventin' again, you promise me?'

Demelza felt a slight pang of guilt somewhere in the pit of her stomach knowing that she had no real intention of nodding off, but she couldn't change her mind now – she had a scientific operation to undertake! 'Yes, Grandma,' she said, crossing her fingers behind her back. 'I promise.'

'Oh, and Demelza,' called Grandma Maeve as her granddaughter made for the door, 'can we have a little chat tomorrow mornin'? Nothin' to worry about, just need to talk to you about somethin', that's all.'

Demelza frowned. 'Erm . . . OK . . . Is everything all right, Grandma?'

Grandma Maeve cleared her throat. 'Yes, yes, everything's fine. You just toddle off to bed, and we'll speak tomorrow. Love you more than teapots!'

'Love you more than circuit boards!'

For the next hour Demelza waited patiently in the attic for Grandma Maeve to retire to her room too. To stop herself from falling asleep, she'd decided to work on her mental arithmetic and had just reached number 67,231 in the Fibonacci sequence when she heard the landing light clicking off and the sound of her grandmother's door closing.

Demelza leapt out of bed and pulled on her thinking cap and lab coat. She crept over to her trap and was just about to give it a final test run when a sound came from the window. It was a strange *tap-tapping*, as if something was being pelted at the glass.

Demelza gasped. *Abseiling atoms! Has the intruder arrived already?*

Thinking fast, she grabbed a wrench from her desk and raised it above her head, ready to attack. She whipped open the curtains and—

What on earth?

There, looking up at her from the front garden, with a stone in one hand and a torch in the other, was Percy. He was wrapped up in his pyjamas and dressing gown, a pair of fluffy pink bunny slippers on his feet.

He gave Demelza a little wave and she felt a huge grin spread across her face and a rush of excitement shoot through her body. Percy'd changed his mind! She had a partner in crime after all!

Demelza flitted downstairs and, having triple checked that Grandma Maeve was nowhere to be seen, unlatched the front door. It was freezing outside and under his torchlight Percy's pale skin was almost aglow, like that of a ghostly apparition.

'I thought you weren't coming,' whispered Demelza sarcastically, trying to hide the joy she actually felt at seeing her friend.

'Well, you didn't think I'd really let you do this all on your own, did you?' said Percy. 'You might need me to protect you if anything bad happens.'

Demelza let out a dismissive snort. 'In *those* slippers? Oh yes, I forgot how scary ickle pink bunny wabbits are.'

Percy's face crumpled and Demelza gave him a playful smile. 'Only joking, silly. And sorry if I was a bit mean earlier. You know what I'm like when I get an idea into my head.' She ushered him through the front door and closed it as quietly as possible. 'How did you sneak out, anyway?'

'I waited until Dad was watching one of his boring news programmes then slipped out of the back door. I stuffed some cushions under my duvet to look like my body in case he comes to check up on me.'

'Brilliant!' whispered Demelza. 'Captain Thalasso would be proud! Now come on, I want to show you my booby trap!'

As the pair tiptoed up the cottage's rickety old staircase and the wooden floorboards creaked beneath their feet, their torchlight swept across the walls, giving eerie glimpses of Grandma's antiques and strange collections.

'It's a bit creepy,' whispered Percy, looking over his shoulder as they approached the top of the stairs. 'And it's ever so dark.'

'Of course it's dark!' replied Demelza curtly. 'It's the middle of the night – you know, the bit of the day when the big ball of light disappears from the sky? What did you expect?'

Percy looked to the floor. 'I don't really know. Dad doesn't usually let me stay up past seven p.m.'

Demelza rolled her eyes and was just about to come back with a witty retort when all of a sudden she froze.

'Wh-what's wrong?' asked Percy, peering over her shoulder. 'Why have we stopped?'

Demelza didn't answer.

She shuffled to the window overlooking the back garden and, without saying a word, pointed to Grandma Maeve's greenhouse. A figure was moving around inside, its form silhouetted under the moonlight.

'Th-there's someone there!' whimpered Percy, the ears on his bunny slippers trembling as his knees knocked together. 'Someone's inside!'

Demelza strained through the darkness, trying to make out who it was, but it was no use. All she could see was a dense black shadow.

'What should we do?' asked Percy.

Demelza turned to him. 'I'm going down there. I need to see who it is.'

'Are you sure?'

Demelza nodded. 'Are you coming?'

Percy sighed heavily. 'Well, I guess I've already broken pretty much every other rule in my dad's book . . .' He puffed out his tiny chest. 'Let's go.'

Demelza smiled and the pair headed straight out into the garden. Across the moonlit lawn they went, Demelza moving from tree to tree like a spy, with Percy following behind, trying his best to avoid muddying his cotton pyjamas. The night sky was inky blue and somewhere in the distance an owl hooted sharply.

'Right,' whispered Demelza as they snuck up to the greenhouse. Its panes of emerald glass were spangled with frost, and it was impossible to see much of what was inside. 'Keep your voice down and move slowly. We don't want to scare whatever it is away.'

She pushed the door with her fingertips and it opened with a long, drawn-out creak. Inside, the air was damp and close. She flashed her torch from side to side, throwing pale yellow light across the rows of plants, flowers and vegetables. Demelza had been in the greenhouse a thousand times before, but tonight somehow something felt different, almost as if she were a stranger navigating the shadowy space for the first time. As her imagination went into overdrive, the spiralling fronds of Grandma's exotic blooms became the tentacles of strange and terrifying monsters, the overhanging foliage, the web of a poisonous spider. In her mind, she saw the tomatoes beginning to sprout limbs and teeth like little red beasts waiting to attack.

'Hello?' Demelza muttered, inching forward slowly. A strange knot started to coil in her tummy, the kind of fluttering sensation you might get when walking through a dark forest. 'Is anyone there?'

Silence.

'Come out! I know you're in here!'

Still nothing.

'W-well, it doesn't look like anyone's here,' said Percy with a nervous laugh. 'Maybe we jumped to conclusions? Maybe what we saw was just a shadow or—'

Demelza put up a hand, demanding silence.

Her torchlight had illuminated a corner at the very back of the greenhouse, and there, in the spot where Grandma's cabbage patch usually stood, was a trapdoor.

CHAPTER 7
Through the Trapdoor

Demelza dropped to her knees and shone her torch on the trapdoor. 'Sizzling circuit boards!' she gasped. It was carved from a thick piece of dark wood and engraved with a labyrinthine pattern of symbols painted in shimmering gold. There were triangles, stars, hands, moons, arrows, and in the centre was a ruby-eyed skull with a circular handle clenched between its teeth.

'No! No way!' Percy quavered, quickly dashing behind a nearby row of beanpoles. 'I know I said I wanted my life to be more exciting but I'm not going through there. *Please* don't tell me you want to go through there?'

With trembling hands, Demelza let her fingers trail across the symbols, and to her surprise there was a heat to them, a strange warmth as if she was skin to skin with a living creature. '*Wow ...*'

'What?' said Percy, peeking out from his hiding place. 'What is it?'

Demelza beckoned to him, and taking a deep breath he slowly inched towards her, as if traversing the edge of a clifftop. He looked down at the discovery, agog. 'Oh, Demelza, please don't open it. Why don't we just come back tomorrow when it's not so dark? It's probably locked anyway.'

But Demelza couldn't tear her eyes away from what she'd unearthed, and with curiosity pushing her forward like a hot poker she curled her fingers around the handle. She was just about to turn it clockwise when—

'*Owwwwww!*'

A fierce shock of white heat shot through her hand like lightning, and the trapdoor flung open on its own as if spring-loaded. Demelza stumbled backwards, wincing with pain. '*Ouch! Ouch!* And *ouch* infinitum!'

'Demelza?' said Percy, rushing to her side. 'Are you OK? What happened?'

'I . . . I don't know,' said Demelza, looking towards the trapdoor in confusion. 'The handle got really hot and then it just . . . it just opened on its own . . .' She squirmed in pain, nursing her burning palm.

'Oh, I don't like this,' Percy said with a gulp. 'I don't like this at all!'

'I'm . . . I'm sure there's a perfectly logical explanation,' said Demelza, getting up and trying to convince herself as much as her friend. She peered through the frame of the trapdoor and saw that there was a rickety ladder leading into the darkness below. She slowly put a foot on the top rung, as if testing the water of a hot bath. 'And I guess there's only one way to find out.' She took a deep breath and began to lower herself down. 'I won't be long, I promise. Stand guard up here. And if you see anything weird just shout, OK?'

'Demelza, no—!' Percy shouted.

But it was too late.

Down and down Demelza went, her palms clammy against the metal rungs of the ladder, her heart pounding hard against her ribs. With every descending step the air grew thicker, filling with the smell of spices, smoke and old parchment. How far down was she going to have to go? And what would she find at the bottom? Demelza breathed deeply, coaxing each foot to take her deeper and deeper into the unknown.

At the bottom she found herself in a small stone cavern. It was completely empty apart from a single wooden door which had been left slightly ajar. Demelza teetered towards it, and with both curiosity and fear coursing through her veins, pushed it open the tiniest bit.

She instantly sprung back in shock. *Oscillating orbits!*

A cave-like room, lit only by candlelight, stretched out in front of her as far as her eyes could see. It seemed to be part junk shop, part apothecary, with shelves of peculiar objects stretching from floor to ceiling like displays in the most magnificent of museums. The few bits of wall that could be seen were covered in an ornate wallpaper that was peeling in places, and the whole room gave off a sweet, musty smell.

Demelza didn't know what to think. Of all the things that she'd imagined discovering tonight, not one could have come close to this. What *was* this place? Did Grandma Maeve even know that it existed?

Demelza let her gaze bounce from wall to wall, trying to take it all in. Exotic masks sat next to sparkling crystals, and rows of prosthetic eyeballs stared out from glass cabinets. Gigantic speckled eggs (that would have made the grandest of omelettes) were arranged in order of size, and what appeared to be luminescent sea creatures floated around in pickling jars. There were piles of old books, bottles of ink and faded maps which hung skew-whiff in heavy frames.

But the most shocking sight of all was the copper

crucible which bubbled away over the open fire in the grate, surrounded by a circle of human skulls. Their teeth were crooked, their cheekbones sharp, and they kept watch over the room like hideous bone gargoyles.

'Demelza!' Percy whispered from above. 'What's going on? I don't like being up here on my own. Come back up!'

But Demelza didn't offer a reply.

Because from the pantry at the very back of the room, a figure had appeared through the shadows. It was wearing a golden mask shaped like a skull, which glimmered in the candlelight like a shiny second skin.

Demelza's hand shot to her mouth.

Even though she couldn't see the figure's face there was no doubt about who it was.

The long grey hair, the wrinkled hands . . .

It was Grandma Maeve.

CHAPTER 8
Minced Blobfish Brains

Demelza fiddled with a strand of her hair. Confusion, panic and disbelief all swirled around in her tummy at once. Even though logic told her to burst through the door, something held her back, rooting her feet to the ground as if she were wearing an antique diving suit.

She watched as Grandma Maeve hobbled to a three-legged wooden table next to the fire, on which stood a stone pestle and mortar nearly as large as her head. 'Now, what do I need first?' she muttered, consulting a large leather-bound book before stretching up to a glass cabinet above. It was filled with jars, bottles and tinctures of all shapes and sizes, and she eyed each one intently. 'Woodland fungus fuzz? . . . No . . . triple-distilled appendix pus? . . . No . . . Ah! Minced blobfish brains! Yes, they'll work nicely for someone who died at sea.'

She reached for a hexagonal jar and took out a handful of something pink and slimy, which she then threw into her mortar. Next, she selected a round pot containing what looked like bumpy, dark-green stones and dropped in a fistful. 'Then a few pickled bunions from the year he died. There we go . . .'

As Grandma Maeve pounded her ingredients together, Demelza shuddered. Whatever was being cooked up, she had a sinking feeling that it wasn't the beginnings of a delicious lamb casserole. What was her grandmother up to? Was she planning some kind of Halloween surprise? But why was she doing it hidden down here?

'Right, let's have a little taste,' said Grandma Maeve, putting down her pestle. She lifted a teaspoon of the concoction to her wrinkled lips and slurped noisily. 'Mmm . . . yes . . . the perfect balance.' She emptied the contents of her mortar into the crucible and stepped back. 'Now, just a little somethin' which belonged to the man himself and we'll be ready to start.'

With that, Grandma Maeve reached into her apron pocket and pulled out an oil-black feather that looked like it might have come from the tail of a crow. She let it fall from between her fingers and it hit the contents of the crucible with a popping, crackling hiss.

Almost immediately, the candlelight in the room twisted and flickered, and Grandma Maeve started to sway back and forth. She slowly pulled her arms through the air as if conducting a large imaginary orchestra. After a throaty cough, she began to chant, quietly at first, then louder and louder:

'Spectre, spectre, hear my cry!
I summon you from the other side.
We all live and we all die,
Come forth across the great divide . . .'

Demelza bit her lip. Spectre meant ghost, did it not? As Grandma Maeve's voice rose, the air turned cold. It was as if something was sucking every molecule of warmth from the atmosphere, as if a winter frost had come early. An overwhelming chill flooded Demelza's body, each one of her muscles stiffening like raindrops being turned to ice. Her nerves were ragged, her head full of nightmarish thoughts. Was Grandma Maeve some kind of witch or sorcerer? And whatever she was doing, did it have something to do with the noises Demelza had heard the night before?

A thin turquoise vapour had begun to twist its way upwards from the crucible. Demelza watched as it looped around Grandma Maeve's body like it was being pulled by some invisible force. It settled above the old woman's head in a psychedelic cloud, its hue changing to ochre then ruby then white.

Demelza clamped her teeth around her knuckles to keep herself from shouting out. *No, this isn't really happening*, she told herself. *This is just your mind playing tricks on you. An optical illusion. You're a scientist. Think scientifically. Think scientifically...*

But as much as Demelza tried to convince herself that she was just seeing things, the vapour cloud started to spin and Grandma continued to chant:

'Spectre, spectre, hear my cry!
I summon you from the other side.
We all live and we all die,
COME FORTH ACROSS THE GREAT DIVIDE!'

Grandma Maeve's voice reached a mighty crescendo and all of a sudden she froze, her eyes rolling back into her head. Then, like a snake being charmed from a basket, two threads of bright-white fluid began to appear from her nose. They oozed out of her nostrils like mucoid ropes, writhing through the air in front of her.

Demelza's knees buckled. Was Grandma ill? Did she need help? Demelza couldn't restrain herself any longer.

'GRANDMA!' she shouted, bursting through the door.

'What's happening? Are you OK?'

Grandma Maeve spun around and instantly the vapours plummeted from the ceiling. 'Demelza? What on earth are you doin' down here? You're meant to be tucked up in bed!'

'What am *I* doing down here?' screeched Demelza. 'Shouldn't I be asking *you* that question, Grandma? *You're* the one that's been sneaking around at night! *You're* the one that's doing . . . whatever it is that you're doing!'

'*Shhh!*' hissed Grandma Maeve, clamping a hand over Demelza's mouth. 'Keep your voice down.'

An elderly woman appeared from a chair in the corner and Demelza jumped. She hadn't realized that her grandma had company.

'Mrs Catchpole?' the woman said, stepping towards Grandma Maeve. 'What's happened? Where's my Benjamin? Is everything OK?'

'Yes, yes, everything's fine, Myrtle,' replied Grandma Maeve with a nervous laugh. 'It's just my granddaughter. She's had a bad dream and wants tucking back into bed, that's all. Go and sit yourself by the fire and I'll be with you in a minute.'

The old woman shuffled away and Grandma Maeve pulled Demelza close.

'Who was *that*?' demanded Demelza.

'That don't matter now,' replied Grandma Maeve, bringing her voice to a whisper. 'Now tell me, Demelza, are you alone?'

Demelza loosened herself from her grandmother's grip and shook her head. 'No. Percy's up there in the greenhouse. We came to investigate the noises I'd been hearing. The ones *you* insisted were just bad weather. They were something to do with this, weren't they?'

'Oh, deary me. Oh, deary, deary me!' Grandma Maeve pulled her hands through her ashen hair as she moved towards the door. She took off her golden mask and laid it on a nearby side table. 'Right, come with me. I'll explain everythin' later, but we have to get Percy home immediately. He can't see what's down 'ere.'

She ushered Demelza back up the ladder to where Percy was sitting cross-legged on the greenhouse floor. On seeing his friend, he leapt up. 'Oh, there you are, Demelza! I've been waiting ages. Are you OK? You look like you've seen a—'

'She's fine, thank you, Percy,' interrupted Grandma Maeve, her head popping up through the trapdoor. 'Nothin' to worry about.'

Percy shot Demelza a confused look. 'Mrs Catchpole?

It . . . it's *you*!'

'Well, of course it's me,' said Grandma Maeve. 'Who did you think it was, the Queen of Sheba?'

'We thought you might have been an intruder! A burglar!'

'A burglar? Good gracious me, no. Down there is where I brew my ginger wine. Our family's secret recipe, so I like to keep it all hidden.' She gave Demelza a stern look. 'Demelza was just helpin' me bottle it up and we lost track of time. Ain't that right?'

Demelza knew from the tone of her grandmother's voice that it was best just to agree, and she nodded. 'Yeah, that's right . . . ginger wine . . . I was helping . . . got distracted.'

'Oh, thank goodness for that,' said Percy, a relieved smile breaking across his pale face. 'See? I told you there was probably nothing strange going on.'

Demelza glowered at Grandma Maeve, her mind a twisted coil of confused thoughts. 'No. Nothing strange at all.'

'Right, well, let's be gettin' you home, young Percy,' said Grandma Maeve, clapping her hands together. 'I'd hate for you to be gettin' into trouble with your pa.' She ushered him to the greenhouse door and smiled. 'Demelza's a lucky girl to have a friend like you. A stubborn girl, but a lucky one! Head on back to the cottage and I'll be with you in a minute.'

Percy skipped back across the garden, and when he was safely out of earshot, Grandma Maeve sighed deeply. 'Well, it looks like your old grandma has a bit of explainin' to do, Demelza,' she said, fiddling with the hem of her cardigan. 'Let me deal with Myrtle downstairs, then after I've walked Percy home, we'll talk. Why don't you head on up to bed and I'll bring you a nice cuppa in a while?'

Demelza looked deep into her grandmother's eyes. 'And then you'll tell me everything, Grandma? You promise?'

Grandma Maeve's chin dipped down. 'Yes, I promise.'

CHAPTER 9
The Truth
Revealed

Twenty minutes later a storm had begun to rage, and claw-fingered raindrops tapped violently at the attic window. Demelza was tucked up under her patchwork quilt, Shiver nestling at her feet like a furry, brown hot-water bottle. In his cage, Archimedes was nibbling on a piece of apple, squeaking in terror every time a clap of thunder struck. And the Incredible Intruder Incarcerator was still set up in the middle of the floor, its spiky iron jaws wide open, as if hoping for prey.

Demelza waited restlessly, images of the mysterious cavern, the circle of skulls and the bubbling crucible burnt into her mind's eye. She couldn't stop replaying how Grandma's eyes had rolled back, and how the strange white strands had snaked their way out from her nostrils. What had Grandma Maeve been hiding from her all this time?

'Here we go! Strong, sweet tea all round,' came Grandma Maeve's voice from the staircase. The attic door creaked open and she hobbled inside, placing a silver tea tray down on the bedside table and her carpet bag on the floor. She sat in the adjacent rocking chair and poured out two steaming cups. 'And I thought you might need a little something to keep your strength up,' she said, taking a plate of biscuits and nudging them towards her grand-daughter. 'Go on, tuck in.'

Demelza took the plate, but nothing, not even a custard cream, could ease her mind. She felt queasy, on edge, her tummy fluttering as if it were full of moths.

For a while neither of them said a word, the air heavy with secrets yet to be told.

'Demelza,' began Grandma Maeve eventually, her voice trembling, her eyes damp, 'before I start, I need you to know that I never wanted to keep any of this from you. Not a day's gone by when I haven't wanted to tell you the truth. It's just that, well . . .' Grandma Maeve paused. She was struggling to find the words she needed and tears were gathering in the wrinkled corners of her eyes. 'It's just what with everything that happened with your mum and dad, I didn't want to cause you no more stress unnecessarily. You've had so much to deal with already . . .'

'Grandma, you *have* to tell me,' said Demelza, leaning forward and taking her grandmother's hand. 'Whatever it is, I *have* to know what's going on.'

Grandma Maeve took a lace handkerchief from her cardigan pocket and wiped her eyes. 'I know, I know. And I've waited far too long already.'

She took a deep breath and reached into her pocket. She pulled out a small purple business card and handed it to Demelza. One side was embellished with a golden skull, and on the other, the gilded calligraphy read:

Maeve Catchpole : Spectre Detector
Over fifty years' experience in summoning
the dead and comforting the bereaved.

Their home phone number was listed, and below that, in larger letters, was the phrase:

'Death Needn't Be The End'

Somewhere in the distance there was the call of a nocturnal animal and Demelza let out a shaky laugh. Had Grandma Maeve lost her marbles, or was she pulling her leg? 'Yeah . . . good joke, Grandma . . . very funny. Summoning spectres, that's a good one!'

'Demelza, I'm deadly serious!' replied Grandma Maeve curtly. 'A Spectre Detector is someone who's able to detect the spirits of those who have passed. We're able to communicate with 'em and summon 'em too. We do it to help people in mourning, you see, those who've lost a loved one and are findin' it difficult to cope. The room underneath the greenhouse is my summoning chamber, and a summoning is what you saw me doing down there tonight. Well, the beginnings of one . . .'

Demelza opened her mouth to speak, but all that came out was an incomprehensible stammer. She didn't know what to say.

'We reach out to those who might benefit from our services and they come to us to commune with those they've lost,' continued Grandma Maeve. 'Seeing the spectres of those who've passed can give 'em comfort, closure. Can help with the grievin' process.' Grandma Maeve took a sip of her tea. 'Take Myrtle, who you saw earlier, for example. She lost her only son a few months ago. Fell overboard while fishin', he did. Just dreadful. So Myrtle came to me this evening to say a proper goodbye. It helps the spectre too, of course, to know that someone is still thinkin' about 'em even though they've moved on from the livin' world.'

Demelza fell silent. Surely this had to be a wind-up?

Some kind of elaborate practical joke? Yes – any second now Grandma Maeve would burst out laughing and admit that it was just an early Halloween prank.

But Grandma Maeve's face was solemn, serious. 'You don't believe me, do you?'

Demelza huffed. 'Grandma, you can't communicate with dead people. And there's *definitely* no such thing as ghosts! It's scientifically impossible. Research has shown that—'

'Oh, research smesearch!' interrupted Grandma Maeve. 'Not everything can be proved by big numbers and clever formulas, you know. Some things are just . . . unexplainable. Part of the mysteries of the universe. And we don't use the term *ghosts*, by the way. Very old fashioned, that is, and extremely offensive. Spectre is the correct term, OK?'

Demelza let out a frustrated sigh. She was a scientist, and scientists *definitely* didn't believe in supernatural hocus pocus. It was inconceivable that there could be any kind of life after death. Impossible! But at the same time, she had no other rational explanation for the things she'd seen in the greenhouse an hour earlier.

'OK, Grandma,' she said. 'Supposing you *are* telling the truth – and this is purely hypothetical, of course – how do you summon a spectre?'

'Well, I'll explain it all to you in more detail another

time, but basically we boil a special brew in our crucibles and then chant a summoning incantation. That stuff you saw comin' out of my nostrils is spectoplasm. It's a paranormal energy that us Spectre Detectors create, and it gives spectres their physical form when they arrive back in our world.'

'And where do you summon these spectres from?'

Grandma Maeve leant forward in her chair, her pebbly eyes pinned on Demelza. 'Well, after someone's popped their clogs they head off to Inn Memoriam—'

'In where?'

'*Inn Memoriam.* It's like a big hotel where all spectres go after they've moved on from the living world. Once you've checked out of our world, you check in there! We don't know what it's like inside though, as spectres temporarily lose all recollections of their stay once they've crossed the veil. Spectres stay at Inn Memoriam while they're still in living memory, and that's where we summon them from. But once they've been forgotten, they move to their final restin' place and can no longer be reached.'

Demelza snorted. 'And when they've been summoned, how do spectres travel back here from Inn Memoriam? On their *last legs*, I suppose?'

'Don't be ridiculous!' said Grandma Maeve sharply.

'You ain't takin' this seriously, Demelza.'

Demelza slumped back in bed, trying to line up her thoughts. She felt as if she was going mad, as if she were caught up in a surreal nightmare. She liked things that could be explained with a formula or an equation or empirical evidence, not silly spiritual nonsense! She ran a hand through her hair, not knowing what to say.

'Look, my darlin', I know this is a lot to take in,' said Grandma Maeve, looking into her granddaughter's eyes. 'But you *have* to believe me. People have been summonin' the dead for thousands and thousands of years, for as long as there's been life on earth. There ain't many of us practisin' in this country these days because less and less people are willing to believe, but there are still plenty of us around the world. Look, I'll show you.'

Grandma Maeve reached into the patterned carpet bag that she'd brought with her and took out a large book bound in what appeared to be purple snakeskin. A golden skull was embossed on the front cover along with the words: *Grimoire of the Dead*. 'A Grimoire is a book of knowledge, a sacred text.'

Demelza sat back, resigning herself to the fact that her grandmother was going to show her this weird book, whether she wanted to see it or not.

'Right, let's have a look . . .' Grandma Maeve flicked through the pages and stopped on an illustrated world map entitled, *Spectre Detectors Across the Globe.* She extended a crooked finger towards the continent of Africa. 'In Johannesburg they call their Spectre Detectors *Spookzoekers*,' she said, pointing to an illustration of people in skeleton masks, whose hands reached upwards towards the stars.

Next she moved over to Asia. 'The Spectre Detectors of China are known as the *Shamans of Xian*, and they was possibly the first people in the world to practise our craft. You see?'

Demelza leant forward, pulling her patchwork quilt around her shoulders, and as she took in the images she flinched. A spark of recognition had ignited in her mind, like a match being lit. Somehow, the pictures felt familiar, as if she'd seen them somewhere before. But where?

'Why do they all have those creepy skull masks on, Grandma?' she asked. 'You had one too.'

'They're our Masks of Facelessness. We wear them during a summoning to block out distractions from the outside world and to help us mediate with spectres.'

Grandma Maeve moved her finger to a photograph of a woman in thick furs, whose mask was adorned with antlers and leaves. 'Now this lady is one of the *Nordic Necromancers*, who mostly live in Greenland . . . Then there's the Russian *Yagas of Mort* . . . and *Meibion y Meirw* from Wales.'

As Grandma Maeve continued to talk, Demelza hugged Shiver closer, trying to take everything in. It was strange – even though everything that her grandmother was saying sounded like the stuff of myth or legend, somehow it felt as if she were listening to information that she'd known all her life. It was like she was rediscovering something she'd lost years ago. It was like a memory . . .

'MY PARENTS!' Demelza lurched forward in bed and grabbed Grandma Maeve's hand. '*They* had this book, didn't they? Back in our old house! I remember it now!'

Grandma Maeve's eyes began to twinkle. 'That's right, my darlin'. You were too young to understand it all back then, but your parents was Spectre Detectors too. Your dad didn't spend all that time in his shed just choppin' firewood; that was where the trapdoor to their summonin' chamber was hidden.

'Your parents were two of the most dedicated and able Spectre Detectors I ever met. And now . . .' Grandma Maeve cleared her throat. 'Well, now it's time for *you* to carry on the family tradition, Demelza.'

71

Demelza swallowed. 'Me? You . . . mean . . . I . . . ?'

Grandma Maeve nodded. 'Mmm-hmm. Usually, if someone's gonna inherit the powers of the Spectre Detectors, things will start to happen some time during their tenth year. With you bein' eleven I thought that the powers had skipped a generation. That's why I was so shocked when you started talkin' about them night-time noises this mornin'. I was so taken aback, I didn't know what to say.'

'But what *are* the noises, Grandma? What was I hearing? What was I feeling?'

'It was your powers arrivin', my darlin'. I know it don't feel very nice, and if I hadn't been caught so off guard when you told me, I would have been a lot more supportive. I'm so sorry . . .'

Demelza's body stiffened, the cogs in her brain turning in overdrive. This time yesterday she hadn't even believed in the paranormal – she'd always thought that spiritualists were nothing more than circus acts, fraudsters, cheats – and now she was being told that she had the power to communicate with the dead herself? It seemed ridiculous! But as Demelza looked down at the *Grimoire of the Dead* she couldn't shake off the memory of her parents' copy, and the strange sense of familiarity that was now whirling inside her. What if maybe, just maybe, this could all be true? What if she really *did* come from a family of Spectre Detectors? After all, what was it that the famous astronomer, Ignacio Dimitrov, had once said? *All truths are easy to understand once they are found, the point is to find them.*

Shiver stirred on Demelza's lap. His body was warm and she stroked his ears, trying to calm herself. 'So, if I really do have these special powers, Grandma – and again, this is still purely hypothetical – what am I meant to do with them?'

Grandma Maeve reached for a fig roll and nibbled at its edge. 'Well, you see, Demelza, a Spectre Detector's powers are strongest during youth, and they get weaker with age. I obviously ain't gettin' any younger and won't be able to do what I do for ever. Soon I'm gonna need someone to take over.' She smiled wistfully. 'Demelza, I'd like you to become my apprentice Spectre Detector. I want to teach you everything I know.'

Demelza felt her heart freeze momentarily – she was lost for words. She wanted to believe everything that Grandma had told her, but the scientist in her needed proof. She needed concrete evidence.

Grandma took Demelza's hand and stroked it gently. 'Well?' she said meekly. 'What do you say?'

'I need to see one,' Demelza replied. 'I need you to summon a spectre.'

CHAPTER 10
The Summoning Chamber

The following night, as the moon settled in the inky sky, Grandma Maeve led Demelza down the winding garden path to the greenhouse. As a reminder to keep thinking scientifically, Demelza had put on her thinking cap, and she pulled it down firmly. The air was chill, and the earthy smell of autumn hung thick and smoky on the breeze.

Demelza had been in her room for most of the day, Grandma Maeve's supernatural revelations thrashing around and around in her mind. Usually she'd have spent a Saturday dreaming up new inventions, or testing herself on the decimal digits of Pi, or looking at creepy crawlies under her microscope, but there was no way she could focus on such things with all that had happened. The logical part of her brain still couldn't quite believe that it could all be true

– after all, no scientist had ever proven that there could be life after death. But as Demelza had delved deeper into the passages of the *Grimoire of the Dead,* she couldn't stop thinking about her parents reading to her from its pages when she was a little girl. She began to piece together the tiny fragments of memory she had from that time – there had been a chapter about Spectre Detectors in the Jurassic ages, intricate drawings of skulls and skeletons, passages about crucibles, cauldrons and candles. Somehow each sentence felt more and more like a familiar lullaby, a slice of her childhood being given back to her. These pages had been her bedtime stories all those years ago . . .

'So, are you ready?' Grandma Maeve asked Demelza as they reached the trapdoor. The ruby-red eyes of its skull glimmered under the moonlight as if trying to hypnotize her.

Demelza looked deep into her grandmother's eyes, and even though she wasn't quite sure, she nodded. There could be no going back now.

Down the ladder they climbed, the intoxicating scent of herbs and spices wafting up Demelza's nose once again.

Inside the summoning chamber, Grandma Maeve lit a few of the many purple candles that were scattered around. They were mottled with drips of hardened wax, and looked like little twisted stalagmites. 'There you go, my darlin',' said Grandma Maeve, plumping up some cushions on the leather armchair by the fireplace. 'You park your posterior on there and I'll go get some kindlin' for the fire. It's gonna get a bit chilly in 'ere once we start summonin', as you well know!'

Grandma hobbled over to the store cupboard at the far end of the room and Demelza sunk down in the doughy seat, sending dust particles floating into the air like glitter. She'd expected to feel anxious, unsure, but somehow the place seemed far less frightening than she'd remembered. In fact, it now felt oddly comforting, as if it were somewhere she'd been visiting her whole life.

She gazed around, taking in the collections of curiosities, strange masks and exotic maps which adorned the walls. Fusty books bound with cobwebs were stacked high in higgledy-piggledy piles, and Demelza let her eyes wander down their spines. There was *Speaking to the Dead: Volume 666* by Virginia Wang, *Supernatural Studies for Beginners* by Dr Una O'Brien and *Graveyards of Great Britain* by Jonah Maddocks.

Demelza wriggled as a bolt of excited anticipation zoomed through her body, only to quickly remind herself to continue thinking like a scientist. Professor Heinsteene had always said that 'during an experiment, no concrete conclusions should be drawn until a set of qualitative observations has been made using a large enough sample'. She had to keep that firmly in mind!

Once the fire was crackling, Grandma Maeve clapped her hands together. 'Right,' she said, stretching up to a high shelf in a nearby alcove. 'First things first.'

She pulled down a small wooden coffin fastened with a brass padlock and put it on the workbench in the middle of the room. As she blew on its lid a cloud of thick grey dust was sent into the air. 'This here is your ghoulbox. It's a bit like a toolbox, but less DIY and more RIP!' Grandma Maeve chuckled at her own joke. 'It first belonged to your great-great-grandmother, Octavia, and inside is everything you're gonna need to become a fully fledged Spectre Detector. I have my own, of course, so this is yours to keep. Now, I know it might seem a bit gruesome, it bein' in the shape of a coffin and all, but that's just to stop nosy parkers from wantin' to look inside.'

'Like who?' said Demelza.

'Well, like I said before, what we do is somewhat frowned upon these days, and there are some people who'd like nothin' more than to try and prove that we're frauds. Then there are others out there who want to exploit our powers for–' Grandma stopped herself and coughed. 'Well, we'll speak about that another time.'

She quickly pulled out a little key strung on a piece of purple ribbon from her pocket and put it in Demelza's hand. She gestured to the ghoulbox. 'Go on, open it up. See what's inside.'

With shaking hands, Demelza pulled the little coffin towards her. Just like the trapdoor, it was warm to the touch, almost purring with life. 'Why is it warm?' she asked. 'The trapdoor was too.'

'That's because they're carved out of the wood of the yew tree.'

'Like the ones you find in graveyards?' asked Demelza.

Grandma Maeve nodded. 'That's right. Otherwise known as Reaping Trees. Their roots and branches suck up some of the spectral energy from the graves, you see, and keep it in their fibres. That's what you can feel.'

Demelza, still fascinated and sceptical in equal measures, put the key into the lock. It felt as though she was about to open the door to a completely new world; one twist of her wrist and her old life might be gone for ever!

She turned the key clockwise, slowly pushed the lid upwards and–

'ARGHHHHHH!' Demelza screamed and jumped

backwards. 'Grandma! Inside! It's . . . it's . . .'

'What on earth's the matter?' said Grandma Maeve, hobbling towards the ghoulbox. She peered inside and rolled her eyes. 'Oh, you weren't frightened of Lord Balthazar 'ere, were you? Goodness gracious me!' She reached in and pulled out a large human skull, which she began to stroke as if it were a kitten. The black hollow of its nose was shaped like a diamond, its eye sockets the deepest, darkest of caves. 'You ain't nothing to be scared of, are you, my dear?'

'Good gracious me, no!' replied the skull, his teeth clacking together as he talked. His voice was clipped, almost regal. 'But I do prefer to be addressed by my full title, Lord Balthazar III of Upper Loxworth, if you please. One may not have a body but one can still have one's dignity.'

Demelza felt her cheeks burning. 'But . . . it . . . it talks. The skull talks!'

'Well, of course I talk, girl!' tutted Lord Balthazar. 'I'm a Talking Head. Oh, the youth of today!'

'Will you stop being such a crosspatch?' said Grandma Maeve to the skull with a chuckle. 'I thought you'd be pleased to be out of that box and finally meetin' your new owner.'

79

Lord Balthazar harrumphed and Grandma Maeve put him on to the table next to the fire. 'You see, Demelza,' said Grandma Maeve, 'occasionally when someone dies, their spectre gets stuck in their mortal body and they never make it to Inn Memoriam.'

Demelza pondered this for a moment. 'So that's what Lord Balthazar is? The spectre of a dead lord, inhabiting his former skull?'

'Exactly!' said Grandma Maeve. 'Every apprentice Spectre Detector has a Talking Head to keep them company while they prepare for summonings. I had one when I was your age too. Madame Babineux her name was. It can get a bit lonely at times down here, so it's nice to 'ave someone to chat to while you work.'

'Especially someone with an IQ of one hundred and fifty-six, no less,' added Lord Balthazar. 'I'm not just a pretty face, you know.'

Grandma Maeve rolled her eyes and brought her voice down to a whisper. 'He can be a bit of a grumpy grogs sometimes, but you'll be glad to have him with you when you start taking clients on your own.'

Demelza swallowed and looked to the floor. She'd heard of people having 'skeletons in their closets', but this brought a whole new meaning to the phrase.

Suddenly everything felt painfully overwhelming. This world was a million miles away from the comfort of her inventing desk and her notebooks and her scientific apparatus. How she wished that she could just scuttle back up to the attic and delve into an encyclopaedia with a nice cheddar cheese and peanut butter sandwich.

Grandma Maeve, obviously sensing her granddaughter's worry, held out a hand. It was warm, soft. 'Look, my darlin', I know this probably feels a bit scary to you at the moment; after all, it's not every day that you get given the hundred-year-old skull of an Edwardian English lord—'

'Quite!' interrupted Lord Balthazar. 'Consider yourself lucky!'

'But this ain't a fairy tale we're dealin' with. This is life and death. And it ain't always gonna be easy. Now, are you ready to carry on?'

Demelza took a deep breath and nodded. *It's all in the name of scientific discovery*, she told herself. *It's all in the name of science.*

Grandma Maeve reached into Demelza's ghoulbox again. This time she pulled out a worn but clean apron, some candles, a copper crucible, a pocket copy of the *Grimoire of the Dead* and finally a plain skull-shaped mask fashioned from pale wood.

She held the mask up to her face, and under the candle-light it was an eerie sight. 'The more summonings you do, you get fancier and fancier masks. Once you've done one hundred summonings you get one made from copper, after two hundred that changes to bronze, and so on and so forth. You should see the ones our Spectral Sages wear! Beautiful, they is. Covered in feathers, bones, gemstones . . .'

'Spectral Sages?' replied Demelza, confused. 'Who are *they*?'

Grandma Maeve chuckled. 'Sorry, m'dear, I keep forgetting that you've got a lot to catch up on. The Spectral Sages are the wise elders who run the Quietus. That's the governing body of the spectre detecting world. We swear our allegiance to the Quietus, and in return the Spectral Sages give us any help we might need. You'll become a member once you've finished your apprenticeship too.'

The fire had begun to wane and Grandma Maeve picked up a pair of brass bellows. As she blew air into the fire's depths, Demelza tried to organize all of the new information she'd just been given – *Mask of Facelessness . . . the Quietus . . . Spectral Sages* – there was so much to take in.

When the fire had been stoked, Grandma Maeve picked up the pocket copy of the *Grimoire of the Dead.* She flicked through the pages, their golden edges fluttering like the wings of a moth. 'Now,' she said, propping it up on an ornate metal bookstand on the table. 'Have a little listen to this chapter here, Demelza. Don't worry, it ain't as long-winded and boring as it sounds. Lord Balthazar, will you do the honours and read it out?'

'With pleasure.' The skull coughed as if clearing his throat for an after-dinner speech and began to read aloud:

'The sacred statutes of spectre summoning.

'One. A spectre may only be summoned as an act of true altruism and a Spectre Detector must never use their powers for personal gain or profit.

'Two. Summonings can only take place between the hours of dusk and dawn.

'Three. A summoning can only take place in a licensed summoning chamber or a location authorized by the Quietus.

'Four. A spectre may spend no more than a total of three hours within the mortal world. It is a Spectre Detector's duty to ensure their safe return to Inn Memoriam within this timeframe. Failure to do so will result in the spectre being trapped in the limbo between life and death for ever.

'Five. A spectre can be summoned once, and once only.

'Six. A Spectre Detector is responsible for the safety and wellbeing of both the mourner and the spectre at all times.

'Seven. Apprentice Spectre Detectors may only practise under the strict supervision of their mentor.'

Once he had finished, Lord Balthazar tipped forward as if taking a bow, nearly tumbling off the edge of the table.

'Thank you,' said Grandma Maeve, taking a seat in one of the armchairs by the fire and gesturing for Demelza to join her. 'Now, I know that rules ain't your favourite thing, Demelza, but these ones must be followed to the letter, you hear me?' Her eyes darted to the scar on her hand and she quickly pulled down the sleeve of her cardigan. 'Any fooling around or lapses in concentration can have horrible consequences. This process can be extremely dangerous, in more ways than one, if you don't pay proper attention to what you're doing at all times. You understand?'

'Yes, Grandma,' answered Demelza, and for some reason a chill shot down her spine like lightning. What sort of dangers did she mean? What kind of horrible consequences could there be?

'Right, we're nearly ready to start,' said Grandma Maeve. 'These last things I'm gonna show you are perhaps the most important things that a Spectre Detector owns.'

'Apart from their Talking Head, of course!' interjected Lord Balthazar.

'Are you quite finished?' said Grandma Maeve, rolling

her eyes. She pulled herself up from the depths of her chair and stretched to the cabinet of jars and bottles above the fireplace. It was the one from which Demelza had seen her taking the minced blobfish brains the night before. She unlatched it and ran a finger along the bottom shelf. 'These are the Ingredients of Awakening that help us to summon every spectre. Whether it be adult, child or animal.'

'Animal?' asked Demelza. 'People want to bring back dead animals?'

'Well, you'd be surprised at how attached people become to their pets, Demelza. Or perhaps you wouldn't, what with Shiver and little Archimedes. Only last week I was asked to summon the spectre of a pet tortoise. And very pleased the owner was too to be able to see little Shellby once more. Wept with joy, she did!'

Demelza stood up and looked at the cabinet. Every jar and bottle had a label, each one beautifully handwritten in dark purple ink. There was a decanter housing some kind of black herb known as *Moon Parsley*, and a hexagonal jar was filled with *Dehydrated Frogspawn*. A phial contained a viscid goo labelled *Badger Bogies: Cold Pressed* and another bore the words *Indian Fire Water*. Demelza's eyes widened; she was used to combining phosphorus, sulphur and copper with her chemistry set, but Grandma's set of ingredients was definitely a little more unusual. Badger bogies? *Yuck!*

'For each summoning you choose three Ingredients of Awakening,' explained Grandma Maeve. 'Each related to the person whose spectre you want to communicate with.' She flicked to another page in *the Grimoire of Death*, and pointed to a particular passage:

The Three Ingredients of Awakening
1. An item deriving from the deceased's decade of death.
2. An item representing the trade, profession or interests of the deceased.
3. An item belonging to the deceased themselves.

'As you get more experienced, you'll see how some ingredients are more suited to a spectre than others,' said Grandma Maeve. 'You just get a feel for it. But these are the basic requirements. You understand?'

Demelza nodded, and as a thought suddenly occurred to her she jostled from foot to foot. If everything Grandma Maeve was saying was true, then . . .

'I could meet my parents!' she blurted out. 'If I got hold of something belonging to Mum and Dad then I could summon their spectres!'

Grandma Maeve shook her head and frowned. 'Are you forgetting statute number one already? You can't just summon the spectres of whoever you fancy willy-nilly. We work for the benefit of other people, never our own, OK?'

Demelza felt a lump form in her throat – the hope of being able to see her mum and dad again was dashed completely.

Grandma Maeve seemed equally as crestfallen. 'I know it's a hard thing to come to terms with, my darlin'. I want to see them myself, of course I do. I can't tell you the amount of times I've been tempted to break the rules and summon them . . .' Grandma Maeve squeezed Demelza's shoulder before clapping her hands together. 'Now come on, you need to start preparing.'

Demelza's nose wrinkled. 'Preparing for what?'

'Well, your first summoning, of course! There's no time like the present after all. Your client is arrivin' in half an hour.'

CHAPTER 11
Summoning the Circus

'**B**ut are you sure I'm ready to do a summoning, Grandma?' asked Demelza as the pair stood boiling up water in the crucible ten minutes later. 'I . . . I thought you were going to show me how to do it first!'

'Like I said before, Demelza, a Spectre Detector's powers are at their strongest during youth,' replied Grandma Maeve. 'There ain't no reason why you won't be able to perform this summonin'. And don't worry, I'll be here to guide you through it.'

Demelza sighed. Grandma Maeve had shown her how to lay out her circle of skulls and tie the ribbon of her Mask of Facelessness in a good double knot, but she still wasn't sure if she was ready to communicate with the dead quite so soon.

'Who's the spectre I'm going to summon?' she asked.

Grandma Maeve took a long wooden spoon and began to stir the crucible. 'Well, it's the late brother of a woman named Miss Carlotta Tombolini. His name is Giacomo, and the siblings come from a family of travelling circus performers. Miss Tombolini heard about my services through a bearded lady she met at a clowning conference last week, and decided to get in touch.'

'I had a beard back in the day,' interrupted Lord Balthazar, who was now sitting atop the hearthstone. 'I didn't like it at first . . . but then it grew on me!' He guffawed at his own joke. 'Get it? Grew on me! *Grew* on me!'

Demelza shook her head and groaned. The talking skull was starting to get on her nerves.

She let the steam from the crucible warm her face as she took in what Grandma Maeve had just said. So she was going to summon the spectre of a circus performer! She *loved* going to the big top – the lights, the tricks, the smell of popcorn, the freshly whipped candyfloss. *But how had Giacomo died?* she wondered. Maybe he'd been gobbled up by an escaped tiger, or squashed by one of the strong men!

As if reading her granddaughter's mind, Grandma Maeve quickly said, 'Now remember, don't go askin' no personal questions to Miss Tombolini tonight, Demelza.

No wisecracks, no jokes. And definitely don't start chattin' about your inventions, you hear me?'

'I don't know what you're talking about,' replied Demelza, looking at the floor with a wry smile. 'I'm the personification of sensitivity.'

'I don't even know what that means,' replied Grandma Maeve. 'But I doubt very much that you're it, young lady. Oh, and one more thing, Demelza – when a spectre arrives through the crucible, they arrive in their birthday suit . . .'

Demelza frowned. 'In their what?'

'In their . . .' Grandma Maeve puffed out her cheeks. 'They don't have any clothes on! So just be courteous and I'll hand them a gown to wear, OK?'

Just then a tinkle of a bell sounded from the corner of the chamber. 'Oh! That'll be Miss Tombolini now,' said Grandma Maeve, giving the crucible a final stir before pulling on her golden mask. She reached into her cardigan pocket and pulled out a thick envelope, which she handed to Demelza. Inside was a piece of parchment titled: *Giacomo Tombolini – Spectography*. 'Now, here's the information I have about her brother. Have a gander, then why don't you see if you can find the first two Ingredients of Awakening we're gonna need for his summoning, hmm? Don't forget to put your mask on too.'

Demelza nodded, and Grandma Maeve toddled up the ladder to the greenhouse.

'I can do this,' muttered Demelza, pulling on her own mask. The wood felt smooth against her skin and there was an earthy smell to it, as if she was breathing in the scent of an ancient forest.

As she looked up at the glass cabinet above the fireplace she thought back to what Grandma Maeve had said about Ingredients of Awakening earlier on. 'Right, I need to find an ingredient from the decade Mr Tombolini died, then something which represents his profession, trade or interests.' She ran a finger down the spectography, searching for the information she needed. 'Ah! Here we go . . . so he died three years ago . . . and his job title was . . . trapeze artist!'

Demelza scoured through the various glass vessels on the shelves and within five minutes she'd returned to the workbench carrying a tall bottle of *Bumble Bee Wee-Wee*, which Grandma had collected a few years ago, and a phial of *Powdered Chalk for Aerial Acrobatics*. Choosing what she needed hadn't been that different from choosing the right components for an invention really, albeit involving more weird animal fluids and fewer bolts and cogs!

'I hope you've chosen your ingredients carefully,' said

Lord Balthazar, eyeing up the things that Demelza had put on the workbench. 'You don't want to go making any silly mistakes before you've even started.'

'Well, maybe you'd like to fetch them for me?' replied Demelza. 'Oh no, you can't, you don't have any hands!' She was really starting to feel annoyed by this smug skull. The thought of having to spend night after night in his company was a prospect worse than a run-in with the Smythe twins!

Just then there was the sound of footsteps coming down the ladder from the greenhouse, and the door to the summoning chamber creaked open. Demelza turned and in came Grandma Maeve, followed by a tall, slender young woman. She was wearing a bright-red leotard spangled with stars, and her dark hair was styled into neat little pincurls.

'Here you go, Miss Tombolini, do take a seat,' said Grandma Maeve, plumping up a cushion on the small settee before gesturing for Demelza to come over. 'Now this 'ere is my apprentice, Demelza, who will be performin' the summoning tonight. She's in the process of trainin', you see.'

Remembering her manners, Demelza gave a small awkward wave. 'Nice to meet you, Miss Tombolini. Would you like a cup of bumble bee wee? I-I-I mean, tea?'

Grandma Maeve shot Demelza a stern glare. Oh dear, this was already going badly.

'No, no, thank you,' replied Miss Tombolini, taking her seat. As she took in the skulls and crucible, she clutched at her handbag tightly, clearly full of anticipation.

'In which case,' continued Grandma Maeve, 'I think we should get started. Just to confirm, it's the spectre of your late brother that we're going to try and communicate with tonight, is that correct, Miss Tombolini?'

'Please, call me Carlotta,' replied the woman. 'And yes, that's right, it's my brother, Giacomo. It's been a few years now since he passed and I still miss him so much. We were double-trapeze partners, you see – The Death-Defying Tombolinis. One day Giacomo's hand slipped from the bar and . . .' She smiled sadly. 'Well, he certainly failed to live up to our stage name, didn't he?'

Demelza gulped. What an awful thing to have happened.

'When I heard about your services I jumped at the chance to speak with my brother again,' continued Carlotta. 'You see, I'm going to be opening my very own circus soon. It was a dream ever since Giacomo and I were children. I'd love to be able to tell him the good news.'

'Wonderful!' replied Grandma Maeve. 'And congratulations. Mind you, I don't know how you do all of that dangling around upside down in mid-air – I wouldn't be able to keep my false teeth in.' She clapped her hands together. 'Now, before we start the summoning, Carlotta, did you remember to bring one of Giacomo's personal possessions for us to use?'

'Yes, I did,' Carlotta replied. Her eyes began to twinkle, the desire to be reunited with her brother burning bright within them. She reached into her bag and brought out a pair of black-and-white polka-dot underpants. 'These were his lucky pair. I know they didn't bring him much good fortune in the end, but he never did a performance without them. Will they do? They have been washed . . .'

'Perfect,' said Grandma Maeve. She turned to her grand-daughter. 'And, Demelza, did you manage to find the other ingredients we need?'

Demelza nodded proudly and pointed to the things on the workbench that she'd collated.

'Mmm-hmm . . . very good . . . yes . . .' muttered Grandma Maeve, nodding in approval as she inspected the things her granddaughter had picked. 'Couldn't have chosen better myself.' She smiled and whispered in Demelza's ear, 'I knew you'd have a good nose for this!'

For the next part of the process, Demelza followed Grandma Maeve's lead, preparing everything she'd need for the summoning with the same meticulous care she'd give to one of her inventions.

Before long she was standing at the crucible with her concoction bubbling away in front of her. As she caught a glimpse of her masked reflection in its copper surface, a prickle of nervous excitement shot up the back of her neck.

'All right, Carlotta, I think we can begin,' said Grandma Maeve. 'Are you ready?'

The trapeze artist nodded furiously. 'Oh yes! More than ready!'

'In which case, Demelza, will you start to recite the incantation in chapter ten of the *Grimoire of the Dead*? Make sure you're nice and clear, OK?'

Demelza flicked to the right page and took a deep breath. She concentrated as hard as she could on the words in front of her, focusing on every sentence, every syllable. She'd always hated public speaking in school, the way that everyone's eyes bore into you, urging you to stumble and stutter. But just then, as if a forgotten part of her brain had suddenly been switched on, Demelza opened her mouth and the incantation began to flow confidently from her lips, like the words of a familiar poem:

'Spectre, spectre, hear my cry!
I summon you from the other side.

We all live and we all die,
Come forth across the great divide . . .'

Her words echoed around the room like the notes of a singing bowl, and astonished at the confident sounds she was making, Demelza began to say them louder and more stridently.

'That's it, Demelza!' encouraged Grandma Maeve. 'You're doin' it! I knew you could! Now just keep on focusin'!'

Demelza's pulse quickened. As she continued to chant she could feel her fingers getting warmer, tingling as if a flame were dancing on the tip of each one. The heat crept over the back of her hands and up her arms, and soon her whole body felt as if it was being powered by volts of electricity. She felt as if she could do a trillion somersaults followed by a trillion more!

'Spectre, spectre, hear my cry!
I summon you from the other side.
We all live and we all die,
Come forth across the great divide . . .'

She glanced at Grandma Maeve, who indicated for her to raise her arms through the air. Demelza did so, and with her fingers reaching out above her, Demelza watched in wonder as a turquoise vapour began to rise up from the crucible, just like it had for Grandma Maeve the previous night! It followed the path of her fingers as if she were a magician, its colour slowly turning ochre, then ruby, then white. The summoning was happening, it was *actually* happening!

'That's it, Demelza! You're nearly there!' said Grandma Maeve, her voice vibrant as she spurred her granddaughter on. Up in the rafters the vapour was swirling and twirling, showering the chamber with luminescent sparks. 'Don't stop saying them words. Don't let your focus drop!'

But Demelza was starting to feel tired.

Her limbs were aching and her throat was dry from all of the chanting. It was as if the summoning was draining her body of its energy. She felt her arms beginning to fall, her voice fading with every passing second.

'You can do it!' yelped Grandma Maeve. 'Don't let your mind get the better of you. You have the strength, I know you do!'

Demelza felt her grandmother's supportive hand land on her shoulder and she took a deep breath. She pictured Carlotta's face, and how happy it would make her to see her brother. She pictured her parents and how proud they would be if they could see her now.

She had to carry on!

Screwing up every last ounce of energy, Demelza began to chant again. She battled through the ache pulling at her muscles and the wrench on her vocal chords, and to her astonishment, before long she felt the first strands of spectoplasm beginning to twist up her throat and through her nostrils.

Grandma Maeve whooped with joy and clapped her hands. 'You've done it, Demelza! You've done it, my darlin' girl!'

Demelza tried to keep calm, watching as the strands of spectoplasm looped and twisted towards the vapour cloud before her very eyes. She'd thought the process would be uncomfortable, as if she were choking or gasping for breath, but it wasn't. She felt contented, in control.

And then it happened.

BOOOOM!

A burst of shocking white light illuminated the summoning chamber.

Demelza stumbled back, exhausted, panting as if she'd just completed a cross-country race. But soon enough her nose started to twitch, as all at once the scent of buttery popcorn, the tang of elephant dung and the cloying sweetness of candyfloss wafted through the air – the smells of the circus!

'Giacomo!' gasped Carlotta, her hand shooting to her

lips as she leapt from her seat. 'Oh, my dear Giacomo! You're here!'

Demelza looked up and, like a vision from a dream, the spectre of a muscly-armed trapeze artist had appeared before her, floating just above the crucible. Not quite solid, but not opaque either, he looked like a figure in an old photograph which had desaturated over time. Grandma Maeve had already cloaked him in a long gown and Demelza stared at him as if hypnotized, unable to take her eyes away.

'Carlotta? Is-is that really you?' he stuttered. For a moment he seemed lost, confused, but as his eyes focused on his sister, he gasped. 'No! It can't be!'

'Yes, it's me, Giacomo! It's really me!' Carlotta ran forward, her eyes sparkling, her face aglow. She stood face to face with the spectre of her deceased brother. 'Oh, Giacomo, I've missed you so much.'

As the siblings began to talk, Grandma Maeve grabbed Demelza's hand and squeezed it tight. Demelza wasn't sure if it was her own heartbeat or her grandmother's that she could feel pulsing through her fingers, but it was so strong it felt like a drumroll. She'd done it! She'd summoned a spectre!

'I'm so sorry for not believing you, Grandma,' she whispered. 'Really I am.'

'That's all right, my darlin',' replied Grandma Maeve with a wink. 'You wouldn't be you if you hadn't demanded *scientific evidence*! I hope that this is proof enough?'

Demelza nodded. It was more than enough!

'But Carlotta, how am I here?' asked Giacomo, floating out into the room. He looked down at his pale white hands, then over to Demelza and Grandma Maeve. 'And who are these people? I fell from my trapeze . . . I died . . . I was staying somewhere . . .'

'I'll explain everything later,' replied Carlotta gently. 'But it's all down to this wonderful girl.' She turned to Demelza, beaming. 'She brought you back! She's a Spectre Detector!' Carlotta went to stroke her brother's face, but as soon as her hand made contact with his cheek it disappeared right through it. It was as if her brother was made from smoke. 'I . . . I can't touch him?' she asked, turning to Grandma Maeve.

'Unfortunately not,' she replied with a frown. 'Even though spectres look solid enough, human flesh can't connect with spectoplasm. Spectres can touch inanimate objects, though – pick things up, wear clothes, relax in an armchair – in fact, why don't you both make yourselves comfy?'

The siblings sat down in front of the fire and, as Demelza watched them bask in each other's company, a comforting warmth spread through her body – as if she'd just drunk a mug of the most delicious hot chocolate. It was like the cosy feeling she got when giving a Christmas present, or the joy of testing out a new invention for the first time.

'Let's give them some space, shall we?' whispered Grandma Maeve, tugging at Demelza's shirt. She turned to the Tombolini siblings, who were chatting away as if they'd never been separated. 'We're going to leave you both now. You have three hours together and after that Demelza will return to reverse the summoning, OK?'

'Thank you! Thank you!' spluttered Giacomo. 'I don't know how I can ever repay you both. I never got to say goodbye to my Carlotta and now . . .' He looked to his sister and beamed. 'Now we can take a final bow, together.'

CHAPTER 12

Grandma Maeve's Warning

Demelza and Grandma Maeve sat eating breakfast at the old oak table as the sun rose. Shiver was curled up by the stove, his nose twitching as the pair tucked into plates of crispy bacon, mushrooms and fried tomatoes. As a special treat, Grandma had even made a batch of crumpets, which were piled up high and oozing with butter and honey.

'So did you enjoy your first summonin', my darlin'?' asked Grandma Maeve.

'Grandma, it was amazing!' replied Demelza, reaching for the pepper pot and shaking it liberally over her food. 'Astonishing! Astounding! No scientist has ever been able to conclusively prove that there can be life after death before! This is a revolutionary breakthrough!' Her knee began to jerk up and down as visions of winning a Nobel

Prize for Physics zoomed through her mind. She pushed back her chair and reached for the pen and paper on the dresser. 'In fact, as soon as I've finished eating I want to start studying the summoning process. It needs to be monitored, researched, verified. When people learn about this I'm going to be the most famous scientist in the—'

'NO!' Grandma Maeve slammed her teacup on to the table, making Demelza jump. Her brow was as dark as a thundercloud and her body was shaking. 'No! You can't tell *anybody* about this, Demelza. I thought I'd made that very clear. No one can know about what we do, you hear me? We ain't lab rats to be poked and prodded. Everything we do must be kept under lock and key.'

'But, Grandma, I—'

'BUT NOTHING, DEMELZA!' Grandma Maeve shot to her feet, and Shiver let out a frightened yelp. 'NOTHING! YOU HEAR ME?'

The pen Demelza was holding fell from her grasp. She'd never seen Grandma Maeve so angry before, so serious. In the blink of an eye the atmosphere in the room had changed completely, and there followed a thick and uncomfortable silence. The ticking of the kitchen clock suddenly sounded louder than it ever had before. Demelza didn't know what to say.

'Look,' said Grandma Maeve after a while, holding out a hand. 'I didn't mean to shout at you, my darlin'. It's just –' she looked to the floor – 'well, it pains me to say it, Demelza, but I fear I must. I didn't want to worry you without no need, but I think you need to understand exactly just how dangerous bein' a Spectre Detector can be.'

Her normally rosy cheeks had paled, her small hands trembled. 'You see, Demelza, there are people out there who want to exploit our powers for evil rather than good. Bad people, dangerous people.'

A lurch of apprehension rose in Demelza's tummy and she quickly swallowed down a mouthful of mushroom. 'What do you mean, Grandma? What dangerous people?'

Shiver stirred and Grandma Maeve scooped him up, caressing his long, velvety ears. 'Well, there *is* a way for us Spectre Detectors to bring someone back from the dead completely. A forbidden step which turns a spectre into a living, breathing human being again. We call it the Conjuring of Resurrection.'

Demelza paused, trying to figure out exactly what her grandma was implying. 'You mean, a spectre can be brought back into the living world as a real person . . . ?'

'Can, but mustn't,' said Grandma sternly. 'The Conjuring of Resurrection is completely forbidden by the

Quietus. You wouldn't want to attempt it anyway. You see, Demelza, if a Spectre Detector gives a spectre another chance at human life, their own life is forfeited in the process.'

Demelza bit her lip. 'So . . . if I performed the Conjuring of Resurrection, then I'd die?'

Grandma Maeve nodded. 'Yes. A life is traded for a life.'

Demelza pulled at a strand of her hair. She was only getting used to the idea of spectres, and now Grandma was saying it was possible to completely resurrect the dead? To give someone a second chance at being alive?

'But how do you do the Conjuring, Grandma?' she asked. 'Is it very different to a normal summoning?'

Grandma Maeve put down her crumpet and sat back in her chair. 'There are a few differences. The Conjuring of Resurrection can only be performed at midnight on Halloween – that's when the veil between worlds is at its thinnest. You also need a fourth Ingredient of Awakening – a fragment of bone from the body of the deceased. And because a Spectre Detector's powers get weaker with age, the Conjuring is best performed by a detector in the prime of youth.'

Demelza felt worry rising in her voice. 'But . . . but . . . what's the Conjuring of Resurrection got to do with those evil people you were talking about before? The ones who want to exploit what we do?'

Grandma Maeve edged forward in her seat. 'Well, it all started about five years ago. One day, just before Halloween, an apprentice Spectre Detector named Willy Priddle went missin' from the village of Skippingworth. He wasn't much older than you, actually. One minute he was on his way back from school, and the next he'd vanished. Never seen again.'

Demelza reached for her mug and grasped the handle tightly. 'Wh-what had happened to him?'

'We don't know exactly, but over the years other apprentices went missing too. About one a year, in fact, and always around Halloween.' Grandma Maeve cleared her throat. 'They was never found, but because they was all young Spectre Detectors, and because of the time of year, the Quietus figured it was someone wanting them to perform the Conjuring. Someone they call the Snatcher.'

Demelza's mouth went dry. 'So you think the children must have done as the Snatcher asked? They performed the Conjurings, and by doing it they died?'

'Either that,' said Grandma Maeve, 'or they refused, and were murdered by the Snatcher to stop them divulging his or her plans.'

106

On hearing the word *murder*, Demelza felt her mouth open into a gigantic 'O' of horror. 'Grandma, this is awful! Why did the Snatcher want them to perform the Conjuring of Resurrection? Who did they want to bring back to life?'

Grandma Maeve shrugged. 'No one knows.'

Demelza felt her heartbeat treble in speed as her mind began to swirl with horrible, nightmarish thoughts. 'But what if the Snatcher is still at large? What if they're still on the lookout for young Spectre Detectors? It's nearly Halloween! They could come for me!'

Grandma Maeve leant forward and stroked her granddaughter's head. '*Shhh*, my darlin', I didn't mean to scare you. But that's why it's so important that we keep our identities hidden. As long as you keep all that we do to yourself, everything will be absolutely fine, I promise. And besides, I ain't the only Spectre Detector round here. There's others lookin' out for you.'

Demelza's brow furrowed. 'Really? Who, Grandma?'

'That I can't say. I don't want to go puttin' no one else in danger.' She poured some more tea from the pot. 'Now, finish your brekkie, then we'll both go get forty winks. I don't know about you, but I'm absolutely cream-crackered!'

'OK,' said Demelza. But as she speared the last of her bacon on to her fork, her heart was heavy with worry.

CHAPTER 13
The Notebook

That week, Demelza stayed home from school to continue with her apprentice training. Daytimes were dedicated to theoretical areas of study – collecting Ingredients of Awakening, incantation elocution, and the very important process of scrubbing your crucible to avoid cross-contamination. ('A clean crucible equals a clean mind,' Grandma Maeve had stressed. 'It's very difficult to concentrate if your crucible is still tainted with dog food from the time you tried to commune with someone's pet chihuahua.')

Demelza enjoyed the studies, but it was the night-time summonings that she looked forward to most. Grandma Maeve said the best way for her to gain confidence in her powers was to practise, and as such had filled every slot in their appointment book with mourners. Night after night new spectres would appear from the crucible, the sight of their pearly white forms leaving both their loved ones and Demelza lost for words. This time last week, the most impressive thing she'd seen was the collection of antique safety goggles displayed at the Museum of Scientific Apparatus in London, but this now paled in comparison to the otherworldly wonders she was witnessing. Even though thoughts of the Snatcher were niggling at the back of her mind, Demelza looked forward to reaching her one hundredth summoning, when she'd be able to apply to become a member of the Quietus and receive her new Mask of Facelessness fashioned from copper.

But by the following Monday, and much to Demelza's discontent, Grandma Maeve had declared that it was time for her to return to school.

'Now, remember, not a word to anyone about what we've been doin',' she said, as Demelza reluctantly packed up her satchel on the kitchen table. 'Just say that—'

'—that I've been very ill with an incredibly contagious bout of Monkey Pox,' interrupted Demelza. 'I *know*, Grandma. We've been through this a squillion times.' She rolled her eyes as she put her lunchbox into her bag. 'I still don't understand why I have to go back to school anyway. I've learnt more from you this week than I ever learnt from

Ms Cardinal.'

'Because I don't want none of them busybody school inspectors knockin' on my door!' she replied, escorting Demelza to the front door.

'But I haven't done any inventing all week!' protested Demelza. 'I wanted to spend today testing out my robotic hand. It would be ever so useful for picking out Ingredients of Awakening . . .'

'Ha! You ain't bringin' any of your dubious contraptions near our summoning chamber, young lady,' replied Grandma Maeve, adjusting Demelza's school tie. 'Federica ain't laid anythin' since you used her coop as an electrical conductor for that thingamajig you made last month.'

Demelza giggled as she thought back to her failed Heated House for Happy Hens. It had brought a whole new meaning to fried eggs!

'Now, off you go,' said Grandma Maeve. 'And remember, no talkin' to strangers. Cycle straight to school and straight back. There'll be toad in the hole with pumpkin mash waitin' for you when you get home. Got enough gourds to last me until Christmas.'

She opened the front door and the wind brought in a gust of richly coloured autumn leaves. 'Oh! Hang on a minute. Be a poppet and put these in the postbox for me, will you?' Grandma Maeve turned to the sideboard and picked up a bundle of letters tied with twine. 'Important they get sent today.'

'OK,' said Demelza, and having sneakily re-loosened her tie, she stuffed the letters into her satchel and headed out into the crisp morning sun.

Demelza couldn't concentrate during morning assembly. The hall was stuffy, and the smell of Friday lunchtime's tripe stew still lingered in the air like a thick, meaty veil. Instead of listening to Ms Cardinal's boring talk on corridor etiquette, Demelza was amusing herself by secretly doodling in the little notebook she'd hidden beneath her hymn sheet. As the headmistress droned on about *decorum* and *posture* and *courtesy*, Demelza let her pen dance across the page. In one corner she drew Shiver with fanged teeth, howling at the moon as if he was a werewolf. In another she plotted out a design to carve on to her Halloween pumpkin. Even though it hadn't been her intention, it wasn't long before some inky depictions of the summoning chamber began to appear too. She drew tiny spectres floating around, strangely shaped bottles, bubbling crucibles. Demelza was just about to ink in the eye of a human skull when–

'Miss Clock! Perhaps you might like to share with the school whatever it is that you're doing, and which you obviously consider more important than listening to your headmistress?'

Demelza jerked to attention to find Ms Cardinal towering over her like a grey pillar. Her spiky frame was stiff in her heavily starched clothes, and sweat glistened on her hairy upper lip, the way it always did in the heat of the packed school hall.

'I-I was just doing some extra reading,' Demelza lied, quickly snapping her notebook shut. 'About . . . corridors . . . and etiquette . . . fascinating stuff!'

Titters of laughter echoed around the hall and Ms Cardinal harrumphed. 'Coming from you, Miss Clock, I find that extremely difficult to believe. Now give me what you're holding immediately.'

Demelza's body tensed, her fingers clawing around her notebook. 'Ms Cardinal, it's nothing! It's just a—'

But the headmistress had snatched the book from her grasp. Demelza watched with horror as she inspected its cover, running her fingers along the spine. *Please don't look through it*, she thought to herself. *Please don't look through it . . .*

Ms Cardinal already had her nose inside the book, and as

she took in the drawings her face began to contort, as if she were sucking on an extremely bitter gooseberry. As she flicked through the pages, Demelza squirmed with panic. What if Ms Cardinal showed the notebook to the other members of staff? What if she showed the other pupils in the hall? Grandma Maeve would be furious if half the village saw drawings of what they'd been up to. How could she have been so careless?

'As I'd expected,' snapped Ms Cardinal eventually, slamming the notebook shut before slipping it under her arm. 'Just more evidence of a ridiculously overactive imagination and a complete lack of self-discipline. You will collect the notebook from my office at the end of the day.'

'No, Ms Cardinal! Please!' protested Demelza. 'Let me have it back. I promise to keep it in my satchel, I won't let it distract me again.'

'Enough!' Ms Cardinal hissed. 'My office, the end of the day.' She threw her nose into the air and paced back to her lectern on the stage.

CHAPTER 14
The Telephone Conversation

'Demelza, you know running is forbidden in school!' said Penelope, blocking Demelza's way as she ripped down the corridor later that afternoon. The end-of-day bell had rung and she was desperate to get to Ms Cardinal's office to retrieve her notebook as soon as possible. It was imperative that no one else saw her drawings.

'Oh, for goodness' sake, just let me pass,' said Demelza with a huff. 'Surely you want to be getting home to be with your precious ponies or something?'

'I think we should tell Ms Cardinal on her, don't you?' said Persephone, who was glued to her sister's side.

Miranda, quiet as usual, watched on.

'Of course we should,' jeered Penelope. 'Especially after this morning's assembly on corridor etiquette. Maybe you should come up with an invention that will stop you from misbehaving so much, Demelza?'

'Oh, I'm far too busy at the moment,' replied Demelza with a sarcastic smile. 'I'm dedicating all my time right now to a new contraption that will obliterate annoying twin girls. Want to be my first guinea pigs?'

The twins' faces dropped in unison, but Miranda spluttered.

'You think that's funny, do you?' Persephone hissed, turning to Miranda with eyes like daggers.

'Of-of course not,' said Miranda, choking back her laugh. She thumped her chest as if trying to clear it. 'I was just coughing . . . I have a bit of a tickly throat.'

But Demelza could see her eyes still glistening with mirth. She'd often wondered if Miranda *actually* enjoyed being Penelope and Persephone's personal bodyguard. She was an incredibly strong shot-put thrower, and had won the county cup three years in a row. Surely she dreamt of being something greater than just the twins' flunkey?

'Well, don't just stand there, Miranda!' ordered Pene- lope, with a stamp of her foot. 'GET HER!'

But Demelza was already on the move. She ripped down the corridor before taking the winding staircase to Ms Cardinal's office three steps at a time.

As she approached, something made Demelza stop short. Through the creak in the office door she could hear the headmistress talking to someone on the telephone, and in the silence of the corridor Demelza couldn't help but overhear what was being said.

'Yes, I'm certain,' said Ms Cardinal. 'Yes, earlier on today in assembly . . . It came as a bit of a shock, to be honest . . .'

Demelza's brows furrowed. There was something odd about the headmistress's tone of voice – she was speaking in a hushed, frantic whisper, the kind that you use when you're trying to tell someone a secret but want to keep it quiet.

Unable to quash her curiosity, Demelza tiptoed closer and put her eye to the crack in the door. Ms Cardinal was sitting at her desk, piles of assignment papers stacked up in front of her, no doubt waiting to be sullied by her signature red ink.

'I'm telling you, Wilfred, I'm certain,' she continued, gripping the receiver so tightly that her knuckles were turning white. 'I took it from her and it's all there as plain as day! . . . Yes! . . . Spectres, skulls, crucibles . . .'

Demelza's heartbeat spiked. *Spectres? Skulls? Crucibles?* Was Ms Cardinal talking about what was in *her* notebook?

Feeling the hairs lifting on the back of her neck, Demelza watched as Ms Cardinal's expression became increasingly intense.

'I guess her powers must have come late,' said the headmistress. 'Yes, it can happen on occasion . . . but at least now I know for sure that she's a Spectre Detector.'

Demelza's hand shot to her lips.

Ms Cardinal knew all about the Spectre Detectors? She knew about her powers? The thought should have been enough to make Demelza run away at once, but she listened on, desperate to know what the headmistress would say next.

Ms Cardinal wound the coil of the telephone wire around her hand. 'I'll do it soon,' she said with a grin. 'At the end of this week. I've waited years for this and now I might finally get what I want. But this will be my final attempt, Wilfred. I can't keep on going on like this . . .'

Gallivanting gamma rays! Demelza stumbled backwards, feeling the blood rush from her face. Ms Cardinal's words crashed through her mind like molecules colliding.

At the end of this week.

Waited years.

Final attempt.

Surely it didn't mean . . . ?

The idea hit Demelza like potassium hitting water. Was Ms Cardinal the Snatcher?

'I must go,' said Ms Cardinal finally. Her tone was brusque, clipped. 'We can speak more about it later, but remember, not a word to anyone.' She put down the phone with a clatter, before her gaze darted towards the door as though she somehow sensed that she was being watched.

Demelza jumped back.

'Who's there?' said Ms Cardinal.

Demelza's instinct was to run, but she was in such a state of shock that her feet stayed rooted to the spot.

'I said, who's there?'

Demelza squirmed. 'It's . . . It's me, Ms Cardinal . . . Demelza Clock.'

There was a screech from inside as Ms Cardinal pushed back her chair, followed by the *click-clack* of her court shoes coming towards the door. She pulled it open, her face flustered.

'Demelza, what have I told you about loitering?' she said, her eyes darting to the telephone. Her normally pallid cheeks were flushed and she seemed nervous, obviously caught off guard. 'W-what do you want?'

'You told me I could come and get my notebook back at the end of the day,' Demelza replied, trying to remain calm despite the fear clamping at her body. 'The one you took from me in assembly.'

'Oh . . . oh yes . . .' stuttered Ms Cardinal nervously. 'I'd forgotten all about that little notebook of yours.'

You haven't stopped thinking about it, more like, thought Demelza.

Ms Cardinal pulled the notebook out of her jacket pocket and coughed loudly. 'Now, I don't want to see this in school ever again, Miss Clock. Stricton is not a place for you to be indulging your overactive imagination and ridiculous juvenile fantasies.' The headmistress turned away, barely able to look Demelza in the eye. 'Am I making myself clear?'

Demelza nodded, adrenalin seething behind her clenched teeth as she took the notebook from the headmistress.

'Good. Now be off with you. And for goodness' sake, girl, straighten your tie at once!'

Demelza turned and quickly made her way back downstairs. What had she got herself into? She felt panicked, overheated, faint. She needed to sit down.

Seeing that the girls' toilets were still open, she darted inside and locked herself in one of the cubicles. She slumped against the door, a feeling of terrible foreboding washing over her like a torrent. All of the things she'd heard

Ms Cardinal say on the telephone *can't* have just been a coincidence, surely?

Demelza's tummy was in knots.

It all pointed to one thing: the headmistress of Stricton Academy was the Snatcher, and she was coming for her next!

CHAPTER 15

A Problem Shared
is a Problem Halved

'You're very quiet tonight,' said Grandma Maeve as Demelza pushed a half-finished Yorkshire pudding around her dinner plate later that evening. Gravy was sloshing over the sides, dripping down on to the flowery cotton tablecloth. 'And you ain't eaten much of your toad in the hole. Everythin' all right?'

Demelza put down her fork with a clink. She'd been worrying about Ms Cardinal's telephone conversation all evening and it was obviously showing. But if she told Grandma Maeve about what had happened with her notebook, she'd be so angry, so disappointed. And besides, there was no point in worrying her grandmother unnecessarily, especially not until she had concrete proof about Ms Cardinal's intentions.

'I'm fine, thanks, Grandma,' she lied, throwing the

untouched sausage from her plate into Shiver's mouth. 'Just tired, that's all. We had double phys ed today and had to run twenty laps around the hockey pitch.'

'Is that all?' said Grandma Maeve, forking up the last of her peas. 'We had to do at least forty laps in my day, and that was while wearing a rucksack full of rocks.' She pinched Demelza's cheek and smiled. 'But your day was OK apart from that? You didn't go blabbing about *you-know-what*?'

Demelza's hands suddenly felt clammy. She gulped. 'Of . . . of course not. The secret's safe with me.'

Grandma Maeve nodded. 'Good. Well, you'll be glad to know that we ain't got no summonings booked for tonight. A nice hot bath's in order for you, I think. You ain't had one since last week and I could make candles with the amount of wax in your ears, young lady!' She pushed back her chair and began to clear the gravy-smeared plates from the table. 'But first, how about a nice bowl of raspberry ripple ice cream? Got some orange jelly in the fridge too. You think you can manage that?'

Demelza sighed. As delicious as it sounded, pudding was the last thing on her mind. All she could think about was what she was going to do about Ms Cardinal. If she really was the Snatcher, whose spectre did she want to summon through the Conjuring of Resurrection? Was it an old colleague, or friend or family member? Whatever the headmistress's motives, Demelza needed to stop her before she struck. But how?

'Heeelllooo! Earth calling Demelza!' said Grandma Maeve, looming over her with a carton of swirly pink-and-white ice cream. 'Pudding?'

Demelza shook herself from her trance and looked up. 'Erm . . . maybe later.'

Grandma Maeve sat down next to her. 'My darlin', are you sure you're OK? You really don't seem yourself. Come on, you can tell me. A problem shared is a problem halved, you know.'

Demelza sighed. She knew Grandma Maeve was right. This wasn't something that she could resolve on her own with a mathematical equation or a scientific formula. But she really didn't want to admit to Grandma what was going on. Not yet, at least. If only she could talk to someone else about her suspicions. If only she could tell—

A thought suddenly pinged into Demelza's mind.

Surely it would be OK for her to confide in Percy? He rarely left his room, after all, and he had no other friends. Who was he going to tell, his teddy bears and stuffed animals?

'Well?' said Grandma Maeve. 'Are you gonna tell me

what's goin' on in that coconut of yours or are you gonna just sit there starin' into space all night?'

'Really, it's nothing,' said Demelza, getting up. 'I . . . I think I'll go and run that bath like you suggested.'

Grandma's hands shot to herself in faux-horror. 'Demelza Clock havin' a wash voluntarily! Call the papers!'

Demelza's mind was too preoccupied to react to Grandma Maeve's joke. She made her way out of the kitchen and ran upstairs, a plan of action hatching in her brain. Later tonight, when both Grandma Maeve and Mr Grey would be sound asleep, she'd sneak out of the cottage and talk to Percy.

A problem shared *would* be a problem halved.

CHAPTER 16
Telling Percy

'Demelza, this is *not* a very good idea!' grumbled Lord Balthazar as Demelza made her way down the hill towards Percy's just before midnight. She had the skull wrapped up in a jumper under one arm, and had her ghoulbox tucked under the other. 'You know you aren't meant to show me to anyone. And that includes young Percival.'

Demelza stopped, and having checked that there was no one around, peered under her jumper. '*Shush!*' she hissed. 'I told you to keep quiet. And besides, I thought you hated being locked up in the summoning chamber all day?'

'I do! But I don't much like being carried around under your sweaty armpit like a football either. And you know your grandmother wouldn't approve of all this. Wouldn't it be easier just to tell her about your suspicions instead of

125

traipsing around after hours like a vigilante?'

Demelza felt a heaviness spreading across her chest as she walked briskly through the night. She'd be lying if she said that she had no concerns about going against Grandma Maeve's wishes. She'd spent so long mulling it over in her bath earlier that by the time she got out, her fingers were as wrinkly as raisins. But she needed to talk it over with someone. If she didn't, she feared that her brain might spontaneously combust.

'I don't want to worry Grandma Maeve until I'm certain my hypothesis is correct,' she said curtly. 'I know she pretends to be as fit as a fiddle, but she's getting old. The last thing I want is to give her a heart attack. Now be quiet, otherwise you'll *really* feel what it's like to be a football!' She covered up the skull again, and continued down the sloping path towards Percy's.

When she got there, Demelza pulled down her thinking cap and held her head low. She tiptoed up to the picket fence and peered through the slats. Yes! All the lights were off!

She snuck in through the side gate. Moving quickly and silently, she navigated her way across the back garden, avoiding Mr Grey's beds of immaculately preened pansies and prize-winning hyacinths. She knew that there was a spare key hidden underneath the ornamental cherub statue next to the back door and, as silently as possible, she let herself in.

Percy's room was right at the very top of the house and, remembering to remove her boots, Demelza crept up the thickly carpeted staircase towards it. Family photographs in gilt frames adorned the walls at every level, lit up in the bright moonlight: Mr Grey at the golf club's Christmas ball, Mr and Mrs Grey on their wedding day, Christenings, birthdays and Christmases. But there was something strange about the collection of pictures which Demelza hadn't noticed before – there weren't any recent ones of Percy. There was one of him on his first day in junior school, and one showing him blowing out the candles on his ninth birthday cake, but nothing since then. Demelza shook her head. *Mr Grey is probably too worried that the camera flash will damage his son's delicate little eyes*, she thought.

At Percy's door, Demelza quickly shot a backwards glance across the landing. The coast was clear! She slunk inside to find her friend snoring softly under his thick feather quilt, one of his comics lying open on the floor beside him.

'Percy,' she whispered, carefully closing the bedroom door behind her. 'Percy, wake up.'

Percy stirred but his eyes stayed closed. 'Just one slice of chocolate cake,' he muttered, obviously deep in a dream. '*Please*, Dad, just one little slice . . .'

Demelza knelt down by his bed and shook him through the thick duvet. 'Percy, it's me, Demelza. Wake up! Come on, wake up!'

'*Urhhh!*' Percy jerked upwards with a gasp and looked around in the darkness. 'Who is it? Dad? Fräulein von Winkle?'

'*Shhh!*' Demelza hissed. She flicked on his bedside lamp, illuminating her face. 'It's me. It's Demelza.'

'Oh, Demelza,' he said, letting out a relieved sigh. 'You scared the life out of me.' He shook his sleepy head and rubbed his eyes. 'What are you doing here? What time is it?'

'I need to talk to you,' said Demelza. She made sure that Lord Balthazar was still completely covered by her jumper and came to perch on the end of the bed. 'It's important.'

'Something so important that it couldn't wait until morning?' replied Percy, pulling his covers around him. 'I was having such a nice dream.'

'Yeah, I know,' said Demelza, rolling her eyes. 'But you'll have to go back to your chocolate cake another time.' She glanced quickly towards the bedroom door.

'I don't understand,' said Percy. 'What's going on?'

Demelza cleared her throat. 'Well, it's a long story,' she began. 'And to be honest, I don't think you'd believe me if I just told you. So I'm going to show you something. But you have to promise not to scream, OK?'

'Erm . . . OK,' said Percy, looking confused. 'But it better not be one of those weird snail-hamster hybrids that you were breeding in the summer. My dad still moans about finding their droppings in his geraniums.'

Demelza frowned. 'They were called *snamsters*, and they were completely toilet trained, I'll have you know . . . well . . . most of them anyway.' She got up and stood by the desk. 'Now, are you ready?'

Percy nodded, and with a deep breath Demelza whipped back her jumper to reveal her Talking Head.

Lord Balthazar coughed dramatically, as if he were choking. '*Urgghh!* Thank goodness for that. I thought I was going to suffocate to death under that disgusting, pongy jumper.'

'You're already dead,' muttered Demelza under her breath. 'Anyhow, Percy, I'd like you to meet Lord Balthazar III of Upper Loxworth. Lord Balthazar, this is my friend Percy.'

The skull's gaze shifted towards the boy and he nodded.

'It's very nice to make your acquaintance, Percival, even though I fear we might have interrupted you at a somewhat ungodly hour. How do you do?'

Percy didn't answer. His face slackened, and before Demelza could stop him, his mouth dropped open and he let out an ear-piercing scream. 'ARGHHHH! IT'S ALIVE! IT'S ALIVE!' He leapt from his bed, and with arms flailing, ran across the room to the door. 'Keep it away from me! Keep it away from me!'

'Percy, be quiet!' hissed Demelza. 'I told you not to scream! Your dad will hear!'

Percy threw his hands over his eyes, trembling like a jelly.

'Goodness gracious me, boy!' exclaimed Lord Balthazar. 'Is there really a need for such histrionics? I'm a talking head, not a poisonous cobra!'

'Oh, I must be going mad,' Percy muttered to himself. 'I'm seeing things! Maybe I'm having one of my allergic reactions.'

'Percy, calm down,' said Demelza, looking into his eyes. 'I promise, you're not going mad or having an allergic reaction. Come and sit down and I'll explain everything.'

Percy peeked through his fingers and, when he realized that he wasn't hallucinating, he muttered, 'Only if you get rid of that . . . that thing.'

'*Thing?*' spluttered Lord Balthazar, almost gagging. 'How very rude! The *thing* of which you speak is actually an esteemed member of the British aristocracy! Demelza, I will *not* be spoken to in such a manner!'

But Demelza had already picked up the skull, and before he had a chance to protest any further, she'd shut him in Percy's wardrobe. 'That better?' she asked.

Percy nodded, and when he'd finally stopped shaking and was tucked up in bed again, Demelza told her story.

She began by going back to the night when they'd crept into the greenhouse together and discovered the trapdoor, and told Percy all about what she'd *actually* discovered beneath it. She talked about her new-found powers, the Spectre Detectors, the Snatcher and finally her suspicions about Ms Cardinal.

Percy was silent throughout, his chin dropping lower with every word Demelza spoke.

'S-s-so let me get this straight,' he stuttered after she'd finished. 'You're telling me that you and your grandma c-c-can talk to ghosts?'

'Well, technically we call them spectres,' said Demelza, as if she'd been practising all her life. 'But yes, that's right. We summon them to help people deal with their grief. I'm only an apprentice at the moment, but when I'm ready I'll take over from Grandma Maeve.'

Percy shook his head. 'But . . . I didn't think you believed in stuff like that, Demelza. I thought you only trusted things that were *scientifically proven*.'

Demelza hesitated. 'This time a couple a weeks ago I *wouldn't* have believed it. But I guess there's no better proof than seeing something with your own eyes, than summoning something with your own hands. Detecting spectres is in my blood, Percy. Always has been.'

Percy shot a quick glance at the wardrobe and shuddered. 'But why didn't your grandma tell you about all this before? It's a pretty huge thing to keep quiet.'

'Grandma just wanted to protect me for as long as possible, especially as my powers didn't show up on time,' answered Demelza. 'Like I said, being a Spectre Detector is dangerous. And I think it's about to get even more so, with a murderous criminal as my headmistress.'

Percy plumped up his pillows. 'You really think that your headmistress is this Snatcher person?'

'I'm fairly certain,' said Demelza. 'But I don't know what to do about it. I can't tell Grandma without letting slip that I was super careless. I don't want to disappoint her.' She picked up the copy of Percy's comic and pointed to the front cover. 'What would Captain Thalasso do?'

Just then a loud creak came from the landing and the children spun towards the door.

'Quick!' Percy hissed, gesturing to the space below his bed. 'Under there! It'll be my dad!'

Demelza scrambled under the bed, and as the door creaked open she held her breath, expecting the worst. If Mr Grey caught her then she'd be grounded for weeks . . . months . . . years!

But it wasn't Mr Grey's feet that appeared in the threshold.

Four ginger furry paws padded into the room and crossed the carpet with a high-pitched miaow.

'Tiger, it's *you*,' whispered Percy. 'Panic over, Demelza. It's just the cat.'

Demelza poked her head out from under the overhanging duvet and pulled herself to her feet. Tiger was purring on Percy's bed, a red leather collar around her neck.

'She's probably just come back from one of her night-time strolls,' said Percy. 'You gave us a fright there, girl.'

But even though Demelza was relieved, a feeling of guilt had begun to swell in her tummy. That had been *way* too close for comfort, and she was suddenly very aware of all the information she'd revealed to Percy; the promises that she'd broken. Had she done the right thing, confiding in her friend?

'Percy, you do promise not to tell anyone about any of this, don't you?' she said, hoping for reassurance. 'This is our little secret, yes?'

'Little?' scoffed Percy. 'That's the understatement of the century! But of course I promise.' He picked up his comic and a look of newly found determination twinkled in his eyes. 'I tell you what, why don't you come over tomorrow and we can put together a plan to confront Ms Cardinal? You know how formidable I look in my bunny slippers!' He flexed his non-existent arm muscles and gurned.

Demelza laughed. 'OK, but if you see anything suspicious before then, you can let me know using this . . .' She reached into her satchel and pulled out a set of her home-made walkie-talkies. They'd originally been created when Demelza had been bedridden with a twisted ankle the previous year – whenever she'd needed another hot-water bottle, or bunch of grapes, or Danish pastry, she could make the request to Grandma Maeve without having to move from the comfort of her room.

She handed one of the handsets to Percy and showed him how to use it. 'But don't use your real name over the airwaves, OK? Anybody could be listening in. I'll be known as Clever Cog, and you'll be the Comic Book Kid. Do you understand?'

Percy smiled. 'Loud and clear, Clever Cog!'

Demelza got up and opened the wardrobe. 'Come on, Lord Balthazar, it's time to go home.'

'Well, thank goodness for that,' spluttered the skull as Demelza lifted him into the air. 'I have never been treated with such contempt! I am a lord, not a pair of smelly old boots!'

'Yes, yes . . .' said Demelza, silencing him with her jumper once again. She tucked him under her arm and made for the bedroom door. 'I'll see you tomorrow, then, Percy. Or later today, I guess. And remember, not a word to anyone.'

CHAPTER 17

Dancing with Death

'Ah! There she is!' said Grandma Maeve as Demelza stumbled into the kitchen later that morning. 'I was just about to come and wake you, sleepy head.' The old woman was standing at the stove and she gave her frying pan a gentle shake before tossing a fluffy pancake into the air. It landed back in the pan with a sizzle, golden side up.

Demelza looked at the clock and gasped. It was gone noon! She must have been so exhausted after her midnight expedition to Percy's that she'd completely slept through her alarm! 'Grandma, why didn't you wake me up? I've missed half of school!'

'Well, you looked so peaceful,' said Grandma Maeve, flipping the pancake on to Demelza's plate with a satisfying *flump*. 'You was all curled up like a little koala. And besides, I need you well rested for tonight.'

Demelza's nose wrinkled. '*Uh?* What's happening tonight? Has someone booked in for a summoning?'

'Nope! We're goin' on a little outing,' said Grandma Maeve, putting the plate down on to the table and gesturing for Demelza to sit. 'So it's important to 'ave a big brekkie.' She looked at her watch and chuckled. 'Or should I say lunch?'

Demelza's eyes widened as she took her place at the table. *A surprise?* What on earth could it be? Had Grandma Maeve finally got the hint, and was taking her to buy the new Astro 250 telescope that she'd been wanting? She *had* been dropping hints into conversation every week for the past year!

'So, what is it, Grandma?' she asked, dipping her spoon in the pot of syrup and drizzling it over her pancake. 'What's the surprise?'

'You'll just have to wait and see, eager beaver,' said Grandma Maeve, coming to join her with a pot of tea. 'But we've got a long walk ahead of us this afternoon, so make sure you fill ycr belly. And get yer winter coat and scarf out from the closet. It's gonna be a chilly one.'

It was already getting dark when the pair slipped out of Bladderwrack Cottage later that afternoon. Aided by her walking stick, Grandma Maeve hobbled down the garden path. Demelza followed, and did up the toggles of her duffel coat before pulling on her thinking cap. She still had no idea what Grandma Maeve had in store, and a nervous anticipation had been brewing in her stomach all day to the point where it was almost bursting. Was it wise to be going out with Ms Cardinal possibly on the prowl? Demelza decided that she wasn't taking any chances, and had packed her satchel with a few of her inventions that could possibly double up as weapons if need be: a box of Bogey Bombs, a set of Stay-Away Brass Knuckles, and a handful of her Fantastical Fizzing Firecrackers left over from last year's Bonfire Night.

'Now, you must stay close at all times,' said Grandma Maeve as they reached the front gate. She was wearing a long velvet cloak and had a battered portmanteau hoisted over one shoulder. Under the fading light her green eyes twinkled, cat-like. 'No wandering off, and keep that loud voice of yours down. We can't have anyone following us: we're on Spectre Detector business.'

Spectre Detector business? *Oh no!* Demelza's head began to spin with worry. This would be the perfect opportunity for Ms Cardinal to strike! Her mind filled with horrible visions of her headmistress stalking them across the countryside, but she nodded, and the pair set off down the winding country lanes, the darkening sky slowly becoming embroidered with stars. She'd just have to keep her wits about her.

Eventually, they reached the outskirts of the village and made their way into the surrounding hills. As Demelza looked back towards Little Penhallow, the buildings seemed minuscule and the street lamps were mere flickers in the distance. She could see the spires of the church and, further away, the crumbling deserted turrets of Crooke-scroft Castle – the village's oldest relic – rising upwards like knobbly fingers.

Grandma Maeve took a couple of lanterns from her portmanteau and handed one to Demelza. With the strike of a match their wicks were aflame, and they illuminated the path ahead with a dancing orange light.

Demelza gasped as she realized where they were heading. A thick wood stretched out in front of them, the dark stems of its trees jutting up densely, like prison bars. Demelza shivered, anticipating Ms Cardinal appearing through the trees to steal her away into the night. This was *not* the kind of surprise she had been hoping for. 'We're . . . we're going in there?' she asked.

Grandma Maeve just nodded and pulled their Masks

of Facelessness from the bag, signalling for Demelza to put hers on.

They walked silently through the trees in single file. Underfoot, the ground was brittle and each of their footsteps sent a crunchy echo through the tangle of branches around them. Every now and then Grandma would stop, as if listening for something or someone, and Demelza grew more and more anxious by the second. Thoughts of Ms Cardinal commandeered her brain, and the longer they walked, the more she felt that it was best just to come clean. She hadn't wanted to worry Grandma Maeve, but then again she hadn't anticipated that they'd be walking through a forest in the middle of the night, just before Halloween!

'Grandma . . .' she began, looking down at her feet with nerves as they walked. 'I . . . I need to talk to you about something. It's important. You see, I think I might have got into a bit of bother. It happened at school yesterday. Ms Cardinal got hold of my notebook. She saw some doodles that I'd done in it of the summoning chamber . . .'

Demelza looked up, but to her dismay, the old woman hadn't been listening. She'd walked on ahead and was now standing under a sprawling oak tree, surrounded by undergrowth. A soupy mist was swirling all around it, almost as if it were the opening to another dimension.

'Come on, slowcoach, we're here,' whispered Grandma Maeve, gesturing for Demelza to come closer. She rapped out a complex rhythm on the tree's knotted trunk and waited.

With the suddenness of a jack-in-the-box, a woman popped her head through some of the surrounding branches. She was wearing a Mask of Facelessness, adorned with lustrous black pearls. 'Password?' she whispered.

'None of your business!' answered Grandma Maeve curtly.

Normally, Demelza would have been shocked to hear Grandma Maeve answering someone in such an impolite way, but what was happening in front of her was far more pressing. As if by magic, the branches surrounding the oak had begun to part, and a large grassy clearing stretched out before them for acres and acres!

All around its edges the trees were aglow with lights and jack-o'-lanterns. At its centre, a bonfire encircled with skulls cast an amber glow over the throng of masked people huddled around it. The night breeze brought with it a sweet, smoky smell – cinnamon and cloves and spice. It felt like the curtain had been drawn back on the most magnificent of stages.

'Grandma, what *is* this place?' Demelza asked, wonder-struck.

Grandma Maeve put an arm around her granddaughter as they stepped out into the clearing. 'This, my dear, is the Dance with Death. It's the Spectre Detectors' autumn gatherin' and the highlight of our calendar. It's always held in a different place, so we're lucky that this year it's so close to home. People have travelled from all over the country, and tonight, spectres and detectors alike will celebrate! Look!'

She pointed upwards, and it was only then that Demelza noticed the most impressive sight of all. The night sky was filled with hundreds upon hundreds of historical spectres, who flew among the stars like wisps of bright white smoke. Amazonian warriors floated next to Ancient Egyptians, Edwardian men mingled with Victorian ladies, and supernatural children from yesteryear hopscotched together through the moonlit clouds. It was a sight like no other and Demelza felt her eyes glistening. 'Where have they all come from? I thought spectres could only be summoned to help others?'

'These are the staff of the Quietus, my darlin'. They're all spectres that were summoned at some point in history, and for whatever reason didn't get sent back to Inn

Memoriam in time. The Spectral Sages keep them busy now. There's one of them over there, in fact.'

She pointed to the bonfire, where a dark-haired man had appeared, his face masked, his body cloaked. His skull-shaped mask was more ornate than any Demelza had seen before. It was adorned with feathers, shells, glass beads, bits of mirror and, as the firelight fell upon it, it sparkled like the most bounteous of treasure troves.

'Now remember,' said Grandma Maeve, 'it's very important to keep your mask on at all times. Even though everyone here is a Spectre Detector, we need to maintain our anonymity in case of intruders. You understand?'

Demelza answered vacantly – she wasn't really listening any more. There was so much going on around her and she was desperate to explore! Any thoughts of Ms Cardinal had completely vanished, all of her concerns suddenly felt like a distant memory. She'd be safe here.

'Let's go warm up and get something to eat,' said Grandma Maeve, pointing towards the bonfire. 'The feast is always something special. I hope you're hungry?'

She took her granddaughter's hand and led her through the jostling crowd. The air was thick with a smoky miasma, and all around, long, wooden banqueting tables were laden with scrumptious-looking food. Hot pies were nestled next to mounds of golden jacket potatoes, and buns decorated with currants were piled high in sugar-coated towers. Demelza's mouth began to water.

'I suggest we start here,' said Grandma Maeve, wandering over to a small pavilion. It was decorated with strings of golden pumpkins and gourds, and inside, a woman wearing a horned mask was ripping pieces from a dark loaf of bread.

'What *is* this?' asked Demelza, reaching for a piece and popping it into her mouth.

Grandma Maeve smiled. 'This, my dear, is one of our oldest recipes. It's what us Spectre Detectors call Bread of the Dead, and it's a very special food indeed.'

'*Yuuuuuck!*' Demelza nearly spat out her mouthful. 'You mean . . . it's made from *dead* people?'

Grandma Maeve chuckled. 'Oh no, don't be daft! It's just a symbolic name. It's called Bread of the Dead because we eat it to remember everyone who has passed.'

Demelza let out a sigh of relief as she took another piece of the loaf and contemplated a plate of familiar-looking chocolates, but as she spotted the trays of ladyfingers on the next table she could only hope that their name was purely symbolic too.

As the night progressed, the clearing filled with music. A small band of spectres played jigs on fiddles, bells and whistles and the crowd danced merrily around the bonfire. Flagons of Howling Jack – a honey mead so strong that even the tiniest whiff was enough to make Demelza dizzy – were passed around and swigged in abundance. Grandma Maeve must have had at least a litre's worth, and soon enough she'd flung her walking stick into the trees as she and Demelza tapped their feet to the music.

'I think I'll just go and get some more pudding, Grandma,' Demelza said after a particularly fast-paced dance led by the spectre of an ancient samurai warrior named Toyotomi. 'This dancing malarkey is hungry work!'

'That's your third helping, ain't it?' said Grandma Maeve, ruffling her granddaughter's hair. 'But I suppose it's good to see a young girl with such an appetite. Be quick, though, and come straight back.'

'Will do!' said Demelza, and off she skipped across the clearing to the dessert table. She was just picking up a bowl of delicious-looking treacle sponge and custard when something caught her eye. Over in the trees at the edge of the clearing, branches were stirring and an owl suddenly launched from its nest with a shrill hoot.

There was a flash of movement.

A crunch of footsteps.

A cough.

Demelza edged forward, and as she squinted through the darkness, her dessert bowl fell from her fingertips.

Even though the trees were shrouded in shadow, the light spilling from the bonfire was just enough to illuminate a pair of eyes hidden under a pointed hood.

Someone was watching.

CHAPTER 18
Firecrackers

With her heart in her throat, Demelza careered back across the clearing as quick as a flash. Even though she hadn't seen the watcher, it *had* to be the Snatcher. Ms Cardinal had followed them here, just as she'd feared!

Not daring to look back even for a second, Demelza bounded over to Grandma Maeve, breathless. 'Grandma, Grandma!' she panted, tugging at the old woman's cloak. 'Over there! Look!'

'Excuse me, young lady!' snapped Grandma Maeve. 'What have I told you about interruptin' when I'm in the middle of talking to someone? It's very rude!' She turned back to the spectre of the wild-haired cave woman who floated beside her. 'I'm sorry about that, Edwina, you were saying . . . ?'

'Grandma, you don't understand!' Demelza persisted. She snatched a quick glance to the edge of the clearing, and to her horror the hooded figure was still there. 'We're being watched! In the trees! I think it's the Snatcher!'

Grandma Maeve turned with a huff. 'Demelza, if this is one of your practical jokes I'll—'

She didn't finish her sentence.

As she clocked what Demelza was pointing at, a sharp gasp came from behind her golden mask. 'Demelza, wait here and don't move!' she ordered, and within an instant she'd run into the crowd and was screaming at the top of her voice. 'Intruder! Intruder!' she cried, her arms flailing in the air. 'Intruder in the trees!'

All around, faces were suddenly awash with panic. Within seconds, the clearing was a whirlwind of Spectre Detectors, all packing up their possessions and trying to locate family members and friends. People began to copy Grandma Maeve's words and soon shouts of 'Intruder' echoed around the clearing.

Caught up in the scramble of arms and legs, Demelza looked around, not knowing what to do. This was all her fault. She'd caused all of this!

'Spectre Detectors!' bellowed the Sage she'd seen earlier. He'd climbed atop a table near the bonfire and was striking the wood with his foot. 'Pack up your things immediately and leave not a speck of evidence! Keep your apprentices close! Spectres, return to the Quietus!'

The sound of feet trampling across the cold ground rang through the air as Spectre Detectors fled in all directions, like a colony of ants. Spectres began to disappear too, speeding off through the trees like bright white comets.

It was then that Demelza heard the scream.

She spun around and saw the hooded figure pelting across the clearing with something bundled under its arm. Demelza pushed her way through the moving throng of people and gasped. The *something* was a child – an apprentice Spectre Detector, probably only a little younger than herself! Her hair was red and curly, and her mask had fallen from her face, revealing pale, freckled skin. She was writhing around and yelping in fright.

Demelza scanned the jostling crowd for assistance, trying to catch someone's attention, but it was a tornado of chaos. Grandma Maeve was nowhere to be seen either. 'Help!' she called into the crowd, but under the tumult of the exodus, her cries were useless.

What now? She couldn't leave the young girl in the hands of Ms Cardinal! In the hands of a potential killer! She *had* to do something, and fast.

Demelza set her jaw and pushed her way through the stampede. With no time to lose she grabbed one of the lanterns from the base of the bonfire. It was crackling and hissing ferociously now, smoke twisting from its flames in dark feathery fronds. Demelza took a deep breath, and sheltering the lantern from the wind, pelted as fast as she could in the direction of the hooded figure.

Across the grass she ran, the night wind whipping through her hair. At first, Ms Cardinal's strides were long and fast, but the weight of the struggling girl began to slow her down. It didn't take Demelza long to catch up, and soon she was only a few metres away.

But what now? There was no way she could bring down an adult all on her own. Especially one whose favourite pastime was murdering young Spectre Detectors . . .

But then she remembered!

Still running, she reached to the bottom of her satchel and pulled out one of her Fantastic Fizzing Firecrackers. Its cylindrical shape was smooth in her palm, and with a trembling hand she held its wick to the flame of her lantern. It ignited in a flash of sherbet-like orange, and with all the strength she could muster, Demelza propelled it through the night air.

BOOOOM!

It landed at Ms Cardinal's feet, exploding with a crackling shower of sparks. She fell to the ground, the young Detector tumbling from her grip.

'Quick!' shrieked Demelza, beckoning to the girl frantically as Ms Cardinal lay, dazed. 'Get over here! Run!'

With tears and snot streaming down her face, the girl scampered through the grass on her hands and knees. She cowered behind Demelza, trembling uncontrollably.

'What's your name?' asked Demelza, not taking her eyes off Ms Cardinal for a second.

'It's . . . it's Hazel,' sobbed the girl.

'OK, Hazel, don't worry. My name's Demelza. You're safe with me. No one's going to hurt you now.'

But Ms Cardinal had already begun to stir, and was pulling herself up. As she looked around for an escape route, Demelza stepped forward. 'Don't move!' she hollered, trying to sound as fearless as she could. 'I know who you are! I have more explosives and I'm not afraid to use them!'

Just as she was reaching into her satchel for another firecracker, she was jostled out of the way. Two burly Spectre Detectors in bronze masks came rushing past, each yielding flaming torches. Ms Cardinal instantly started to run away.

'STAY WHERE YOU ARE!' shouted one of the Spectre Detectors.

'YOU WON'T GET AWAY WITH THIS!' bellowed the other.

As they gave chase and disappeared into the darkness, Demelza dropped to the floor. She gulped in deep lungfuls of air, trying to calm herself. This had all been her fault. *She'd* led Ms Cardinal to the biggest gathering of Spectre Detectors, and a young girl had almost been taken as a result. She was in so much trouble.

Hazel pulled her knees into her chest, shivering.

'Are you OK?' asked Demelza, taking off her coat and wrapping it around the girl's shoulders.

Hazel nodded. 'Y-y-yes, I think so. Thank you for helping me.'

Demelza smiled. 'Well, us redheads have to stick together!' she said, nodding to Hazel's curly auburn hair, which was nearly the same shade as her own.

'There they are!' came a sudden shout from behind them. 'I see them!'

The girls turned to find a group of Spectre Detectors hurrying towards them, led by the Spectral Sage Demelza had seen earlier and a woman wearing a carved bone mask.

'Mummy!' squealed Hazel, leaping to her feet and

tossing Demelza her coat.

The woman ran forward with arms outstretched, scooping her daughter into her bosom.

Hazel began to cry again, clutching tightly to her mother's neck like a bear cub.

'Oh, my precious girl,' said her mother, stroking her daughter's face and wiping away her tears. '*Shhh*, *shhh*, don't worry. Mummy's here now. Daddy too.' After a few moments Hazel's mother passed her daughter to her husband and turned to Demelza. 'My dear girl, thank you so much! You saved our daughter's life! How can we ever repay you?'

'It's . . . it's OK,' replied Demelza, suddenly lost for words. She shrugged on her coat and fiddled with the cuff. 'Anyone would have done the same. It was nothing.'

'Nothing? NOTHING?'

Grandma Maeve came striding forward, her voice harsh and her body visibly shaking. 'Demelza, what on earth was you thinkin', runnin' off like that? You could have been killed!'

'I-I-' stuttered Demelza, a tightness spreading across her chest. 'I thought that it was the right thing to do. I thought that—'

'You didn't think! That's the problem! YOU DIDN'T

THINK AT ALL!' Grandma Maeve burst into tears, her masked face falling into her hands. 'Don't you ever, *ever* do anything like that again, you hear me? I was so frightened. I thought I was gonna lose you.'

Demelza looked to the ground. 'I'm sorry, Grandma. I just wanted to help. That girl was terrified. I couldn't leave her.'

Grandma Maeve sighed deeply as she drew Demelza apart from the rest of the group. 'I know, my darlin'. And you was ever so brave. But that person was the Snatcher – did you think you could fight them on your own?'

Demelza ran her hands through her hair. Even though she knew it would mean getting into lots more trouble, she couldn't keep her suspicions quiet any longer. She *had* to tell Grandma Maeve about Ms Cardinal. She'd waited too long already.

'Grandma, I think I know who it was,' she began.

'Oh?' said Grandma Maeve. 'You managed to get a glimpse of them?'

'No, but I think . . .' Demelza faltered, not knowing how to come out with it. 'I think it's Ms Cardinal.'

Grandma Maeve scoffed. 'Oh, Demelza, don't be ridiculous! This ain't no time for larkin' around.'

'I'm serious!' protested Demelza. 'Ms Cardinal got hold

of my notebook in assembly yesterday and saw some doodles that I'd done of the summoning chamber. Then later on I heard her talking about me on the phone, saying something about *finally getting what she wanted*. She must have followed us here. I'm sorry, I should have told you earlier, I know.'

Grandma Maeve's eyes widened and Demelza braced herself, expecting the worst. She'd have her soldering iron confiscated, there'd be no more pancakes for breakfast, and worst of all, she'd let her grandma down.

But the old woman put a hand on Demelza's shoulder and smiled. 'My darlin', I appreciate you tellin' me all this, but that definitely wasn't Ms Cardinal out there. I know she's a bit of an old battleaxe but she ain't a kidnapper. And you ain't exactly a model student – she was probably talking about you to another teacher or somethin'.'

Demelza frowned, confused. 'But, Grandma, the things she was saying, she—'

'She ain't our culprit,' Grandma Maeve cut in. 'That vivid imagination of yours has been workin' in overdrive again. Now come on, let's get you home. It's been a long night.'

Demelza sighed, and as they trekked back through the forest with some of the other Spectre Detectors, she couldn't help thinking about Grandma Maeve's reaction to her revelation. Why hadn't she taken it seriously? She ran through the conversation she'd overheard again and again. Ms Cardinal had definitely been talking about spectre detecting. She had definitely said, 'I've waited years for this and now I might finally get what I want.'

It wasn't just her imagination. She knew it wasn't.

CHAPTER 19
Boris and Gregor

Demelza awoke with Grandma Maeve's hands on her shoulders, shaking her from her sleep.

'Demelza, you have to get up!' she hissed. 'Quickly, out of bed!'

Demelza rubbed her eyes. The blurry shape of her grandmother was standing over her. She was in her nightdress, a candle illuminating a face full of panic.

'Grandma . . .' Demelza groaned, putting on her spectacles before looking at her bedside clock. It was 4.15 a.m. 'What's wrong?.'

Grandma shot a glance towards the attic window and brought her voice down to an urgent whisper. 'Someone's tryin' to get in. We have to hide!'

'What? Who is it?'

'Demelza, there's no time for questions,' Grandma

insisted, backing towards the attic door. 'We could be in danger! Now come on!'

With adrenalin suddenly shooting through her veins, Demelza jumped out of bed. Was it the Snatcher? Had Ms Cardinal followed them home from the Dance with Death?

She quickly pulled Archimedes from his cage, the little mouse wriggling as he was put into her pyjama pocket.

Demelza scampered downstairs behind Grandma Maeve, and on the landing the pair knelt down and peered through the wooden spindles of the bannister. Demelza's body stiffened in an instant. Through the smoked glass of the front door she could see two shadowy figures walking up the garden path. Had Ms Cardinal brought someone with her?

'Grandma, what shall we do?' she whispered.

'You need to hide, quickly!' hissed Grandma Maeve. She handed Demelza her candle and pointed downstairs. 'Hide somewhere in the summoning chamber and don't come out until I say so.'

'But, Grandma, what about you? I can't leave you here—'

'Don't worry about me,' interrupted Grandma. She put a trembling hand on Demelza's shoulder and looked deep into her eyes. 'I'll come and join you, don't worry. But if this *is* the Snatcher, then I need to try and get a glimpse of them.'

The latch of the front door began to rattle. There was the pounding of fists on the glass. A heavily booted foot kicked against the front door . . .

'Go!' hissed Grandma Maeve. '*Go now!*'

Demelza jumped to her feet. She had no choice but to follow Grandma's order.

With rasping breath, she ripped down the staircase, through the kitchen and out into the garden. The night was bitter and she could feel the dampness of dew seeping through her bed socks as she ran. Archimedes had curled himself up into a ball in her breast pocket and his tiny heart was pounding next to hers.

Demelza fled through the trapdoor, pulling it closed behind her. Inside the summoning chamber she looked around frantically for somewhere to hide. She moved her candle around, using its pale glow as a spotlight.

Under the table?

Behind a cabinet?

No, too obvious!

Her only hope was to tuck herself away inside the pantry at the back of the room and pray that in the darkness its door wouldn't be visible. She took a quick look over her shoulder before scampering inside, leaving the door ajar just enough to hear if anyone was coming.

It was stifling inside, the heady scent of Grandma's spices, herbs and balsams oppressively potent. Demelza sank into a corner and held her knees close to her chest. She could feel her pulse racing. She hated not having her satchel full of inventions with her – she felt unprotected, unprepared. Why hadn't she picked it up?

Trying to calm herself, she started to count the number of cinnamon sticks in a large jar in front of her. *One . . . two . . . three . . . four . . .*

Would she be found down here?

Five . . . six . . . seven . . .

Would she be kidnapped?

Eight . . . nine . . . ten—

A crashing sound erupted from the greenhouse above. Feet hammered across the floor and Demelza could hear the muffled din of deep male voices. Who were they? She couldn't make out what they were saying but they sounded angry, and she snuffed out her candle in anticipation of them venturing downstairs.

'Oi! Gregor, over here!' came a grunt from above. 'Look what I've found! It's a trapdoor!'

Demelza gasped in horror. They'd discovered the summoning chamber!

All of a sudden there was the clang of boots on metal,

and as softly as she could, Demelza shuffled towards the crack in the cupboard door. Grandma Maeve might have told her to hide, but she wanted to see who these men were. She *needed* to. Were they working for Ms Cardinal?

With terror rippling through her, she watched as an ape-like figure lowered himself through the hatch, followed by another man, slightly smaller in stature. When they reached the bottom of the ladder they flicked on their torches, and Demelza winced as their faces were uplit, like something out of a nightmare.

The taller man was bald with a neck as thick as a tree trunk, and his arms bulged from his shirt like slabs of sinewy roast meat. His face was pock-marked and two sharp snaggle teeth protruded over his upper lip, like those of a rottweiler. The other man was shorter but no less frightening, with greasy hair and eyes so bloodshot that the whites were almost completely red. There was mushed-up food stuck in his teeth.

Demelza gasped. There was something strangely familiar about these men. She was sure she'd seen them before, but couldn't for the life of her place where.

'This must be where they do them magic spells!' said the taller man, sniffing around the room like a wild beast. His voice was low and guttural, as if he were wrenching his words from the very pit of his throat. 'Turn it over, Gregor! Leave no place unchecked.'

'All right, bruv!' Gregor replied.

And without even pausing for a moment, the pair began their attack. With every *crash* and every *bang*, Demelza's stomach turned, and she could feel Archimedes wriggling around in her pocket, his little body vibrating with fear.

'Hey, look at this, Boris,' said Gregor, putting one of Grandma's masks to his face and stomping around like a monster. 'It's like a better lookin' version of you!'

'Oi! Give me that!' shouted Boris, wrenching the mask from his brother's hand before giving him a clout over the head. 'We've got work to do, stupid! Especially as it was *you* who snatched the wrong girl in the forest earlier and made the boss so angry. If you hadn't made such a big mistake in the first place then we wouldn't have had to come 'ere at all.'

Gregor frowned. 'Well, all kids seem the same to me – small and smelly. And besides, she had red hair, didn't she? It was hard to tell who was who with those stupid masks they all had on.'

'There's always an excuse with you! Now let's hurry up and find Demelza. I'm starvin'.'

Demelza clenched her fists to her mouth to stop herself

from gasping. *Somersaulting satellites!* Gregor was the hooded figure at the Dance with Death, and he'd been attempting to kidnap *her* all along. So, these brothers must be working for Ms Cardinal! How else would they have known to pinpoint her? How would they have known her name? Ms Cardinal was the only person, except for Grandma Maeve and Percy, who knew about her new powers.

Demelza desperately wanted to fling open the door and stop the brothers in their tracks. She knew that would be reckless, though – these men might sound stupid, but they were obviously extremely vicious.

'Well, it don't look like she's 'ere,' said Boris after a while. 'Let's go and 'ave one last look up in the cottage. But if we don't find her it's gonna 'ave to be Plan B.'

'And after that we can raid the pantry!' said Gregor, licking his dry lips. 'I fink I saw a nice piece of pork pie in there earlier.'

The two men retreated, and as they made for the ladder Demelza breathed a huge sigh of rclicf. She leant back against the shelf, allowing her body to relax for a second. But as her legs stretched out, her foot made contact with one of the glass jars on the floor and—

SMAAAASH!

'Hang on! What was that?' came Gregor's voice. 'I fink I heared somefink back in there.' He scuttled back into the summoning chamber and pointed in the direction of the store cupboard. 'There's someone in there!'

Demelza's chest tightened and she edged backwards. It suddenly felt as if there was no door between her and the men at all, as if Gregor's bulging arm was a gun pointing directly to her head. She frantically looked around for an escape route, but there was nowhere to turn.

'Come on, little girl,' said Boris. 'You don't need to hide. We just wanna have a little chat, that's all.'

'Yeah, why don't you come out?' added Gregor, rubbing his hands together. 'We've got a nice little dolly-wolly for you to play with.'

On any other occasion, Demelza would have made it perfectly clear that she'd rather eat her own eyeballs than play with stupid dolls, but she felt that perhaps now wasn't the time to be self-righteous. Instead, she inched backwards to the large sack of flour which was slumped against the furthest wall, and cowered behind it.

'OK,' said Gregor. 'I'm gonna give you to the count of ten, and if you don't come out nicely, I'm comin' to getcha. One . . . two . . . three . . .'

Demelza's stomach turned as she listened to the sinister

pleasure in the man's voice. Realistically, she only had two options – either stay put and *definitely* be kidnapped, or try and make a run for it and *possibly* be kidnapped.

'Four . . . five . . . six . . . erm . . . what comes next, bruv?'

'Seven, you bozo!'

Demelza raised herself on to her haunches and breathed deeply. As soon as Gregor opened the door she'd make a dash for it. It was her only hope.

'Eight . . . nine . . .TEN! Ready or not, here I come!'

Footsteps approached and a large hairy hand reached around the door. With blood pounding in her ears, Demelza prepared to move.

But all of a sudden she felt something scratching against her skin. She glanced down to find Archimedes clawing his way out of her pocket, and before she could push him back he'd scrambled down her body on to her trouser leg. 'Archimedes, no!' she whispered, trying to make a grab for him. 'Come back!'

It was too late.

The little mouse slipped through the crack in the door, his long pink tail twisting in the air, as if waving a final goodbye. Demelza's face fell into her hands. *Archimedes, what have you done?*

Then something surprising happened.

One of the brothers began to scream.

'ARGHH! GET IT OFF ME! GET IT OFF ME! ARGHHHHHHHH!'

Demelza quickly put an eye back to the crack in the door, and couldn't help but choke back a laugh. There, flailing his arms around as if doing some kind of celtic jig, was Gregor, and gnawing down on the little finger of his right hand was Archimedes!

'Help me, you idiot!' he cried to his brother. 'Get this rat off me! It's massive!' The colour had drained from his cheeks, and his voice had risen so many octaves that it had taken on the falsetto tones of a church choirboy.

'I ain't touchin' it!' said Boris, leaping to the other side of the room. 'It might have rabies or somefink!'

'Bleedin' 'eck!' cried Gregor. With a violent jolt of his beefy shoulder he catapulted Archimedes across the room, where he hit the opposite wall with a thump.

Demelza's hands shot to her mouth, her eyes stinging with the saltiness of tears.

'There – that showed 'im!' stuttered Gregor, cracking his knuckles as he edged proudly towards the limp creature. He tapped Archimedes with the tip of his boot, making sure that he wasn't moving. 'No vermin messes with me. Now let's get outta here. The girl's obviously not here,

166

and this place is givin' me the creeps.'

The two brothers scrambled back up the ladder, and as soon as she heard them leave the greenhouse, Demelza flung open the store-cupboard door. 'Archimedes!' she cried, running across the room and scooping the little ball of fur into her arms. 'Oh, please be OK! Please be OK . . .'

At first the animal didn't move. His eyes were closed, his pink tongue hanging from the side of his mouth like a tiny limp sausage. But as Demelza stroked the fur on his back, his whiskers began to twitch and he eventually let out a muted *squeak*.

'Oh, Archimedes, thank goodness!' said Demelza, giving him a kiss on his nose. 'You definitely deserve some extra-crunchy carrots for breakfast. But first, let's go and find Grandma Maeve.'

She made to stand, but Archimedes had begun to wriggle again, and with a little yelp he hopped from Demelza's grasp once more and dashed across the stone floor. His whiskers were guiding him like the prongs of a divining rod, and soon enough he stopped at the bottom of the ladder. His nose quivered upwards towards the rungs, as if he were trying to tell Demelza something.

'What? What is it, boy?' she asked, striding forward and bending down. 'What have you—?'

Demelza stopped mid-sentence. There, dangling from a piece of black ribbon which had caught on one of the lower rungs, was a key!

Demelza quickly untangled it and let the key hang in front of her eyes. It was aged and weighty, with two crescent moons engraved into its rusted metal. 'They must have dropped it,' she whispered excitedly. 'Those two buffoons have left a vital piece of evidence! Ha!'

She popped Archimedes on to her shoulder and when she was certain that the coast was clear, she ran back across the garden.

'Grandma,' she whispered, opening the door to the kitchen. 'Grandma Maeve, it's me . . .'

But no sooner had Demelza stepped inside than she came to a halt.

The kitchen looked as if it had been whipped up by a tornado. Pictures had been ripped from the walls, chairs lay in pieces, and Grandma's recipe books were strewn across the floor like paper birds. The pantry had been completely ransacked, its shelves now bare.

Demelza inched forward slowly, crunching across an icy tundra of shattered glass. A broom lay across her path, and she picked it up, ready to bring it down on to someone's head if necessary.

'Grandma? Shiver?' she whispered, making her way into the hallway. But there was no sign of anyone – human or dog. Her voice was trembling, barely there. 'Grandma. If you're here, please say something, please–'

Then she saw it.

On the floor, snapped in two, was Grandma's walking stick.

Chapter 20

The Ransom Note

Under the broken walking stick was a note. As if in a dream, Demelza unfolded it and read:

FOR THE ATTENTION OF DEMELZA CLOCK,

IF YOU WANT TO SEE YOUR GRANDMOTHER AND DOG ALIVE AGAIN, COME TO SOURBANK BRIDGE AT 11 P.M. ON 31 OCTOBER.

BE PREPARED TO PERFORM THE CONJURING OF RESURRECTION.

DO NOT CONTACT THE POLICE, AND COME ALONE. FAILURE TO COMPLY WITH THESE INSTRUCTIONS WILL RESULT IN VERY UNPLEASANT CONSEQUENCES FOR BOTH YOUR GRANDMOTHER AND YOUR CANINE COMPANION.

Demelza's stomach turned. The words in front of her began to swell in and out of focus and she felt as if she might vomit at any second. This was the Plan B that Boris had talked about earlier! Plan B was to kidnap Grandma Maeve and Shiver! To use them as leverage!

'Oh, Grandma . . .' Demelza cried, dropping to the floor. 'Grandma, what have I done?'

All of her worst fears had come true. Ms Cardinal had struck and it was all her fault. Why had she taken that note-book to school? Why had she drawn those stupid, stupid pictures? Why hadn't she made Grandma believe her suspicions?

'HELP! HELP!'

Demelza flinched. A muffled cry was coming from the corner nearest the front door. She turned to look, but all she could see was the messy pile of coats and hats and scarves which had been thrown from the hooks on the wall.

'Who is it?' she demanded. 'Who's there?'

'It's me!' came the muted voice once more. 'On the floor. Underneath the clothes!'

Demelza groped her way along the hallway and began to rifle through the mess. She pulled back a blue anorak and there, looking up at her, was Lord Balthazar.

'Oh, my goodness!' Demelza yelped, picking up the Talking Head. As she dusted off his scalp, he let out a loud groan. There was a long crack creeping upwards from his left eye socket and a few of his teeth were missing. 'Lord Balthazar, are you OK?'

'Oh, the pain, the pain!' he moaned. 'My poor, poor head! One minute I was in the middle of a lovely dream about having a body and the next I was on the floor.'

Demelza set Lord Balthazar on a side table. She couldn't think straight, fear and worry draining all of her brain-power. Halloween was tomorrow! What should she do? Set out to find Grandma now? Or was it wiser just to follow the instructions on the ransom note and go to Sourbank Bridge tomorrow night?

Just then, the telephone rang. Demelza glanced at the hall clock and was shocked to see it was gone 7 a.m. – she must have been hiding in the store cupboard for far longer than she'd thought.

She quickly righted herself. Maybe it was Grandma Maeve? Maybe she'd managed to escape and had found a phone box somewhere? All of a sudden, Demelza's stomach was a tinderbox waiting for a spark of hope, and she sprinted to the sitting room to pick up the receiver.

'Hello?'

'Oh hello, Demelza dear,' came a crackled reply. 'Mr Barnabas here. Sorry for calling so early, but I'm going to be up near your cottage doing some deliveries in a while, and I was wondering if your grandma had any errands that she might want me to run for her? Any groceries she wanted picking up, any letters that she might need posting? Maybe I could speak to her quickly?'

Demelza gulped, caught unawares. 'Erm . . . no . . . my grandma's not available at the moment, Mr Barnabas. She's . . . erm . . . in bed with flu.'

'Oh dear,' replied Mr Barnabas. 'That's not good. Maybe I should come over with a few bits and pieces to make her feel better—'

'NO!' interrupted Demelza, with a force that she instantly regretted. 'I mean, *no, thank you*. It's highly contagious and I'd hate for you to get ill too. In fact, I think I can hear Grandma coughing now. I'd better go. Thanks for phoning, Mr Barnabas!'

Demelza quickly put down the phone and ran her hands through her hair. She knew that Mr Barnabus meant well, but she couldn't risk him coming over and snooping around. If he found out what had happened to Grandma Maeve then the news would be around the village in no time. She'd already revealed the Spectre Detector secret once, she couldn't do so again! Besides, who knew how Ms Cardinal would react?

No, Demelza had to deal with this by herself. She had to come up with a plan of action!

'Where are you going?' called Lord Balthazar as she dashed upstairs. 'You can't leave an injured soldier behind!'

'Don't worry,' Demelza replied without stopping, 'I'll be back.'

She bolted up to the attic and put Archimedes in his cage before delving into her satchel for a notebook and pen. She always found it helpful to write things down when coming up with a strategy. She was just rummaging around in the inside pocket when her hand brushed across what felt like a bundle of envelopes. *Oh no!* The letters that Grandma Maeve had asked her to post at the start of the week. She'd completely forgotten to put them in the postbox!

Demelza wiped her sweaty palms down her dressing gown and unpicked the twine that bound the bundle together. Most of the letters she discarded immediately – bills, orders, a birthday card to her Swedish penpal – but one envelope caught Demelza's eye. It was plum coloured and the address was written in golden calligraphy which looped and swirled like the path of a kite:

Department of Inhuman Resources,
TQ - East England Branch,
Pitchfork Passage,
Bury Rattlesborough,
England

With her brow furrowing, Demelza reread the address, and then for a third time. What on earth was the Department of Inhuman Resources? And what did TQ stand for?

It was only when Demelza turned the envelope over and found it sealed with a blob of purple wax embossed with a skull that it clicked.

Of course!

TQ was The Quietus, the Spectre Detector governing body that Grandma Maeve had been a member of for over sixty years. She should go there! Didn't Grandma say they were there to help out with any Spectre Detector trouble? Surely one of the Sages would be able to help – they'd definitely want to know what Ms Cardinal had done.

With revived determination pushing her forward like a juggernaut, Demelza grabbed the walkie-talkie from her desk and pressed its button. 'Clever Cog to the Comic Book Kid. Do you copy? Over.'

There was a pause before Percy's sleepy voice came through the airwaves. 'Demelza? Is that you?'

'Yes, it's me,' Demelza replied curtly, wanting to avoid any menial chit-chat. She sat on her bed and brought her voice down to a whisper. 'Now listen carefully. You need to sneak out of your house and meet me outside the village hall as soon as possible. Tell no one where you're going. I repeat, tell no one. Over.'

CHAPTER 21
Pitchfork Alley

By the time Percy had run down to the village hall an hour later, the morning sun was staining the sky in pinks and reds and oranges. He was wearing at least ten items of woollen knitwear, including a scarf, cardigan, mittens and oversized fluffy earmuffs. He came to a standstill, his eyes poking out from under the brim of a bobble hat.

'Nice outfit!' said Demelza, looking him up and down. 'I forgot that we lived in the Arctic. I hope you didn't have to wrestle any polar bears on your way here?'

Percy grimaced and poked out his tongue. 'You know I'm unwell, you know I have to keep wrapped up.'

'But you managed to sneak out OK? Your dad didn't see you?'

Percy pulled off his mittens with his teeth, revealing

(much to Demelza's amusement) another pair of gloves beneath. 'No, he's away on business so Fräulein von Winkle's looking after me. She helped herself to a bottle of red wine from the cellar last night so I think she'll be asleep for a while! But what are we doing here anyway? Why are you up so early?'

Demelza felt a sickening lurch in her tummy. 'Percy, something awful has happened,' she said, looking round to check that they weren't being watched. 'Something really, really awful. And I don't think I can fix it on my own.'

Percy's face dropped. 'Is it to do with Ms Cardinal?'

Demelza nodded.

'Oh no! Oh, Demelza, what's happened?'

Demelza gestured to her bike. Lord Balthazar was sitting in a bed of bubble wrap in the front basket, a plaster covering the crack along his cheek. 'Hop on. I'll tell you everything en route. We need to get to Bury Rattlesborough as soon as possible, and we haven't got much time.'

Percy nodded and swung his legs over the back seat. Putting her foot on the pedal, Demelza pushed off and the pair sped down the cobbled high street.

As they rode, Demelza filled Percy in on everything – the Dance with Death, Boris and Gregor, the ransom note, Grandma's kidnapping – and by the time they'd reached the outskirts of Little Penhallow, Percy had forced her to come to a stop.

'Demelza, this is terrible!' he whimpered, jumping off the bicycle and distancing himself from his friend. He began to fiddle with the tassels of his long scarf, pulling at the bits of wool. 'You *have* to tell someone about Ms Cardinal. We should go to the police immediately!'

'NO!' snapped Demelza. 'I told you what it said on the ransom note. And besides, I've figured where we need to go to get help. It's called the Quietus. It's the Spectre Detectors' headquarters. They'll know what to do.'

Percy groaned. 'Oh, Demelza, not more weird ghostly stuff, please! This could be really dangerous. Why don't we just go back to my house and telephone my dad? I know he's a bit old fashioned but I'm sure he'll underst—'

'Your dad?' interrupted Demelza, her body tight with anger. 'Are you serious? What's he going to be able to do to help? He probably doesn't even believe in spectres!' Demelza's voice had risen considerably and she knew from Percy's trembling chin that he was upset. She took a second to calm herself before talking again. 'Look, I'm sorry for snapping, but this is my only hope. I have to get to the Quietus as soon as possible. Now, are you coming with me or not?'

Percy shuffled nervously under Demelza's gaze before nodding. 'Yes, of course I am. Grandma Maeve needs us.'

The pair hopped back on to the bicycle and Demelza looked into the front basket. 'Are you OK in there, Lord Balthazar?'

Lord Balthazar groaned. 'Yes, but could you please cycle a little bit slower from now on? Going over pot holes at high speed is not conducive for a smooth ride, especially when one's countenance is as prone to fractures as mine!'

It didn't take long to get to the village of Bury Rattlesborough, and when they reached the main street, Demelza stopped and looked around. It was a pokey-looking place, and apart from a handful of run-down shops and a dilapidated train station, it was almost deserted.

'So, I'm pretty sure that we need to be somewhere around here,' said Demelza, taking a pocket map from her satchel and unfolding it.

'Doesn't Lord Balthazar know where we're going?' asked Percy. 'Surely he's been to the Quietus before?'

Demelza shook her head. 'Talking Heads aren't meant to leave their apprentice's summoning chamber.'

Lord Balthazar coughed. 'The last time I had a social engagement, people were still travelling around by horse and carriage.'

Demelza let her fingers trail along the red, vein-like roads before gazing up. 'Ah, yes! Over there! I think I can see it.'

She pointed to a narrow alleyway on the other side of the road that would have barely been visible if not for the eerie yellow glow of the solitary street lamp that still illuminated its threshold. An ancient-looking street sign hung above it, the place name only just visible through the rust.

'The Quietus is down *there*?' said Percy, his voice quaking.

Demelza double-checked the address on the purple envelope and nodded. 'Yup. That's definitely it. Pitchfork Passage. Come on, let's go.'

Down the narrow alleyway they went, the weak morning light fading with every step they took. They crept past shadowy doorways and empty shop fronts, the air around them as thick and stale as a fog.

'Oh, Demelza, I don't like this,' Percy said. 'It's horrible. I want to go home!'

'Hear, hear!' agreed Lord Balthazar from the front basket of the bicycle. 'This is not a place for an English lord! Besides, shouldn't you be getting ready for school?'

'School? Somersaulting synchrotrons! There are more

important things to worry about right now,' said Demelza. 'Now buck up, the pair of you.' But despite her brave words, Demelza's heart was pounding fast.

The children ventured on, and soon enough they were standing in the shadows of a dark gothic building. It was extremely tall and extremely narrow, almost as if it had been forced upwards by the two buildings either side of it. All of its windows had been blacked out with thick curtains and there was a skull-shaped knocker hanging from the front door.

'I think we're here,' said Demelza, taking in every centimetre of the building. 'This is the Quietus – it must be!'

'Are you sure?' said Percy, cowering behind her. 'It doesn't look like the kind of place that helps people. It looks like the kind of place where Dracula might try and suck your blood.'

'I'm-I'm sure it'll be different inside,' Demelza replied, stepping forward. But even as the words came out of her mouth, she couldn't help feeling an overwhelming sense of foreboding. She hadn't been expecting a mug of hot milk and a cuddle on arrival, but this place definitely didn't feel as welcoming as she'd hoped. What were they letting themselves in for?

She stepped towards the door, and with a trembling hand rapped the skull-shaped knocker down hard. The sound of brass on brass echoed all around, bouncing off the brick walls like gunshots.

Nothing happened for a moment, then all of a sudden a letterbox-shaped hatch in the door was pulled open, and a pair of pale eyes appeared through the darkness.

'PASSWORD?' came a deep, rasping voice.

'Erm . . . Hello . . .' muttered Demelza. 'I wonder if you could help me please? My name's Demelza Clock, and I–'

'Password?' interrupted the voice. 'What's the password?'

Demelza shifted her weight from foot to foot. 'Well . . . I don't know the password . . . but this is very important. I really need to–'

The hatch was pulled shut, nearly trapping the tip of Demelza's nose in the process.

'*Owww!* Petrified pie charts!' she cursed, giving the door a sharp kick.

'Don't you know the password?' asked Percy. 'Didn't your grandma tell you?'

'Grandma Maeve never mentioned it. I guess she was waiting for me to finish my apprenticeship. What could it be?'

Percy swallowed. 'Well, I know what I'd choose if I had to have a password. Something that I'd love to eat if I was allowed. Strawberry gateau! Or possibly Victoria sponge . . . no, treacle tart!'

Demelza huffed. 'Not everyone thinks with their stomachs, Percy. I doubt the most powerful Spectre Detectors in the country were thinking of pudding when they were putting their security measures in place.' She looked to her bicycle basket. 'Any ideas, Lord Balthazar?'

The skull scoffed. 'SOS?'

Demelza rolled her eyes. She searched her mind, trying to recall any password that Grandma Maeve might have mentioned. Could it be the name of a famous spectre perhaps? Or an ingredient used in a summoning?

She was just about to give *minced blobfish brains* a go, when she remembered what Grandma Maeve had rudely said to the woman guarding the entrance to the Dance with Death.

'Well, what are you going to do?' asked Percy.

'*MIND YOUR OWN BUSINESS!*' exclaimed Demelza.

Percy's face soured. 'All right, grumpy pants, I was only asking . . .'

'No, you don't understand,' said Demelza. She jumped to her feet and wrapped viciously on the door once more.

'*Mind your own business!*' she shouted as soon as the hatch was open. 'The password is *mind your own business*!'

CHAPTER 22

Inside the Quietus

The front door groaned open, and a bald, thickset spectre floated forward, an eerie yellow light radiating from behind him. He was so tall that his scalp nearly touched the lintel above, and his back was hunched, as if two large boulders were nestling beneath his tunic. 'Enter,' he grunted, and beckoned to the children with a bony white finger.

With Percy at her heel and Lord Balthazar under her arm Demelza stepped inside and scampered to keep up with the doorman, who was already floating ahead with speed. He led them through a labyrinth of candlelit corridors, each swarming with historical spectres of all shapes and sizes. There was a Bronze Age woman with plaited hair, an Ancient Egyptian pharaoh, and a medieval knight wielding sword and shield. Then came a salty sailor with a wooden leg and a Native American chief adorned with feathers. Further ahead a Victorian chimney sweep was busy cleaning one of the many fireplaces, whistling cheerfully as he worked.

'Woooah!' said Percy, his mouth wide open as he took it all in. 'Real life ghosts!'

Demelza gave him a sharp elbow to the ribs and glared.

'Ouch!' he moaned, rubbing his side. 'What did you do that for?'

'Percy, we're trying to get these people to help us,' hissed Demelza. 'They're hardly going to cooperate if you're gawping like you're at a circus freak show! And I've told you before, it's *spectres*, not ghosts.'

'Keep up!' shouted the doorman from ahead, and Demelza quickly picked up her pace, not wanting to get on his bad side.

Before long they arrived at a large, circular hallway. Its walls were panelled with dark wood and the floor was tiled in purple, gold and black, with a large skull motif worked into the centre. Candles in little brass holders lined the walls, filling the space with a dim smoky glow, and narrow passages led off in every direction, like the beams of a shooting star.

'*Ahem!*'

A high-pitched cough came from across the floor and the children looked up. The spectre of a court jester was floating behind an ornate marble reception desk. He wore a diamond-patterned tunic, and a fool's hat adorned with bells sat atop his head. A huge oil painting hung on the wall behind him, depicting a Spectral Sage from yesteryear holding a polished human skull. In front of him was a bowl of toffees wrapped in shiny papers that looked as though they might have been bought from Mr Barnabas's shop.

'May I help you?' snapped the jester as the children approached. His voice was sharp and shrill, almost as if he was talking through his nostrils rather than out of his mouth. Demelza glanced down at the little placard on the desk, which bore the words *Harry Le Quin – Duty Manager*.

'Erm . . . yes . . . hello, Mr Le Quin . . . sir,' she said, trying to sound as assertive and grown-up as she could. 'I'd like to see one of the Spectral Sages, please.'

'Do you have an appointment?' replied Harry Le Quin. 'The Sages are very busy people.'

'Well . . . erm . . . no. But it's very important that I speak with one. You see I–'

'Your membership papers?' interrupted the jester.

Demelza gulped. 'Oh, I don't have any papers yet either.

I'm still an apprentice, you see. But I have a Talking Head. Surely that proves I'm not an imposter. She held up Lord Balthazar who tilted forward in her hands.

'Lord Balthazar III of Upper Loxworth at your service,' he said.

Le Quin rolled his eyes and muttered, 'Charmed, I'm sure,' before opening the large record book in front of him. He dipped a fountain pen in gold ink, and poised the nib on the page. 'The reason for your visit today?'

'It's an emergency,' said Demelza. 'Something awful has happened to my grandma and I need—'

Harry Le Quin butted in sharply. 'Does the emergency concern: a) an escaped spectre, b) a cracked crucible, c) a misplaced ghoulbox, or d) none of the above?'

Demelza's face dropped. This silly spectre obviously didn't understand the severity of her situation at all. 'None of the above!' she blurted out. 'My grandma's been kidnapped!'

The jester looked up from his notes, his lips pinched together as tight as a walnut. 'Kidnapped?' he scoffed. 'Well, that is indeed unusual. Are you quite certain that she hasn't just gone on holiday? Gone to get some peace and quiet?' He leant forward and smiled coldly. 'Emigrated to the Amazon, perhaps?'

'No!' snapped Demelza, her voice rising. 'I'm eleven years old! She wouldn't just go off on holiday without telling me. She's been kidnapped!'

Mr Le Quin sighed loudly and muttered something under his breath about not getting paid enough. 'And what is your grandmother's name?'

'Catchpole. Maeve Catchpole.'

The jester turned to a filing cabinet behind him and brought back a ledger emblazoned with the word 'Members'. He began to fan through the pages until he got to a section headed with the letter 'C'.

'Clatworthy . . . Clements . . . Clinton,' he muttered, trailing a calloused white finger down a list of names. 'Carson . . . Caruthers . . . Ah, here we are, Catchpole, you say?'

Demelza nodded, her body filling with hope. 'Can you help?'

Harry Le Quin took in the information written next to Grandma Maeve's name and shook his head. 'Well, unfortunately our records show that your grandmother hasn't actually re-pledged her allegiance to the Quietus this quarter.' The jester looked to the calendar on his desk. 'You see, her correspondence should have arrived with us yesterday at the very latest. That was the deadline. And no pledge of allegiance means no contact with any of the Sages.'

Demelza shook her head in disbelief. 'But . . . that can't be possible. Grandma Maeve's been a member of the Quietus all her life. There *has* to be some kind of mistake.'

The spectre shook his head. 'According to our records, we've received nothing from your grandmother expressing her wish to continue being part of the Quietus. And no membership means no assistance. Now, I suggest that you and that self-important skull of yours toddle off before I call security.'

Lord Balthazar let out a horrified harrumph. 'Self-important? Now listen here, you brute. I am an esteemed member of the British nobility, I'll have you know, and I will not tolerate some menial member of house-staff speaking to me in such a manner. Now let the girl see one of the Spectral Sages, at once!'

Demelza looked at the jester wide-eyed and pleaded, 'Please! I know my grandmother would have meant to re-pledge her allegiance. You *have* to trust me!'

'Trust is something to be gained over time,' said Harry Le Quin, looking down at his pocket watch. 'And unfortunately for you I'm due on my break in five minutes.' He slammed the members' book shut, and the sound echoed around the circular hall like a clap of thunder. 'Now, if that is all?'

Percy, who had been loitering nervously behind his friend, whispered, 'Come on, I think we should leave.'

'No! They *have* to help us!' said Demelza, her voice thickening. 'Something must have happened to my grandma's letter. Maybe it got filed away somewhere. Maybe it got lost in the–' Demelza's hand shot to her mouth and she froze. She felt the blood draining from her face. 'No! No . . . this can't be happening . . .'

'Demelza, what's wrong?' asked Percy.

Demelza started rummaging frantically through her satchel and from the very bottom she pulled out the plum-coloured envelope addressed to the Quietus that Grandma had asked her to post. She ripped it open, and there, written in her grandmother's unmistakably swirly handwriting, was her pledge of allegiance. It hadn't been lost at all. *She* had forgotten to post it!

'Look, I have it here!' said Demelza, waving the paper frantically at Harry Le Quin. 'My grandma *did* mean for you to get it, but I forgot to post it. This is all *my* fault!'

But Harry Le Quin shook his head. 'Rules are rules, I'm afraid, and I cannot compromise our security measures, especially at this time of year.' He rang a bell on the desk and the doorman appeared from the shadows. 'Brutus will show you out.'

'No!' objected Demelza. She felt the sting of tears in her eyes, panic flooding through her. 'You don't understand! I have to see one of the Sages! I need to help Grandma Maeve!'

As the gigantic doorman approached, Percy whispered, 'Demelza, seriously, we need to go. Come on, we'll think of another way to help your grandma, I promise.'

CHAPTER 23

Confronting
Ms Cardinal

'Are you sure you want to go and confront your headmistress straight away?' Percy called out from the back of Demelza's bicycle. She was peddling back down Pitchfork Alley at the speed of light, her mind set on Stricton Academy. 'Maybe you should calm down a bit.'

'No!' replied Demelza curtly. 'I should have stood up to her right from the start. Ms Cardinal was acting suspiciously and I should have followed my gut instinct! Time's running out!'

Demelza peddled furiously, using every bit of power in her legs. She was livid – livid with Harry Le Quin, livid with the Quietus, but mainly livid with herself. Why hadn't she just posted the bundle of letters when she'd been asked? There was no help available to Grandma Maeve from the

Sages and it was all down to her. All of a sudden, guilt opened the floodgates to a thousand memories of the times she'd had with her grandmother and tears began to well in Demelza's eyes, blurring her vision as if she were looking through a broken kaleidoscope.

'Demelza . . .' began Lord Balthazar from his spot in the front basket, but he was stopped in his tracks.

'Not now, Lord Balthazar,' Demelza snapped. 'I know what you're going to say, but I haven't got time for your "I told you so".'

'I was just going to ask if you were all right,' muttered the skull to himself, rejected. '*Ufff!* This day is going from bad to worse. It's on par with the time that my valet mistook my double-breasted jacket for my tailcoat.'

Demelza picked up the pace, and once they'd reached the grey school building she rested her bicycle against the railings. With the pupils already in lessons, the playground was completely empty. Percy looked up at the spiked turrets and gargoyles with a shudder.

'Well, I never thought I'd say it,' he said. 'But maybe being kept at home with Fräulein von Winkle all this time wasn't such a bad option after all. Is this place a school or a prison?'

'Wait till you see inside,' said Demelza. 'I've seen

dentist surgeries that are more inviting.'

Percy looked back up at the tall, iron gates and rattled them. 'But it's all locked up. How are we going to get over? The last time I checked I was neither a spider nor a flying superhero.'

'I've already thought of that,' said Demelza, plonking her satchel down on to the ground. 'Professor Demelza Clock has an answer for everything!' She rummaged through her satchel before pulling out a length of thick rope with a two-pronged hook attached to its end. 'My newly improved Clandestine Climbing Claw! Perfect for the everyday cat burglar and school trespasser. Now, watch yourself!'

Percy jumped back and Demelza swung the contraption around her head a few times before lassoing it through the air. The hooked end latched over the top of the metal gate with a ringing clang.

'Bullseye!' Demelza exclaimed, pulling the rope taught. 'Follow me!'

'*Ahem*, what about me?' came Lord Balthazar's nasal tones from the front basket of the bicycle. 'Not all of us have the desire, nor the limbs, to pull ourselves up a twenty foot vertical incline.'

'Don't worry, Lord Balthazar,' said Demelza, knowing

full well that what she was about to say would rile the Talking Head even further. 'I wouldn't expect such an *esteemed member of the aristocracy* to endure such a task. I thought I'd just throw you over instead. I've always been good at netball . . .'

The skull's jaw dropped.

'Only joking!' said Demelza, suddenly feeling like a bit of a meanie, and she lifted him into her satchel before beginning her ascent.

All was quiet inside the school as Demelza led the way up the gloomy winding staircase to the third floor. She'd been sent to the headmistress's office so many times that she could have found it with her eyes closed.

They stopped at the dark-wood door bearing the words *Ms Margaret Cardinal – Headmistress*. Taking a deep breath, Demelza knocked sharply and waited.

'Yes?' came Ms Cardinal's harsh nasal voice from within. 'Who is it?'

'Erm . . . It's Demelza, Ms Cardinal. Demelza Clock. I need to talk to you.'

There was a short pause before Ms Cardinal opened the door just wide enough to allow her one good eye to peer through. 'What are you doing here? You should be in lessons,' she snapped. There were crumbs in the corners of her mouth – they'd clearly interrupted her breakfast. 'And who's this? One of your little ruffian friends, no doubt.'

Demelza frowned, puzzled. If Ms Cardinal *was* the Snatcher, then why wasn't she inviting her in with open arms? Maybe it was a double bluff.

'This is my neighbour, Percy,' replied Demelza. 'We need to talk to you. It's urgent.'

The headmistress took a sharp breath. 'Well, I'm afraid you'll just have to wait until the end of the day. Now back to class, immediately!'

She tried to shut the door, but Demelza jammed her foot in the gap just in time. She looked at the headmistress with fiery determination, her face solemn, her eyes steely. All of a sudden she felt fearless, safe in the knowledge that she was about to give Ms Cardinal a nasty shock. 'I wouldn't do that if I were you,' she said. 'Unless, of course, you want everyone in this school to know about your *little plan*?' She took Lord Balthazar from her satchel and held him up.

'Hello, Margaret,' said Lord Balthazar. 'Nice to meet you!'

Ms Cardinal staggered backwards and her cheeks suddenly turned a washed-out shade of green. She tried to talk, but all that came out was an unfathomable series of strange gurgling noises.

'Well?' said Demelza impatiently. 'Are you going to let us in or not?'

'Put that thing away!' she replied, looking left and right down the corridor. 'Inside. NOW!'

Ms Cardinal ushered the children into her office and pointed to the two threadbare chairs in the corner. Percy shot Demelza a worried look, and as they sat down she couldn't help but share his nerves. Suddenly she realized how impulsive it was to have come here with only Percy and a satchel of inventions. They were hardly an army ready for battle, especially with Ms Cardinal being such a dangerous killer. But she had to keep her cool – she couldn't let the headmistress intimidate her. She clutched Lord Balthazar close on her lap.

'So you really *have* inherited the powers,' said Ms Cardinal eventually. She began to pace, her court shoes clacking against the hardwood floor. 'I thought that might have been the case when I saw you drawing those pictures in assembly.' She stopped by the window and looked down at Lord Balthazar. 'And you've started your apprenticeship, I take it?'

Demelza didn't answer. Was Ms Cardinal trying to trick her into giving information? Trying to see if she really was capable of performing the Conjuring of Resurrection?

'I'm not here to talk about my apprenticeship,' she answered sternly.

'Well, what is it, then?'

'Oh, come on, Ms Cardinal,' said Demelza. 'You know what I'm here for. Last night? Your men, Boris and Gregor?'

'My men?' Ms Cardinal's nose shot into the air. 'How very rude! I've never heard of a Boris nor a Gregor, never mind being acquainted with them, thank you very much.'

Demelza snorted. 'Don't lie to me, Ms Cardinal. You sent them to my cottage, after the Dance with Death, didn't you?'

'Demelza, I sincerely have no idea what you're talking about!' said the headmistress. 'In fact, I think I've heard quite enough. You should leave immediately.'

'I'M TALKING ABOUT THE KIDNAPPING!' Demelza blurted out. She stood up, kicking back her chair with a screech. 'I know you've taken my grandma! And I know what you want.'

All of a sudden the headmistress looked panicked. 'K-k-kidnapping? Your grandma? Demelza, if this is some kind of prank you'll be writing lines in detention for the next fifty years!'

'It's not a joke, and you know it!' Demelza pulled out

the ransom note and handed it to the headmistress. 'You wrote this, didn't you? You've taken Grandma to bribe me into doing the Conjuring of Resurrection! I know you have!'

As Ms Cardinal took in the contents of the note a hush cut through the air, the headmistress's eyebrows travelling further towards her hairline with every word she read. She looked genuinely shocked. Was Ms Cardinal really unaware of what had happened to Grandma Maeve, or was she just pretending? Demelza's eyes narrowed and she glanced over to Percy, who seemed equally confused.

Ms Cardinal put down the note. 'Oh, Demelza, this is awful!' she gasped. 'Who would do such a terrible thing? When did this happen?'

Demelza didn't answer. Unless the headmistress was a very good actress, Demelza had misjudged her. 'You mean, you didn't do it? You didn't order Boris and Gregor to kidnap her?'

'Of course not!' said the headmistress. 'Why would you think that?'

'When I came to get my notebook I heard you talking to someone about me on the telephone,' said Demelza. 'You said you were going to "act soon". You said you had "a plan"!'

Ms Cardinal shook her head. 'Oh, Demelza, I was talking to my husband! When I looked through your notebook that day I guessed you'd become a Spectre Detector, and my plan was to use the information as a way to make contact with your grandmother again. To try and get through to her.'

Demelza paused. 'Hang on, what do you mean, *get through to her*? Why would you want to talk to my grandma?'

'Surely your grandma must have talked to you about . . .' Ms Cardinal's voice trailed off and her hand shot to her mouth. 'Oh, my goodness gracious, Demelza. She's never told you about me, has she?'

'Told me what?' said Demelza, her voice suddenly trembling.

Ms Cardinal looked to the floor. 'Well, I'm not sure I should be the person to tell you this, but I fear I must.' She looked up slowly, and as their eyes met, Demelza's tummy began to knot. 'Your grandmother and I . . . we're sisters.'

CHAPTER 24
Sisters

Ms Cardinal let out a heavy sigh. She sat down at her desk and from the top drawer pulled out an old photograph. Its corners were creased and it was yellowed with age. 'Here, take a look.'

'Demelza, no!' shouted Percy. 'It's a trap!'

Demelza took the photograph cautiously before wiping her glasses. It showed two teenage girls – undoubtedly a young Grandma Maeve and Ms Cardinal – sitting under an apple tree in the sunshine. They were smiling, enjoying what looked like an early spring afternoon.

'I was eighteen when we stopped speaking,' said Ms Cardinal. 'Maeve had been a Spectre Detector for some time by then and everyone in the family was so proud of her, so pleased that someone was carrying on the tradition.

'It was always *Maeve's done this* and *Maeve's done that*.

Nobody cared about what boring old Margaret could do. So one night I snuck down to the summoning chamber in our parents' house when I knew my sister would be in there. It was only meant to be a prank. I'd only planned on creeping up and frightening her, but . . .' Ms Cardinal's voice began to quaver and she looked to the ground. 'I didn't realize that she had a crucible bubbling away in front of her.'

Demelza's skin prickled as she anticipated the end of the story.

'In her fright, Maeve dropped the whole bottle of black-bird blood that she was holding into her crucible. There was a terrible explosion and, well . . . this happened.' The headmistress pulled down her eye patch and Demelza and Percy gasped. Her eye was cloudy and void of colour, with scars twisting around it like thick red worms.

'And my grandma's hand?' asked Demelza with a gulp. 'That's how she got her scar too?'

Ms Cardinal's voice lowered. 'Yes.'

All of a sudden, Demelza found herself thinking back to something she'd heard in the summoning chamber – something that Grandma Maeve had said on her very first night of training. *Any fooling around or lapses in concentration can have horrible consequences. Being a Spectre Detector can be extremely dangerous, in more ways than one.* She'd been talking about what her sister had done!

'Good grief!' exclaimed Lord Balthazar. 'Well, I wasn't expecting that. And I thought it was only the aristocracy who kept such juicy family secrets!'

'But why did you stop speaking to your sister?' asked Percy. 'It wasn't like it was really anyone's fault. It was just a horrible accident. Why did you fall out?'

'We had a big argument after that,' said Ms Cardinal sadly. 'Maeve was such a proud Spectre Detector and she said that I wasn't taking her work seriously. I guess I wasn't, if truth be told. She said that she didn't want anything to do with me any more. . .'

Demelza smiled sadly. Yes, that sounded like Grandma Maeve – a devoted Spectre Detector through and through, but as stubborn as a mule.

'For a while, I felt the same,' continued Ms Cardinal. 'I was so ashamed of what I'd done, it was too painful to think of seeing Maeve. But deep down I've always wanted to make up with her. When I got offered the chance to take over at Stricton last year I knew the time was right. I thought that your grandma and I might finally be able to make amends after all these years, Demelza. And I'd have a chance to get to know *you* too.

'But when I got here, your grandma refused to see me.

And she made it very clear that I wasn't to forge any kind of relationship with you either. I was devastated—'

'Well, you have a funny way of showing it!' Demelza blurted out. 'You're always so mean to me. I *hate* school because of you!'

For a moment there was silence, then the headmistress's shoulders started to heave and the sound of her sobs filled the room. 'Oh, I'm so sorry, Demelza. It was the only way I could deal with your grandma's rejection. I just thought it would be easier for me to respect her wishes and keep my distance if I pretended that you were a troublesome student. All I really wanted to do was give you a big cuddle.'

'Well, it sounds like you dodged a bullet there, Demelza,' muttered Lord Balthazar.

Ms Cardinal took a cotton handkerchief from her pocket and blew her nose with a trumpeting honk. 'You *are* mischievous, of course, infuriatingly so at times, but you're one of the smartest children I have ever met. Maeve has done an excellent job in raising – perhaps not quite a *fine young lady* – but certainly a very remarkable girl indeed. I'd love to see some of your inventions one day. They sound wonderful!'

On hearing the headmistress's words Demelza was almost speechless. 'Erm . . . erm . . . thanks,' she mumbled.

'But, Demelza, we can talk about all of this later,' said Ms Cardinal. 'Right now, you really need to tell me exactly what's going on, and why Maeve's been taken!'

Demelza bit her lip and, starting from the very beginning, relayed all that had happened over the past few hours. It was painful to talk about. Horrible images of Grandma Maeve being snatched by Boris and Gregor kept appearing in her mind's eye, like a scene from a film being played over and over.

When she'd finished there was quiet.

'I . . . I don't know what to say,' said Ms Cardinal. She looked stunned, even more so than the day that the school inspectors from the local council had turned up unannounced. 'This is just terrible. And you have no idea who this Snatcher might be?'

Demelza shook her head. 'You were my only suspect. I guess it's back to the drawing board now.'

Ms Cardinal stood up. 'Well, you're not going back to the cottage, that's for sure. I'll get Nurse Miller to make up the spare dormitory for you and you'll reside here at Stricton until we get Maeve back. Percy is more than welcome to stay too.'

Demelza looked to her friend with hopeful enthusiasm. 'Will you stay, Percy? *Please?*'

Percy's shoulders drooped. 'I wish. There's no way that Fräulein von Winkle will agree, she's under strict instructions from my dad.'

Ms Cardinal tapped her nose. 'Oh, you can leave that with me. I'm sure a quick word in the ear from a fellow pedagogue will do the trick.'

Demelza looked at Ms Cardinal with disbelief. Was this really the same woman who viewed telling lies as a crime punishable by a whole term without playtime? The same woman who considered rule-breaking to be the eighth deadly sin?

The headmistress got up. 'Now, why don't you both relax in the common room for a bit? I'll make the phone call to Fräulein von Winkle. Then we have some serious planning to do.'

'But what about lessons?' Demelza said.

'Lessons?' Ms Cardinal blinked. 'Demelza, you have shown no interest in them before – why start? And as much as I think you could benefit from this morning's double history, finding Maeve is your priority right now.'

That evening, as the rest of the boarders headed to the dining hall for supper, Demelza and Percy settled down in the dormitory that Nurse Miller had prepared for them.

The curtains had been drawn, the bedside lamps glowed brightly, and in the corner a set of wooden bunks had been made up with flannel blankets and pillows. Lord Balthazar was already asleep on top of the wardrobe, and much to Demelza's surprise, it actually felt quite cosy.

'Bagsie this one!' she shouted, launching her satchel on to the top bunk as if she were an Olympic hammer thrower. 'I've always wanted to sleep up high! It's like being in a tree house.'

'Fine by me,' said Percy, who just seemed pleased to be somewhere other than the confines of his own room. Ms Cardinal hadn't told them *exactly* how Fräulein von Winkle had reacted to her phone call, but apparently his private tutor had quickly arrived at the school with a bag of his possessions big enough for a round-the-world expedition.

Preparations for staying at Stricton had taken up most of the day. Demelza had been back to Bladderwrack Cottage to pack a bag for herself and to fetch Archimedes. The little ball of fur had been in the middle of running his daily wheel-marathon, but on seeing the lump of Edam that Demelza had brought for him, he'd been quick to abandon his exercise and tuck in. Demelza had taken the big leather suitcase from the cupboard under the stairs and packed her ghoul-box, mask and crucible. Her thinking cap went in her satchel, along with the cleanest of her (not very clean) socks, a screwdriver, some wire and her Remarkable Robotic Hand for Homework Haters. She thought she might tinker with it later on if she felt a bit homesick.

As she'd packed her pyjamas, the strange crescent-moon key that Boris and Gregor had dropped in the summoning chamber fell out of the front pocket. Demelza slipped that in her satchel too, just in case, although she had no idea how she would figure out what door it opened. It had been too painful to stay in the cottage for long, with everything turned upside down and no Grandma or Shiver to keep her company, and for the first time ever, Demelza had actually been pleased to be heading back to Stricton.

'So what's the plan now?' asked Percy, beginning to unpack his things.

'I think I might take a little walk around the field to clear my head,' said Demelza. 'You want to come?'

But just then, the dormitory door creaked open and Ms Cardinal came in carrying a large tray covered with a silver cloche. 'A little something from the kitchens for your supper,' she said with a smile. 'You're probably both absolutely famished.'

Demelza's face dropped as she anticipated the bowls of lukewarm gloop that were probably awaiting them. Mrs

Reid the dinner lady's cooking skills were less *Cordon Bleu* and more *Cordon Bluuuurgh*. 'Erm . . . I'm not actually very hungry, Ms Cardinal,' she said. 'I had a big breakfast. Very, very big.'

'Very well,' said Ms Cardinal. 'I didn't think that you would turn down some special treats, but there we go.' She whipped off the silver cloche to reveal a plate piled high with thickly cut sandwiches, golden pastries and beautifully iced buns. 'I guess I'll just take them back down to the bins and—'

'No, wait!' exclaimed Demelza, jumping up at the sight of the delicious spread. 'Maybe I *could* manage just a couple of mouthfuls. It would be a shame for it all to go to waste.'

Ms Cardinal smiled knowingly, and wasting no time, Demelza began to tuck in to the mountain of goodies.

'And what about you?' Ms Cardinal asked Percy. He was eyeing up the array of tasty treats but his plate was empty. 'Not hungry?'

'He's not allowed,' said Demelza, with a mouthful of doughnut. She scooped up the jam that was dribbling down her chin. 'He's got a very delicate stomach. It's his allergies.'

'Oh dear,' said Ms Cardinal. 'That is unfortunate. You poor thing.'

Percy shrugged sadly. 'I'm used to it. I've got my special tablets in my bag, so I'll have them later.'

'That doesn't mean that you can have double portions, Demelza!' said the headmistress as Demelza went in for second helpings. 'Slow down!'

Demelza scrunched up her nose. 'But Ms Cardinal, where did all this lovely food come from? The school kitchens?'

The headmistress let out a snort of laughter. 'Ha! You don't think I'd actually eat the muck that awful dinner lady cooks, do you? No, this is from my own private cupboard.' She gave the children a wink. 'And private it shall stay, OK?'

Demelza felt her eyes widen with disbelief. Who would have thought that Ms Cardinal was such a rebel?

'Now, once you've eaten, you two should get some rest,' said Ms Cardinal. 'You need to be firing on all cylinders tomorrow if you're going to help your grandma.'

CHAPTER 25
The Fight

But Demelza couldn't sleep that night.

Being in the top bunk wasn't as comfy as she'd hoped, and as she tossed and turned she longed for her patchwork quilt and her hot-water bottle and Grandma Maeve. Even one of her grandmother's silly bedtime stories wouldn't have gone amiss.

As quietly as possible, she lowered herself out of bed and went to the window. She peered through the curtains, and found the moon looking down on her like a great white eye. She sighed heavily. Was Grandma Maeve looking up at it too? Was she awake?

'Demelza, is that you?' said Percy, as the lower bunk began to creak. He rubbed his eyes and pulled himself up. 'What . . . what are you doing?'

'I can't sleep,' said Demelza, turning from the window

and switching on the little desk lamp. She sat down and pulled her hands through her tangle of hair. 'It's no use – I can't wait until morning. I need to be doing something *now*! I need to be figuring out who the Snatcher could be. There must be some clues that I've missed. I just have to sit down and think more thoroughly.' She pulled on her dressing gown and made for the door. 'But first, I need a peanut butter and cheese sandwich.'

Percy threw back his covers and shook his head. 'Are you serious? You already had at least three of Ms Cardinal's doughnuts earlier. And don't think I didn't see you sneaking another Cornish pasty into your mouth when her back was turned.'

'It's necessary thinking food,' Demelza replied curtly. 'All great intellectuals have a preferred nibble to help the ideas flow. Now, I'm going down to the kitchens. You coming?'

Percy groaned and reached for his bunny slippers. 'OK...'

The school was mortuary-still when the pair crept out of the dormitory. They tiptoed down the corridor and descended the winding snake of the main staircase, the creaking of the old steps threatening to give them away with every footstep. When they reached the bottom, Demelza pulled Percy behind a nearby bookcase. 'Right, we're nearly at the kitchens,' she whispered, her eyes darting around to check that they weren't being watched. 'Keep close.'

Percy nodded and followed Demelza through the dim hallways. All of the classrooms were still, the rows of desks like tombstones in a cemetery.

But just as they snuck into the kitchen, the sound of approaching footsteps stopped them in their tracks.

'Well, well, well. Look who it is!' came a familiar voice.

The Smythe twins appeared at the door in matching lilac nightdresses, with Miranda loafing behind them in a dressing gown.

'It seems like Dotty Demelza has become a boarder,' said Penelope, sauntering forward and running a hand through her wavy golden hair. 'We saw you coming in earlier but just assumed that you'd been called in for extra detention.'

'What's happened?' said Persephone. 'Your weirdo grandma finally had enough of you at home?'

Demelza stepped forward, her teeth grinding together. 'What did you say?'

Persephone grinned spitefully. 'I said, it looks like that crazy grandmother of yours has thrown you out. I can't say

I'm surprised. Who would want to share a house with you?'

Anger began to fizz inside Demelza like a chemical reaction. 'My grandma's NOT crazy!' she said, the words almost frothing at her lips. 'Take it back! Take it back NOW!'

'Or what?' said Persephone, breaking off with a cruel laugh

'Or . . . or you'll have *me* to deal with!' Percy shouted. He held up his tiny fists like a boxer and Demelza looked at him with amazement.

'Ooooh, big threats from a little weed!' taunted Penelope. 'Who's your new friend, Demelza? And why would anyone choose to hang around with *you*?'

'Unlike you two,' she hissed, 'people want to be around me for my character and *not* just my parents' cash!'

The twins' faces dropped in unison, but once again Miranda's lips seemed to curl upwards into a tiny private smile. Demelza caught her eye and she quickly looked away.

'You're . . . you're not going to let her speak to us like that, are you?' stuttered Penelope, looking to Miranda for backup. 'Do something!'

Miranda's face dropped. 'Really? But it's the middle of the night. I don't think we need to start fighting—'

'WHAT?' interrupted Persephone. 'Do you want to be our friend or not? Don't tell me you've gone soft, Miranda?'

'Of course not,' said Miranda, quickly backing down. 'I meant . . . she's just not worth the effort, that's all.' And like an obedient, overgrown puppy, Miranda pushed her way forward. Demelza made to flee, but before she had a chance she felt the burn of her hair being pulled, and a knee jabbing into her stomach.

'Stop it!' shouted Percy. 'Leave her alone! Get off her now!'

But Miranda showed no sign of ceasing, and with the twins cheering loudly she landed a punch on Demelza's nose, sending her flying back against the cooker with a crunch.

She slid to the cold kitchen floor, pain pulsing through her body as the air was wrenched from her lungs. For a moment everything went black.

'Demelza?' came a voice. 'Demelza, are you OK?'

Demelza blinked her eyes open to find a fuzzy-looking Percy standing over her. She groaned loudly. 'My nose . . . my nose . . .' She sniffed and felt a warm trickle of blood fill her nostrils.

'Look, just stay there, OK?' said Percy. 'I'll get a first aid kit. Don't move . . .'

But Demelza wasn't going to give up. She wasn't going to let some beefy halfwit get the better of her! With the taste of blood in her mouth she pulled herself up, then, with the last ounce of her energy, she ran full pelt into Miranda, who went stumbling backwards like a skittle. She collided with one of the shelves, sending pots and pans crashing to the floor like cymbals.

'What on EARTH is going on here?'

The children turned to find Ms Cardinal in the threshold, wearing a long flannelette nightgown. Her face was illuminated by the glow of her oil lamp, making her cheeks even more sallow-looking than usual.

'It . . . it was Demelza, Ms Cardinal!' protested Penelope immediately, her voice reverting to its usual sickly sweet tone. 'We heard frightening noises coming from down here so we came to investigate.'

'We found Demelza and this strange boy,' continued Persephone. 'And when we reminded them that they shouldn't be out of bed, Demelza just started attacking Miranda.'

'You liar!' shouted Demelza, warm blood dripping from her nose. 'It was *them*, Ms Cardinal, they started it. Miranda punched me in the face and—'

'ENOUGH!' snapped the headmistress. 'I am fully

aware of who is to blame for this vulgar display of hoodlu-mism. It is quite obvious!'

The twins crossed their arms with gleeful satisfaction, smirking at Demelza and Percy. 'Yes, I think Demelza deserves expulsion for the trouble she's caused,' said Persephone with nauseating pretend distress. 'Don't you agree, Ms Cardinal?'

The headmistress turned to the twins. 'I was actually referring to you and your sister, Persephone Smythe. I will see you both in my office immediately.'

'U-u-us?' stuttered Persephone. Her face was a picture of pure disbelief and her sister looked as if she was on the brink of collapse. 'Surely there has to be some kind of mistake—?'

'No mistake whatsoever,' said Ms Cardinal. 'My office. NOW.'

The twins huffed and with faces like storms they turned on their heels, with Miranda in tow.

'Not you, Miss Choudhury!' ordered Ms Cardinal. 'I shall be taking you and Miss Clock down to the sickbay at once. I cannot have students parading around the corridors with black eyes and bloody noses. Stricton Academy is a respectable school, not a backstreet boxing ring!'

'But, Ms Cardinal, I'm fine,' protested Demelza. 'I don't

need to see the nurse, honestly.'

Ms Cardinal sauntered over to her great-niece, and as she pretended to inspect the graze on her cheek, she whispered, 'Not another word, Demelza. You won't be much help to your grandma if you're suffering from severe concussion, will you?'

CHAPTER 26
A Night in the Sickbay

'Goodness gracious, stay still, girl!' scolded Nurse Miller as she attempted to drop iodine from a pipette on to Demelza's scratched cheek.

In the adjacent bed, Miranda was staring miserably at the ceiling with a bandage around her wrist and a frown across her face.

'There's no need to be such a sourpuss, Miss Choudhury,' said Nurse Miller. 'You've got no one to blame but yourself.' She drew the blinds, and through the slats the moonlight fell in long strips across the bedsheets. 'Now, I don't want to hear a peep from you two for the rest of the night. No talking, no bickering and definitely no more fighting. You understand?'

The two girls eyeballed each other before groaning, 'Yes, Nurse Miller!' in unison.

'Good,' replied the nurse curtly, and she flicked off the light and shut the door.

Demelza closed her eyes and sighed. The room reeked of antiseptic cream and bleach, and more than ever she longed to be tucked up in her cosy attic bedroom in Bladderwrack Cottage. She pined for her encyclopaedias, her inventions and the musky, papery smell of her notebooks. She imagined Grandma Maeve warming her feet by the fire, sipping on ginger wine and teaching Shiver how to bark rude words.

But these comforting thoughts were soon interrupted by the rustling of Miranda's bedsheets and her deep voice cutting through the darkness. 'You're going to pay for this, Demelza Clock! Nobody fights *me* and gets away with it. Especially not a weedy little weirdo like you.'

Demelza ignored her and turned over with a huff. Why oh why had she let herself get into a fight? Why had she let her temper get the better of her? Grandma Maeve needed her help but now she was trapped with this goon until morning.

'Are you listening to me, Demelza?' growled Miranda again. 'I said that nobody fights me and gets away with it!'

Demelza puffed out her cheeks in frustration. 'Look, Miranda, why don't you just drop the tough girl act until tomorrow, eh? I know you don't really enjoy it. I've seen the way you laugh when I stand up to the twins.'

'I-I don't know what you mean,' stammered Miranda. 'It's not an act! Nobody messes with Miranda Choudhury.'

'Fine!' said Demelza, turning back over. 'But you don't fool me.' She pulled the stiff hospital sheets over her shoulders and closed her eyes. If Miranda didn't want to accept an olive branch then that was her choice. At least she could say that she'd tried.

'Demelza, wait,' said Miranda after a while. 'What you said . . . about standing up to the twins . . .'

Demelza's ears perked up. 'Yes.'

'Well, maybe . . . maybe . . .' Miranda sighed heavily. 'Oh, it doesn't matter.'

'No, go on,' encouraged Demelza.

There was silence for a moment, as if Miranda was working herself up to say something important. 'I've always found it hard to make friends,' she said eventually. 'When I was little, we moved around so much because of my mum's job that I never really got the chance to get to know anyone.' Miranda's voice had softened and it began to quaver. 'When I came to Stricton as a boarder last year and I met the twins, I thought I'd actually made some real friends. They seemed to like having me around.'

'But they're *not* real friends,' said Demelza, jolting up. She switched on the bedside lamp. Tucked under her white sheets, Miranda suddenly looked like a frail little girl, her wavy black hair framing huge dark eyes.

'The twins just use you! I bet they don't even know what your favourite colour is, or what you choose for breakfast, or your middle name.'

'*Nobody* knows my middle name,' said Miranda, looking away. 'It's too embarrassing to say.'

'Well, OK,' said Demelza. 'But I bet they never ask you how you are? Or if you're having a good day?'

Miranda shook her head and the corners of her mouth started to tremble. 'Everyone always assumes that because of my height and the shot-put competitions, that all I like doing is showing off my muscles. I've been so desperate for friends that I guess I just started going along with it. I thought that being the twins' bodyguard would be better than being on my own.' Her chin dropped. 'I've been such a coward.'

Demelza shifted under her covers. She knew what it felt like to be misunderstood. Poor Miranda. 'So if you don't really enjoy showing off your muscles, what is it that you like?' she asked.

Miranda looked to the floor. 'Oh, it doesn't matter. You

wouldn't be interested—'

'Try me,' urged Demelza.

'OK,' said Miranda. 'I know you probably wouldn't expect it, but I like writing poems. Haikus, rhymes, but mainly love sonnets.'

Even though she didn't mean to, Demelza let out a shocked snigger.

'*See*? Even you think it's weird!' said Miranda, crossing her arms. 'I knew I shouldn't have said anything.'

'I don't think it's weird, I promise,' insisted Demelza. 'It was just a surprise, that's all. You shouldn't be ashamed of what you like. And slushy, kissy, romance stuff is fine . . . if you like that kind of thing.'

Miranda smiled. 'I wish I could just be more honest about it, like you are with your inventions. Sometimes I get up really early before anyone's awake and sneak into the library to write. I daren't do it when other people are around.' She drew her knees to her chest. 'I've never told anyone about all of this before.'

'Well, your secret's safe with me if you want to keep it that way,' said Demelza. 'Hey, you reckon you can make up a poem now?'

Miranda's eyes widened as if she were being given the loveliest of gifts, and she steepled her fingers in thought.

'Hmmmm, let's see . . . OK! . . . *I know a young girl called Demelza . . . who never does what people tellz 'er . . . she's always in detention . . . for making inventions . . . hold your nose in case you smellz 'er!*'

'You'll pay for that!' said Demelza, putting up her fists playfully. 'Although to be honest it's all pretty accurate.' She plumped up her pillows and lay back. 'So what does your mum do? Why do you have to travel around so much?'

'Oh, it's sooo boring,' said Miranda. 'She's an architectural historian – she investigates old buildings and things. She met my dad while digging up this ancient temple in India. I'm always being dragged around creepy old houses and crumbling monasteries. She wants to study Crookescroft Castle next. Apparently it's a *significant example of Tudor architecture*.'

'Isn't it falling to bits?' asked Demelza.

Miranda nodded. 'But there's all sorts of dungeons and oubliettes and secret chambers preserved deep below ground. Mum took me there once. Can you imagine all the prisoners they probably had locked up there back in the olden days?'

Demelza didn't answer.

The beginnings of an idea had suddenly caught alight in her brain.

Dungeons?

Prisoners?

Secret chambers?

What if the engravings on the key that Boris and Gregor had dropped in the summoning chamber weren't two crescent moons after all? What if they were two letter Cs? Two letter Cs standing for Crookescroft Castle! Could Grandma Maeve be being held there?

Demelza leant forward. 'So what else do you know about Crookescroft Castle? Are the public allowed to look around?'

Miranda pulled her sheets up over her shoulders. 'Oh no, it's too dangerous for that. The roof could cave in at any second apparently. The council locked it up years ago.'

'So no one goes in and out?'

Miranda shook her head. 'No. Apart from the occasional group of people with clipboards and hard hats, like my mum and her colleagues. Why are you so interested anyway?'

Demelza paused and took a sip of water from the tumbler on her bedside table. She still didn't know if she could completely trust Miranda, but if her theory about Crookescroft Castle was true then she needed to go and look around as soon as possible. And if Miranda had already been there she'd be a good person to have on board.

Demelza shot a glance to the door then leant in and whispered, 'Miranda, how do you fancy going on a little trip to the castle with me and Percy tomorrow? A little adventure!'

'Erm . . . OK,' Miranda replied. 'But what's this all about?'

'It's a very long story,' said Demelza, tucking herself back into bed. 'And I don't want Nurse Miller to hear us. So I'll explain everything in the morning when we get out of here, I promise.'

Miranda nodded.

'But I'm trusting you, Miranda, so please, please don't snitch. You can't tell anyone about this. I'm counting on you as my friend.'

On hearing Demelza's last word, a huge grin broke across Miranda's face. 'You can trust me, Demelza, I promise!' An idea flashed in her eyes. 'And I tell you what, to prove it, I'll tell you my secret middle name . . . well, *names* to be precise – I have four of them!'

'OK . . .' said Demelza, raising her eyebrows.

'My full name is: Miranda Jocasta Gwendolina Bluebell Ottilia Choudhury.'

Demelza couldn't help but snort into her pillow. 'Yeah,

I can understand why you wanted to keep that quiet! And I thought Demelza was bad!'

The girls giggled, and finally drifted off to sleep.

CHAPTER 27

Crookescroft Castle

The next morning, having been given another stern warning from Nurse Miller, and with extra-large (and extra-disgusting) spoonfuls of cod-liver oil sloshing around in their bellies, Miranda and Demelza hurried out of the sickbay and made their way back to Demelza and Percy's dorm.

Percy was awake, snuggled up in bed, engrossed in one of his comics.

'Ooh, *The Nautical Adventures of Captain Thalasso*, good choice!' said Miranda, pointing excitedly to the front cover as she walked in. 'And that volume is especially good. The bit where he meets his estranged father is so poetic.'

'*Ufff*, well, you've given the ending away now!' said Percy, jerking forward and eyeing Miranda with contempt. 'What's she doing here anyway, Demelza? Is she threatening you again? Do you want me to fetch Ms Cardinal?'

'Don't worry, Percy,' said Demelza, closing the door behind her. 'We'll tell you all about it later, but Miranda and I have made friends. She's actually a bit of a softy at heart.'

'Yeah, well, she has a funny way of showing it!' replied Percy with a scowl. 'She definitely didn't seem very soft when she gave you that clump on the nose last night.'

Miranda's smile dropped and she shuffled under Percy's gaze. 'I'm really sorry about all that, Percy. I've already apologized to Demelza, and I'd really like to make amends with *you* too.' She held out a hand for Percy to shake. 'Friends?'

Percy crossed his arms across his chest. 'We'll see.'

Demelza pulled Archimedes from his cage and took a seat at the desk. The little creature was long overdue a good tummy tickle, and as she ran her fingers through his fur, his whiskers began to twitch with contentment. 'Anyway, I think Miranda might be able to help us, Percy. So we need to tell her why we're really here.'

Percy's mouth curled. 'What, help us with *you-know-what*? Are you sure that's wise?'

'Erm . . . could one of you tell me exactly what's going on?' interrupted Miranda. 'I still have no idea what I'm meant to be helping you with! Is it one of your inventions, Demelza?'

'I wish!' replied Demelza. She gestured to the chair by the desk. 'Here, sit down and I'll explain everything. There's going to be quite a lot to digest but just try to keep an open mind, OK?'

For the next hour, Demelza got to work, filling Miranda in on the events of the past couple of weeks and her theory about Crookescroft Castle. She knew that it was probably another risky move, but at this point she needed all the allies that she could get.

Much to her surprise, Miranda digested all the information calmly, and even managed a polite hello when Demelza introduced her to Lord Balthazar. 'Wow,' she said, when Demelza had finished. 'Well, I wasn't expecting that. I'm sorry about your grandma. But it's pretty exciting that you inherited those special powers. I've always wanted to see a spectre!'

'So you believe in them?' asked Demelza.

'Oh yes! In India, where my dad is from, a lot of people do. They think that a person's essence can live on in a different realm after death.' She thought for a second. 'In fact, that's a lovely idea for a poem! I could write it in rhyming couplets . . . or maybe free verse . . .'

'Eh? What on earth is she talking about?' asked Percy, his nose wrinkling.

'Miranda's a poet, Percy,' replied Demelza. 'I told you she was actually a bit of a softie!' She gave Miranda a playful elbow and they both laughed.

Percy put his comic on to the bedside table. 'So you want to go and look in Crookescroft Castle?' he asked.

Demelza nodded, and took a lettuce leaf from Archimedes's cage for her pet to nibble on. 'What do you reckon, Miranda? Do you think my grandma could be being kept there?'

'Well, like I said, nobody really goes in and out. There's loads of dungeons. And . . .' Just then a thought seemed to flit across her face.

'And?'

'I can't promise anything, but I think I remember Mum saying that back in the day there was rumour that the lady of the castle had a secret room where she kept all of her jewels and gems. Apparently it's through a concealed door hidden somewhere in her bedroom.'

'Brilliant!' said Demelza. 'You can show us where the bedroom is. It will be a good place to start looking. We'll go this evening!'

'But what about Ms Cardinal?' asked Miranda. 'Should

we tell her?'

Demelza shook her head. 'She might be less strict than we previously thought, but she's still a grown-up! There's no way that she'd be OK with us wandering round derelict buildings late at night.'

'But what if we're caught trespassing?' said Percy. 'We could be sent to prison! We could be locked up with criminals . . . villains . . . murderers!'

Demelza turned to him and, trying to remain calm, sucked in a deep breath. 'Percy, my grandma has been kidnapped. I'd prefer to spend the rest of my life in prison than regretting not doing enough to try and save her. Now are you with me or not?'

Percy pulled at his pyjama cuff. 'Yes . . . sorry . . . of course I am.'

Demelza gathered her friends closer and brought her voice down to a whisper. 'OK, here's the plan. Tonight is Halloween. Everyone will be in costume so it'll be the perfect time for us to sneak through the village and into the castle without being recognized.' She popped Archimedes on the desk and reached for her Mask of Facelessness, which she held to her face. 'And I have the perfect disguises!'

'Brilliant!' said Miranda.

'Spooky!' said Percy.

'And me?' asked Lord Balthazar. 'I could wear a disguise too! A moustache and glasses, perhaps?'

'Oh yes, because nothing says inconspicuous like a bespectacled talking skull with facial hair!' said Demelza. 'No, you should stay here. You can throw Ms Cardinal off the scent if she starts asking questions.'

That evening, darkness fell like a blanket over the village, and Demelza, Miranda and Percy slipped out of Stricton Academy. They were wearing some of Grandma Maeve's skull-shaped masks which they'd snuck back to Bladder-wrack Cottage to collect; Miranda's was blood-red and studded with garnets, Percy's bronze with long crooked teeth. Demelza had put on her own wooden one and, under the moonlight, they looked just like any other group of children who were out celebrating Halloween.

Demelza led the way down to the high street, her satchel rattling with inventions, flying on ahead and dashing in and out of the trees. Pumpkins with jagged smiles lit up every window with their candlelit eyes. And on street corners, children dressed as monsters, witches and vampires huddled together, their excited chatter echoing through the streets. Percy gawped at the little buckets they held, each filled to the brim with toffee apples, caramels, lollipops and gobstoppers.

'Awww, trick or treating looks like so much fun!' he said, his voice forlorn. 'I've never been allowed to go out on Halloween before. Dad's never let me.'

'Oh, the tricking bit is the best!' said Demelza with a naughty grin. 'Last year I invented some home-made stink bombs to post through the Smythe twins' dorm! I mixed ammonia and sulphur with some of Grandma's pongy blue cheese – their corridor smelt like a blocked toilet until Christmas apparently!' She pretended to be wafting away an unpleasant odour from her behind and Percy and Miranda laughed.

'That was *you*?' said Miranda. 'The twins thought it was something to do with Stricton's drainage system! They even got their father to write a letter of complaint to Ms Cardinal. How hilarious!'

Demelza nodded proudly. 'Come on, let's get moving. You never know, if we find Grandma Maeve we might be back in time to play a few pranks later on!'

The trio made short work of the journey, and within no time at all they found themselves standing outside the large front gates of Crookescroft Castle. They huddled together in its shadow, peeking through the railings at the decrepit building beyond. It was just as dark and imposing up close as Demelza had expected, with sprawling balustrades and jaunty turrets which jutted upwards like broken crowns. Ivy snaked its way around rotting window frames, and cobwebs stretched from cornice to cornice like sticky nets of lace.

'Urghh, it's so creepy,' whimpered Percy. He pointed to the large oaks which twisted upwards either side of the building, cradling it in the dark, withered fingers of their branches. 'It looks like something you'd see in a scary film.'

'We'll be fine as long as we stick together,' said Demelza, trying to convince herself as much as her friends. She pulled down her thinking cap, her jaw set. 'Come on, let's go in.'

Over the gates they went, with Miranda leading them up to the shadowy arch of the gargantuan front entrance. Demelza could feel her heart pounding hard and her palms beginning to tingle; not because she was scared of the gargoyles that looked down on them from the cornices above, or the bats that flew in and out of the smashed windowpanes, but because of what she might find inside. Would Grandma Maeve and Shiver be locked up somewhere? Would they be hurt?

Demelza reached for the rusty key in her pocket, and with a trembling hand put it in the keyhole and turned clockwise.

Breath left her in a rush.

The door creaked open, its hinges screeching like the cry of an angry cat. Her theory had been right! The key *had* been for the castle.

Without uttering a word she stepped inside, her friends close behind. A decaying entrance hall lay before them – it looked as if it had been frozen in time. Curtains hung tattered at the windows and the antique furniture was threadbare, as if it had provided a tasty meal for many a hungry moth. Flies buzzed around wonky chandeliers. A thick layer of dust covered every surface like lichen.

Demelza ran a finger along one of the windowsills until her skin was black. 'My bedroom hasn't seen a vacuum cleaner for a while, but this is filthy!'

With their torches pointed low, the children rallied behind Miranda as she guided them up the sweeping staircase which spiralled into the darkness above. The worm-eaten wood of the bannister was damp to the touch, and a musty smell hung thick and close like a cloak. The steps moaned underneath their weight, and more than once Demelza spun around, thinking that someone was following them. *Don't be scared*, she told herself, as she put one foot in front of the other. *Just think of Grandma Maeve. You're doing this for Grandma Maeve.*

'Right, I think this is it,' said Miranda, once they reached a large doorway at the very top of the house. It was intricately carved with patterns and finished with gilt, but its hinges were encrusted with rust. 'The lady of the manor's sleeping quarters.'

Without a moment's hesitation, Demelza reached for the handle. But as much as she rattled it, the door wouldn't budge. '*Ow!* Plummeting protons,' she cursed. 'The stupid thing's locked!'

'Demelza, calm down,' said Miranda, edging forward. 'That's a *good* sign – it means that there might be something hidden inside! Now step back, both of you.'

Demelza and Percy did as they were told and Miranda barrelled shoulder-first into the door like a bull. After a few tries, it crashed open with a clatter.

'Woah! Impressive!' said Percy, looking at Miranda with new-found awe. 'I mean . . . *quite* impressive.'

Miranda blushed. 'Thanks, Percy.'

The children found themselves in a large palatial chamber, its walls adorned with brocade tapestries and gilt mirrors. The floor was covered in a thick-piled carpet decorated with swirling filigree, and at its centre, a large four-poster bed was draped with sumptuous panels. It was in much better condition than the rest of the place, and

Demelza hoped that meant it was still in use.

'Right,' she said, marching inside and corralling her friends like a commanding officer. 'Search every nook and every cranny. We *have* to find the entrance to this secret vault. Percy, you take the shelves. Miranda, you take the cupboards. I'll check behind the paintings and the mirrors. And remember, whatever you do, don't take off your masks.'

The friends nodded and got to work turning over the room from top to bottom. Papers were strewn across the floor, furniture was overturned and mirrors removed. With every *crash* and every *bang*, Demelza hoped that one of her friends might have unearthed something. As she pulled frames from the walls, she tried to picture what Grandma Maeve's reaction might be if they managed to find her. She imagined taking her back to Bladderwrack Cottage, filling up a teapot, and never leaving her side again.

But an hour later, the search party had still found nothing.

'Demelza, I think we should just move on,' said Percy, plonking himself on to the four-poster bed with a huff. 'There's nothing here. Maybe the rumours about the secret vault were just that – rumours. We could check the dungeons?'

Demelza turned to him. 'Let's just keep looking for a bit longer. Grandma Maeve could be only a few metres away from us. We can't give up now!'

'But I'm tired!' groaned Percy, flopping back on to the bed. 'I'm having a rest.'

'Fine!' snapped Demelza, annoyed by Percy's lack of dedication. 'In fact, why don't you just go home? Miranda and I can do this without you. You're even more of a daddy's boy than I thought you were!'

Percy's shoulders drooped. 'Hey, that's not fair. I'm not a daddy's boy!'

'You are!' combated Demelza.

'Am not!'

'YOU ARE!'

'AM NOT!' Percy jolted up and stamped his foot hard on to the floor with anger. 'AM NOT! AM NOT! AM NOT! You're just a massive bossy-boots who doesn't like it when anyone disagrees with her!'

'Oh, come on, you two,' said Miranda, flitting between them. 'There's no need to argue. Why don't you both just apologize and—'

She stopped mid-sentence.

A high-pitched rattling sound was coming from the other side of the room. The three children spun around.

To their complete amazement, one of the bookshelves was opening up like a gigantic hinged door. It swung around, hitting the adjacent wall with a *clunk.*

And beyond it was the hidden vault.

CHAPTER 28
The Vault

The three children stood agog in the middle of the bedroom.

'H-how did that just happen?' said Percy. 'How did that bookcase just open up like that?'

Miranda's eyes darted around the room. 'Look!' she said, pointing to Percy's foot. '*You* opened it! There's a button, right there.'

Percy and Demelza looked down, and indeed a small red button was concealed within the swirly pattern of carpet beneath his shoe.

'When you stamped your feet you must have stood on it and unlocked the bookshelf,' said Demelza. 'Maybe I should make you angry more often?'

Percy scoffed.

Demelza's voice softened. 'Sorry for shouting at you.'

'Me too,' Percy replied.

'Guys, as much as I love the *slushy* stuff, what are we waiting for?' said Miranda with a wry grin. 'Let's look inside!'

Demelza teetered towards the hidden room. It was pitch black inside but an oppressive musky smell was wafting from within it, making her head spin. It was familiar somehow. A scientific chemical, maybe? Or an Ingredient of Awakening?

She fumbled for a light switch and found one on the inside wall.

Click.

The space beyond was illuminated, and for a moment Demelza, Miranda and Percy stood, dumbstruck, as if peering into the entrance of Ali Baba's cave.

For inside the secret room, every centimetre of every wall was covered in photographs of Demelza and Grandma Maeve.

It was like a shrine!

With Miranda and Percy close behind, Demelza crept forward and gazed around. Some of the photos were from as long as a year ago, but some had been taken as recently as last weekend! She pulled one from the wall to take a closer look. It showed her cycling to school, and underneath it a handwritten note said:

TUESDAY 18 June — ZERO Sign OF SUPERNATURAL POWERS
AS OF yet.

Another photo showed her relaxing in the garden with Grandma Maeve. From its viewpoint, it had probably been taken from high up in one of the cherry trees in the back lane, and next to it was scrawled:

SATURDAY 31 August — still no talk of supernatural Activity to DAte.

Demelza screwed up her eyes with both disbelief and horror. It was as if she were seeing her life mapped out in front of her – a collage of all her recent movements, arrivals, departures. Her stomach began to curdle, and she felt her skin tighten with goosebumps. The Snatcher had been following her for months! How hadn't she realized?

'OK, this is *seriously* weird,' said Miranda, looking over Demelza's shoulder. 'Who's been taking all of these pictures? And how haven't you noticed?'

'I . . . I . . .' began Demelza, but she was starting to panic, and she reached for the wall to steady herself. She slumped down onto the floor, her heart racing, her body trembling.

Percy quickly leapt to her aid. 'OK, this has gone far enough, Demelza. We're taking you back to Stricton right now. This crazy person needs to be put in jail! Even if the police don't believe in what you Spectre Detectors can do, this is more than enough evidence to arrest someone for stalking and kidnap!'

Demelza felt too weak to argue. The activities of the past few days had finally caught up with her and this latest discovery was the nail in the coffin. How did she ever believe that she was going to bring down the Snatcher and save Grandma Maeve? She was just a child.

With an arm around her shoulders, Miranda hoisted Demelza back to her feet. 'Come on,' she said. 'It's all going to be OK.'

But just as they were stepping through the threshold, something caught Demelza's eye. Stacked atop the filing cabinet nearest the door was a collection of faded old papers. On the very top was a pamphlet, and on its front, a photograph of a graveyard.

Demelza broke from her friend's grasp and picked it up. She read:

ETERNAL SORROW CEMETERY

A beautifully maintained cemetery in the heart of the English countryside. A place to remember and be remembered.

Demelza flicked through the rest of the pamphlet. There were pictures of weeping willows, headstones, stone angels, and . . .

A loose piece of paper fell out on to the floor.

Demelza picked it up. Typed on it were the words:

Grime & Blair
Funeral Directors & Embalmers

Date and place of burial: 12 NOVEMBER, ETERNAL SORROW CEMETERY

Casket and Services £400.00

Vault Space (Plot No. 10345, Eternal Sorrow Cemetery)....................................£200.00

Opening and closing of vault £25.00

Hire of Hearse...£150.00

Flowers £85.00

PAID IN FULL

Demelza felt her mouth slacken.

'What is it?' asked Percy, coming to stand by her. 'Have you found something useful?'

'I-I think I have,' stuttered Demelza. She pointed to the note and her friends peered down at it. 'It's a receipt for a funeral. What if this is the person that the Snatcher wants to bring back through the Conjuring of Resurrection?'

Miranda looked again at the receipt. 'That could make sense. Eternal Sorrow Cemetery is fairly close to Sourbank Bridge, where you've been ordered to meet. My mum took me there on a historical walk once.'

'And maybe that's where they're keeping your Grandma Maeve too?' added Percy. 'Maybe this room is just their headquarters?'

Demelza looked at her friends with a renewed feeling of hope. They could go and rescue Grandma Maeve!

But her jubilation was short-lived.

'Well, well, well! What's goin' on here then, eh?'

A shadow fell across the secret room and the children turned. The figures of Boris and Gregor loomed in the doorway, terrifying scowls sliced across their faces.

'Erm . . . trick or treat?' attempted Demelza, her voice trembling as she clutched her mask to her face. 'Got any sweets for us?'

'Ha! Nice try, Demelza!' said Boris, lumbering towards the vault. His face was sweaty and slick, like raw gammon. 'But we know exactly who you are and what you're doin' here!' He lunged for Demelza and ripped her mask from her face.

'As we thought!' said Gregor, pulling a bogey from his nose and wiping it on his trousers. 'The boss *will* be pleased to see the little brat so soon. But who are her little friends, I wonder?'

The man advanced and, as Miranda and Percy clutched their masks to their faces, Demelza scuttled backwards, trying to shield them. 'NO! Stay away from us!' she cried. 'Or . . . or . . .'

'Or what?' said Boris. 'A few firecrackers ain't gonna put us off this time, girly! And there's no one here to hear you scream, kiddywinks!' He let out a raspy laugh and flung his fat head backwards.

Boris was right. Demelza knew she'd been lucky at the Dance with Death, but there was no way out this time. Hope left her as she watched the henchmen lurching towards her, flexing their podgy fists . . .

'*You're* the only ones who are going to be screaming!' shouted Miranda suddenly. With almost superhuman strength, she seized the filing cabinet from the ground and pushed it in the brothers' direction with all her might. As if in slow motion, it toppled over like a falling tree, landing across their toes with a blood curdling crunch.

'*Owwwwwww!*' howled Gregor, hopping around on the spot.

'My poor tootsies!' Boris yelped.

The three children looked at each other.

'Run!' shouted Miranda. 'Now!'

The children skirted around the brothers, Demelza stopping to give Gregor a quick kick in the shins. '*That's* for kidnapping my grandma!' she snarled, before moving on to Boris and giving him a wallop across the back. 'And *that's* for taking the last slice of pork pie!'

CHAPTER 29
The Chase

Miranda led the way back through the decrepit corridors and gloomy passageways of the castle. Evening had quickly turned to night and had brought with it a bitter chill that crept through the cracked, grimed windows. Demelza knew that if they just got to the main staircase it would lead them back down to the front door, but every turn they took just seemed to lead them deeper and deeper into the depths of the castle.

'Are you sure we're going the right way?' Demelza called out as they skidded to a stop at the end of an arched passageway. A semicircle of doors lay ahead of them, each identical in colour and shape. 'This doesn't look very familiar!'

'Erm . . . erm . . .' Miranda muttered, panic beginning to set in as she looked around. 'I'm not sure. It's so dark. I think we might have taken a wrong turn . . .'

Worse still, the sound of heavy footsteps somewhere not too far away announced that Boris and Gregor were on their tail.

'They're going to catch us!' Percy whimpered.

Demelza stepped forward, her gaze darting frantically from doorknob to doorknob. 'We'll just have to choose one of these doors and hope it doesn't lead to a dead end!'

Percy squirmed. 'Don't you have an invention in your satchel that could tell us which door to go through? Your fortune-telling toaster thingy or something?'

'Oh yeah, because I always carry huge pieces of kitchen apparatus around in my pockets,' Demelza replied sarcastically. 'Let me just get it out now!'

The sound of footsteps was getting louder, as if a couple of rhinos were charging around in steel-capped boots. Boris and Gregor were now dangerously close!

'Through this one!' said Demelza, pointing to a door at random, and with a firm jolt she turned the handle and the children pushed their way inside.

A high-ceilinged, circular room extended beyond it, its walls covered in gigantic fading tapestries. A dusty grand piano stood in the corner, looking as if it hadn't felt the touch of human fingers in centuries.

'It's . . . it's a dead end!' said Percy, looking around hysterically for an exit. 'We're doomed!'

'Quick, let's try a different door!' shouted Miranda, turning back.

But it was already too late.

Two dark shadows fell across the room as the Neanderthalic shapes of the brothers stumbled inside.

'Oooooh, speedy little fings, ain't ya?' panted Gregor. 'I 'aven't 'ad to run that fast since the police came after me for stealin' that toddler's lollipop last month!'

'Don't worry, bruv, we've got 'em now,' said Boris, bolting the door behind him. His lips curled into a horrible smile, his snaggle teeth protruding from his lower jaw like a troll's.

'Yeah, we certainly 'ave!' agreed Gregor, swiping a rusty axe from the grip of a nearby suit of armour before pacing towards Demelza. 'I 'ope you aren't too attached to those ears of yours, cos they ain't gonna be attached to you for much longer!'

He lifted the weapon high above his head, and as he brought it down through the air Percy let out a scream.

Demelza dived out of the way just in time.

There was a metallic clang as the axe hit the marble floor, which cracked as if it were an icy lake.

'You sneaky little grub!' Gregor growled, scratching his bottom before yanking the axe from the floor. 'Not to worry, it always takes me a little time to warm up. Second time lucky . . .'

'Hey, over here, you big bozos!' called Miranda. 'Ready for some more pain?' She waved to Boris and Gregor before picking up a hardback copy of *Nineteenth-Century Sonnets* from a nearby bookshelf and drawing it close to her ear.

The brothers watched with confusion as she began to pivot on one foot, twirling round and around with the precision of an Olympian, gathering speed with each turn.

'Errr . . . what's goin' on?' mumbled Gregor as he watched the human hurricane whirling in front of him. 'What's she doin'?'

But before his brother could answer, Miranda let go of the book and it went hurtling through the air like a shot put. It smacked Gregor on the side of his jaw, and he fell backwards against the door like a sack of potatoes, groaning in pain.

'Why you little—!' growled Boris, lunging forward and gnashing his teeth. 'You'll pay for that!'

Miranda had already grabbed another book, and before the henchman could react it had smacked him right between the eyes. He fell to the floor next to his brother, flat on his back.

'Oooooh, stars!' he cooed, gazing up into space. 'Pretty, pretty stars!'

'Wow!' Percy spluttered, looking over at the dazed beasts with astonishment. 'Miranda, that was amazing!'

'*Astronomically* amazing!' added Demelza with gusto. '*Astoundingly* astronomically amazing!'

'Thanks,' Miranda replied. 'I'm not sure they'll be out for long, though. We need to get out of here. Fast!'

'But how?' asked Percy, looking at the brothers. 'Those ugly lumps are blocking the door.'

Demelza looked around, and as her eyes fell on a large window draped with heavy curtains, she smiled. It led on to a balcony! 'Follow me!'

Without hesitation she hurried over and pushed open the rusted window, Miranda and Percy close behind her. The cold night air, heavy with rain, whooshed at her like an unwanted guest, and her teeth began to chatter like the keys of a typewriter. They were on the first floor, which felt very high up, but a drainpipe led down the castle wall to the ground.

'Demelza, are you sure about this?' said Percy, peering over the railings.

'Not really, but we haven't got a choice,' she replied. 'Come on.'

Demelza reached for the pipe with both hands, checking its stability. It groaned and creaked but didn't pull away from the wall.

She swung her legs around the pipe, clamping her knees against it like a vice. Her hands followed one by one, and before long she was slowly easing herself down. It was painful – her fingers numb, her thighs burning – but it wasn't too long until she felt the comforting solidity of grass beneath her feet.

She'd made it!

'Well done!' she shouted as Percy came edging down behind. 'You're doing brilliantly! Keep going!' She couldn't help feeling a huge sense of pride in her friend. This time last week he'd barely left his house; now he was shimmying down the drainpipe of an old castle!

Miranda followed, and soon enough the three friends were back on solid ground. They huddled together under the canopy of a nearby tree, their clothes drenched and their hair knotted, as if they'd just been pulled from the sea. Demelza felt her body trembling with both cold and adrenalin.

'Urghhh!' huffed Percy. 'Why didn't the Tudors just

install lifts in their castles? It would have made things a whole lot easier!'

'Well, at least those thugs didn't follow us,' said Miranda, snatching a look back at the balcony.

'Those poetry books to the head must have really knocked them out,' said Demelza.

'Well, they do say that the pen is mightier than the sword,' replied Miranda with a wry smile. 'But what now? What's the plan, Demelza?'

Demelza straightened her thinking cap, her belly aflame with a rekindled determination. 'I need to go to Eternal Sorrow Cemetery immediately. Grandma Maeve, I'm coming to get you!'

Chapter 30
Bonbons

It had finally stopped raining by the time the children arrived back on the high street, but the sky was still masked with clouds. 'Right, this is what's going to happen,' Demelza whispered, gathering her friends together. 'Miranda, Percy – you go back to Stricton and let Ms Cardinal know that we're safe.' She pulled a map from her satchel and studied it. 'I'll go on to the cemetery. If I cut through Hollowbranch Forest, I think I can get there pretty quickly. If I'm not back in a couple of hours, send help.'

'Demelza, no!' said Miranda. 'You can't be walking through forests on your own at this time of night. It's far too dangerous, even for a girl armed with a satchel full of inventions!'

Percy nodded in agreement. 'Miranda's right. Haven't you heard the stories about Hollowbranch Forest? It's full of bears and wolves and monsters!' He took a deep breath and stepped forward. 'I'm coming with you.'

'Me too!' added Miranda.

'Thanks,' answered Demelza. 'But I've put you both in enough danger as it is. Head on back to Stricton and I'll be back as soon as I can.'

'No!' insisted Percy. 'I've always been the sensible one, the one who's obeyed the rules. Yes, the idea of walking through a dark forest in the middle of the night is frightening. *Terrifying!* But we need to do this. We need to bring back Grandma Maeve, together.'

Percy's chin was trembling, his eyes panicked but determined. For perhaps the first time in her life Demelza knew that this wasn't the time to be proud or put on a brave act. She looked to the ground, biting her lip. 'Thank you. I'd love you both to come with me.'

'Well, that settles it,' said Percy. 'Maybe one day the author of *Captain Thalasso* will write a comic book based on our adventures! You'll be Demelza the Daring! Then there'll be Miranda the Mighty. And, of course, not forgetting Percival the Proud!'

'Percival the Pain in the Bottom, more like!' said Demelza with a grin. 'Come on, let's go!'

The trio journeyed up the high street, where the rows of

little shops had long since closed and the trick-or-treaters had gone home. The street lamps cast a spooky light across the cobbles, and even though it was a route Demelza had taken so many times before, it somehow felt different now. It was as if with every step she took she was walking further and further into the unknown, and as they passed Mr Barnabas's shop she couldn't help but stop momentarily to glance at the comforting familiarity of the window display. She let her eyes gaze upon the pumpkins lit up with fairy lights and jars of sweet treats, and a pang of nostalgia melted through her body. She thought back to only a few weeks ago, when the agony of choosing between coconut macaroons and sugar mice had been the worst of her problems. But that seemed like a lifetime ago.

'Demelza? Is that you?' A whisper came from the shop doorway, and there was Mr Barnabas in his nightshirt and slippers. A glowing lamp illuminated his face, picking out his shiny golden tooth.

'M-Mr Barnabas,' stuttered Demelza. 'Yes, it's me. And my friends Percy and Miranda. Sorry, we didn't mean to wake you.'

'No bother, I was just making myself a cup of hot milk. But what are you three doing out after dark? Not causing any Halloween mischief, I hope? No stink bombs this year?'

He flashed Demelza a knowing grin.

Percy looked at his friends and gulped. 'N-n-no! We weren't causing mischief! Definitely not. We were just . . . erm . . . erm . . .'

'We were just returning from school,' interrupted Demelza coolly. 'We had a special night-time class to learn about the feeding habits of nocturnal animals. It's part of the new syllabus.'

Percy looked at her incredulously, but Mr Barnabas nodded without question. 'Right you are, then. But I guess all that studying has probably made you a bit peckish, eh? You could do with something sugary, perhaps?'

Demelza's eyes lit up like the headlights of a car and she nodded without hesitation.

'Well, it's lucky I always carry around a bag of emergency bonbons, isn't it?' The shopkeeper reached into his nightshirt pocket and took out a paper bag. 'And these ones are a new recipe I've been working on. They glow in the dark!'

He handed the bag to Demelza. Sure enough, the round sweets were luminous, aglow like little phosphorescent pebbles. How curious! Any other time she'd have liked nothing more than to quiz Mr Barnabas on the intricacies of the chemical process he'd used to make them, but for now she put the bag in her satchel and made a mental note to question him next time she visited.

As the children left, the shop keeper stood in the threshold and waved them off. 'Now run home quickly and straight to bed. And send my best to your Grandma Maeve, won't you, Demelza? Not seen her in a while . . .'

On hearing her grandmother's name Demelza's heart skipped a beat and, without turning back, she whispered, 'Yes, Mr Barnabas. I really hope I can.'

The night continued to thicken, and by the time Demelza, Percy and Miranda had reached Hollowbranch Forest, an opaque veil of mist had fallen over everything. With only a sliver of moonlight and a smattering of stars as their guide, they stood hand in hand, peering into the spidery depths ahead. The trees twisted above them in charcoal shards, bats hanging from the branches like leathery, black fruits.

'OK,' whispered Demelza, pulling up the collar of her coat before teetering forward. 'Stay close. We don't want to get lost or separated.'

Percy nodded, but before he'd even taken a footstep, he froze. 'Hang on . . . what if we *do* get lost or separated? How will we find our way back out? Shouldn't we mark the path or something?'

'Good thinking, Percy!' said Demelza. 'What can we use?' She took in their surroundings, trying to find something to mark their way, but found nothing. Why oh why hadn't she picked up her Everlasting Ball of String from Bladderwrack Cottage earlier on?

'Hang on, I think I have an idea!' exclaimed Miranda. 'Have either of you ever read the story of Hansel and Gretel?'

'Yeah,' replied Demelza. 'When I was little. But what's that got to do with anything? It's just a fairy tale.'

'In the story the children leave behind a trail of breadcrumbs,' explained Miranda. 'They use it to find their way back home.'

'We don't have any breadcrumbs, though!' said Percy.

'I know that,' said Miranda, reaching into Demelza's satchel. 'But we do have these.' She pulled out the bag of Mr Barnabas's glow-in-the-dark bonbons. 'Ta-da!'

Demelza stood up straight, grinning. 'Miranda Choudhury, you clever, clever thing! As much as it pains me to throw away a perfectly good bag of sweets, it's our only choice.'

Deeper and deeper into the forest they went, with Demelza dropping one of the luminous bonbons on to the floor every minute or so. Underfoot, twigs snapped like brittle bones, and the overhanging growth scratched at their skin and clothes. Every movement, every noise seemed magnified in the thick expanse around them, and with nothing else to distract her, the reality of what lay ahead began to weigh heavily on Demelza's mind. Dark images dominated her thoughts, pushing out hope like a cloud across the sun. She thought longingly of her attic room and her books, and Shiver asleep on Grandma's lap like a little snoozing salami.

But Demelza's thoughts were suddenly scattered.

Without warning, Miranda had grabbed her arm and was ushering both her and Percy behind a nearby tree. She put a cold finger to Demelza's lips, and the three children stood, frozen, listening to the sound of footsteps approaching across the dry leaves and a flurry of escalating voices.

Before long three sets of shoes came to a halt dangerously close to where the children were hiding, their long shadows falling across the ground. Demelza felt her stomach flip.

'I said I was sorry, boss,' pleaded a raspy-sounding man. 'The girl was just too quick for us. But the old woman won't have gone anywhere, that's for sure. Last time I checked it was pretty difficult to run away with rope around your ankles.'

'Yeah!' added another voice. 'Especially when your walking stick's been snapped in half.'

As the men moved off, Demelza peered out from behind the tree trunk. Up ahead she could make out the shape of three hooded figures trundling off into the distance.

'W-w-was that Boris and Gregor?' stuttered Percy.

'I think so,' said Demelza. 'And the one they called "boss" must be the Snatcher!'

Miranda pointed to where the figures were veering left on to the pathway out of the forest. 'Look, they're heading towards the cemetery. You were right, Demelza.'

Demelza nodded. 'Quick, we need to follow them!'

Keeping at a safe distance, the children tracked the figures through the trees, dashing behind branches and bushes with the stealth of three fox cubs. It wasn't long before they came to the edge of the forest, and the dark iron railings of Eternal Sorrow Cemetery appeared up ahead. Stone lions and serpents adorned its gateways, and Demelza watched as the three hoods slipped inside.

'Right, I think it's best if I go on alone from here,' she said to Percy and Miranda. 'You two, stay here and guard the entrance. Hopefully I'll be able to get Grandma Maeve out of there, but if the men try to escape with her, you'll need to do something to stop them going any further.'

'But we can't leave you to go in there alone—' Percy began.

'I'll be fine,' said Demelza. 'I need you to stay here.'

'Well, if you're sure,' said Percy. 'But we'll be right here waiting for you.'

Demelza smiled. 'Thank you. You really are the best friends anyone could wish for. And Percy, whoever it was who called you a daddy's boy earlier really needs their head seeing to.'

Percy crossed his arms in faux-annoyance, but couldn't help smiling. 'Well, as long as they never call me that again I think they can *probably* be forgiven!'

Demelza looked out on to the cemetery, and with her heart thudding in her chest, ventured through the gates. All around, gravestones sprouted upwards like broken teeth, bound together by sprawling tendrils of wilted ivy. It was painfully quiet, and as she walked deeper into the grave-yard, a tide of mist began to swirl about her ankles like water. Soon, to her dismay, she lost sight of the hooded figures entirely. Thinking of the undertaker's bill she'd found in the castle, she decided to try and find the grave herself. Plot number 10345, wasn't it? Where could it be? She knelt down by one of the graves and ran her fingers over the tombstone, but it was covered so thickly in mould that the words were barely readable. As she shuffled to the next one, a familiar voice called out behind her.

'Demelza, is that you?'

Demelza flinched and turned around.

Even in the dim light there was no mistaking the figure that stood over her.

It was Percy's father, Mr Grey.

CHAPTER 31
The Snatcher

'Mr Grey?' mumbled Demelza, slowly getting to her feet. 'What are you doing here? Are you lost?'

'Lost?' Mr Grey shook his head. 'Oh no, I'm very much in the right place.'

Demelza's brows furrowed as she stood silently among the graves. The mist was rising, soupy around her legs. 'Sorry,' she said. 'What do you mean? I thought you were on a business trip.'

'Oh, come on, Demelza!' he replied, running the tip of his moustache through his fingertips. 'You're a smart girl. Do I really need to spell it out? I'm here to see you, of course.'

Demelza's head was spinning . . . he couldn't be . . . could he? He wasn't . . .

'*You?*' she said, her voice hoarse. '*You* kidnapped my grandma?'

Mr Grey nodded, watching her in silence.

Demelza gasped as another realization hit her. *That's* where she'd seen Boris and Gregor before! They were Mr Grey's gardeners!

She stepped backwards, shaking her head. 'No! You can't be the Snatcher! You just can't!'

'But I am,' said Mr Grey. 'I know I'm not exactly the – what was it you said again? – the *murderous criminal* that you had in mind.'

A lump formed in Demelza's throat as she listened to Mr Grey repeating her own words back to her – words she'd spoken to Percy when she'd revealed everything to him in his bedroom the other night. She felt her breath quickening. That creak outside the bedroom door . . . they'd assumed it was the cat, but it wasn't, was it? Mr Grey had been listening all along! Her mind felt like it was about to explode. Demelza lunged forward. 'Where is she?' she shouted. 'What have you done with my grandma?'

'All in good time,' answered Mr Grey calmly. 'But first, let's get down to business.' He began to circle around Demelza, the crunch of his footsteps on gravel cutting through the stillness of the cemetery. 'You know why you're here, don't you?'

Demelza's face was like steel. 'You want me to perform the Conjuring of Resurrection.'

'Exactly!' replied Mr Grey. 'You see, Demelza, there's someone that I've been wanting to bring back to life for a long, long time. I've been looking for a young Spectre Detector to help me for years, but so far no one has had the sense to oblige my request.' He sighed. 'Strange, really. I thought it would be preferable to being killed by my henchmen, but obviously not.'

Demelza clenched her fists. 'All those young Spectre Detectors you kidnapped . . . you got Boris and Gregor to murder them?'

Mr Grey nodded with chilling nonchalance. 'And if you don't do as I ask, your grandmother and that ridiculous sausage dog will be joining them. On the other hand, if you fulfil my request, then I'll promise to spare them both – although, of course, your life will be forfeited as part of the Conjuring. This really couldn't be simpler.'

A sickening feeling rose up in Demelza's tummy as a million conflicting thoughts thrashed around in her head. What on earth should she do? She couldn't make such an awful decision. She needed to buy herself some thinking time.

'Well?' sneered Mr Grey. 'What'll it be? Are you going to come nicely, or am I going to have to get Boris to sharpen his carving knife? He's not in the most forgiving of moods after what you put him through in the castle earlier–'

'FATHER! LET HER GO!'

A voice rang through the night and Demelza turned to see Percy standing under a nearby weeping willow. He was trembling and as pale as frost, but was grasping a large stick which he pointed towards his father. Demelza had never seen him looking so angry.

'Percival?' said his father, quickly distancing himself from Demelza. 'What on earth are you doing here? You're meant to be at home with Fräulein von Winkle!'

Percy's gaze was probing. 'What am *I* doing here? What are *you* doing here, more like!'

Mr Grey cleared his throat. Sweat was pouring down his face and an eel-blue vein had begun to twitch in the side of his head. 'I-I was just on my way back home from a business meeting. I came across young Demelza here, who seemed to be lost. I was just helping her find her way home–'

Percy scoffed. 'Don't lie to me, Father! I heard everything you've said. Now let Grandma Maeve and Shiver go!'

Demelza ran to her friend. 'Percy, I told you to stand guard at the gates with Miranda. What are you doing here?'

'I couldn't just leave you alone,' Percy replied. 'And besides, Miranda's fine on her own. She's tougher than the both of us put together.'

Mr Grey moved towards his son, pushing Demelza aside with unflinching determination. 'Now listen here, Percival, let's not be a silly billy, eh? Demelza's promised to help me with something, that's all. Now come over here with me at once.'

Percy's face crumpled and he looked to the floor. Demelza could see his eyes gleaming and she watched with anticipation, expecting him to give up and submit to his father's wishes. But Percy sniffed and held up his head. 'No! Demelza hasn't promised to help you with anything! Why do you even want her to do the Conjuring of Resurrection anyway?'

'Because . . . because . . .' Mr Grey pushed his fingers through his hair in obvious frustration. 'I'm doing all this for *you*, Percival!'

'Me?' Percy replied. 'What's any of this got to do with me?'

Mr Grey's gaze dropped to the ground and he sighed. For a moment he looked almost defeated, completely lost for words. Demelza swallowed. What was he about to reveal?

'Haven't you ever thought about why I've mollycoddled you so much, Percival?' Mr Grey said eventually. 'Why I don't let you go out to play, why you aren't allowed to go to school? Why you can't eat proper food, or touch other people?'

Percy looked to Demelza then back to his father. 'Because I'm ill, of course. Because I've got a *weak constitution*, or whatever it is that you always say. That's why.'

Mr Grey's chin began to tremble. 'No, Percival, that's not it at all. I'm afraid, son, it's because you're a spectre.'

CHAPTER 32

Percy's Memories

Percy jostled from foot to foot. 'W-w-what are you talking about?' he spluttered. 'How can I be a spectre? That would mean that I'm . . . dead!'

Mr Grey nodded.

Percy looked down at himself, staring in confusion, as if looking at his body for the very first time. 'No,' he muttered. 'No, it can't be true.'

Demelza stood, dumbfounded. She would have *known* if Percy was a spectre, she would have *known* if he wasn't really alive. Mr Grey was lying! She turned to her friend and whispered, 'It's not true, Percy. I've seen spectres and you're not one. This is just some awful trick!'

Percy looked to his dad for confirmation. 'Father?'

Mr Grey sighed heavily. 'Percival, take off your gloves.'

Percy's brows furrowed in surprise. 'But I'll freeze! It's

the middle of the night—'

'Just do it!'

Trembling, Percy put down the stick he was still clutching and began to take off his woollen gloves. He let them fall to the floor, his exposed fingers hanging pale and limp at his sides.

Mr Grey turned to Demelza. 'Now, try and touch his skin. Try and hold your hands against his. You won't be able to.'

Demelza suddenly felt nervous. Surely she'd touched Percy's hand before? Surely they'd arm-wrestled or given each other high fives? But then, Mr Grey had always warned so strictly against making any physical contact.

Demelza edged towards her friend. There was fear in his eyes, desperation. 'Hold up your hands,' she whispered, trying to soothe him. 'It'll be fine.'

'I-I don't want to,' stuttered Percy. 'I'm scared.'

'Don't worry, I had a bath last week,' joked Demelza. She held up her hands and wiggled her fingers. 'There's no bogies on them, I promise!'

Percy smiled meekly and turned his palms towards Demelza's. There were only a few centimetres between them now and Demelza felt the hairs lifting on the nape of her neck. She felt as if she were being made to touch a hot poker or stroke an angry dog.

Don't be dead, she prayed. *You can't be dead . . .*

But as Demelza reached out, she watched as her hands disappeared through Percy's. It was like they were moving through cold air, through a cloud of fog. . .

'No!' Percy yelped. He stumbled backwards, shaking his fingers out in front of him as if they weren't his. 'NO! It can't be . . . It can't . . .' His voice was panicked, desperate. 'If I'm a spectre, then why don't I float around? Why don't I fly?'

'Because you've never known that you could!' replied Mr Grey. 'Why don't you try now?'

Percy laughed nervously and turned on his heel. 'You're crazy!' He glanced at Demelza for confirmation. 'He's crazy, isn't he?'

But Demelza felt the sting of tears. 'Percy, I'm so sorry . . .'

'Even if I think really hard about floating,' Percy murmured. 'There's no way I can . . . no way . . .' Percy gazed down at his feet and his mouth fell open. Demelza followed his gaze: he had lifted a little way above the ground.

For a while all was silent, the long tendrils of the weeping willows moving in the night breeze like trails of tears. Demelza's mind was racing. Why hadn't she spotted it sooner? Her mind flicked back to the photographs she'd seen in their house, how Percy had been curiously missing.

Eventually Percy looked to his father. 'So how did I die?' he whispered.

Mr Grey stepped forward towards his son. 'It was when we were still living in our old house in London. Can you remember it, Percival?'

Percy nodded timidly.

'And what's your last memory of us being there?'

Percy stared at his feet, deep in thought. He looked as if he were panning the rivers of his mind for memories, for any little flash of gold.

'It was that night you took me to the funfair,' he said softly. 'We ate popcorn and went on the waltzers. You got angry because a clown dropped a custard pie in your lap. I remember Mum tucking me in that night, switching off the light . . .'

Silence.

'Go on,' urged Mr Grey.

Demelza could see the cogs of Percy's mind turning again, and he winced as if remembering something unpleasant. 'My chest started to feel tight,' he said. 'It was my asthma. I was having an attack. I was coughing. I couldn't breathe and . . .' Percy paused momentarily. 'The next thing

I remember is waking up in a new house. You said that I'd been in hospital, that I'd been unconscious for a long time but a very special doctor had saved me.' He looked up to his father. 'You lied to me?'

'No, no, I didn't lie!' said Mr Grey. He ran to his son but Percy floated backwards. 'A special doctor *did* save you! He brought you back to me as a spectre . . . so you could have another chance at life. So we could be together again!'

'A special doctor?' Demelza blurted out. 'You mean a Spectre Detector! Percy passed away and you got a Spectre Detector to bring him back, didn't you?'

Percy's cheeks began to tremble, his thin arms tight to his body. 'Is that true, Father?'

Mr Grey nodded. 'I didn't know what else to do. The asthma attack had taken you from me . . .' His voice caught in his throat. 'I had nobody left.'

'You had Mum!'

Mr Grey's shoulders drooped, tears running down his cheeks and into his moustache. 'She left too. She couldn't cope with losing you. She needed to get away. She wanted a fresh start.'

He looked longingly at his son and Demelza could see a deep sadness swirling in his eyes. For a moment she couldn't help but feel sorry for him – he had no wife and his only child had died. No one should have to go through that . . .

No! She couldn't think like that! This was the evil man who'd kidnapped Grandma Maeve and Shiver. This was the man who'd murdered all of the other young apprentices. She *had* to stay strong!

She turned to Mr Grey. 'Why wasn't there a reverse summoning?' she demanded. 'Spectres are only meant to have three hours in the living world. Who was the Spectre Detector you used? Some crook, no doubt!'

Mr Grey sniffed back his tears. Within an instant his face had darkened and he glared down at Demelza with ghoulish eyes. Without answering, he reached into his briefcase and brought out an old photograph. It showed a gentleman with a large moustache standing next to a young, bespectacled man wearing a mortar board.

Demelza's heart sank. It was Mr Grey . . . and her dad!

'I was your father's university professor, you see,' said Mr Grey, reclining against a gravestone. 'We grew close during his studies and stayed friends long after he graduated.

'But after I lost Percival I fell into a state of deep mourning. I thought that I'd never be happy again. Naturally, your father wanted to help me. And so your parents revealed their biggest secret. They took me to their summoning chamber.'

Demelza's stomach flipped as she anticipated what Mr Grey was going to say next.

'Your parents told me all about the Spectre Detectors and what they did to help those in mourning,' continued Mr Grey. 'I couldn't quite believe it at first, but as soon as they performed the summoning and I saw Percival again I—' He breathed out heavily and composed himself. 'Well, for those first couple of hours it was as if I had never lost him.'

'And that's why we Spectre Detectors do what we do!' said Demelza. 'We do it to help people feel better. To let them have a proper goodbye.'

'But it wasn't enough!' snapped Mr Grey. His eyebrows had gathered and anger was rising in his voice. 'As my last hour began, I knew I wasn't going to let Percival go again.'

'So you convinced my mum and dad to let him stay?' asked Demelza. 'They went against the rules of the Quietus?'

'Oh no,' said Mr Grey, his mouth curling. 'Quite the opposite. They'd already said that it wasn't ethical for the deceased to return to this world indefinitely; they said that it was against the principles of being a Spectre Detector. After the three hours were up they were going to send Percival back to Inn Memoriam.' Mr Grey leant forward, the moonlight picking out the glistening pearls of sweat on his brow. 'And that's why, Demelza, your parents had to die!'

For a moment time stood still.

Demelza's body went numb and her vision began to swim. Mr Grey's lips were still moving but his words were now nothing but white noise, like the sound of a radio stuck between stations. 'But they died in an accident,' she whispered. 'They were in a car crash.'

'Crash – yes. Accident? No. They tried to get away from me – but I was faster. I ran them off the road. It's a shame things had to turn out that way,' said Mr Grey. 'I'd offered your parents a lot of money to do as I wished. Your family could have been rich, powerful. What kind of fools would turn that down for the sake of a few potions and a bit of hocus pocus?'

Demelza felt her teeth grinding together, her body a clenched fist. 'My parents were *not* fools! And it's not potions and hocus pocus! It's life and death!'

Mr Grey laughed. 'Oh, you really are just as stubborn as your parents. Just as sanctimonious, just as self-righteous.' He launched forward until he was just centimetres away from Demelza's face, and then stroked her cheek with a clammy hand. 'And if you don't do as I ask, Demelza, your grandma will die, just like your parents.'

'FATHER, NO!' shouted Percy. 'Stop it! You can't ask Demelza to do this! It's not right.'

Mr Grey's eyes were wild. 'But, my darling boy, don't you want to be brought back to life? We can go away, start afresh. It will be just like old times – no more being kept in the house, no more strict rules, no more secrets . . .' He turned to Demelza. 'Just think about it, Demelza, if you do as I ask, you won't *just* be saving your grandma, you'll be giving your best friend another chance to live – to *really* live. Surely you don't want to deny Percival this opportunity? Think of how happy you'd make him. Son, wouldn't that make you happy?'

Demelza watched Percy closely. She could tell he was considering all that his father had said and she couldn't really blame him. After all, if he stayed as a spectre he'd never be able to grow up, never be able to have a family, never be able to see the rest of the world. But at the same time, if she did the Conjuring then *she* wouldn't have a future; her hopes of becoming a member of the Royal Society of Inventors would be taken away, her dreams of winning prizes for her scientific discoveries would be dashed. Her mind was a tangle of conflict.

'We could get that puppy you always wanted, Percival,'

continued Mr Grey. His voice was urgent now, desperate. 'I could take you on holiday! You always loved going to the beach. What do you say?'

Percy fiddled with the edge of his coat and Demelza watched with anticipation, half expecting him to agree to Mr Grey's wishes.

'Father, I know how sad you must feel,' said Percy, drawing himself tall among the gravestones. 'And I know that you're doing all of this because you love me. But I'm dead. And I'm not going to let someone else give up their life for me. Especially my best friend.' He looked at Demelza, appearing more calm and confident than she'd ever seen him before.

Mr Grey's words began to flow out of his mouth uncontrollably. 'But I've been waiting for this moment for so long . . . I want my little boy back . . . I won't lose you again, Percival . . . I won't let her destroy this for us . . .'

Percy edged towards his father. 'I don't want Demelza to do the Conjuring. I want to be left as I am. Now please, let Demelza and her grandma go. Please.'

Mr Grey pinched the bridge of his nose and sighed. For a moment Demelza thought that he was going to do as his son asked. Had he seen sense? Had he realized the awful things he had done?

No.

As a crackle of lightning lit the sky Mr Grey let out an ear-piercing whistle. There was a rustling sound from the trees up ahead and Boris and Gregor came trundling towards him, their shadows stretching as they approached. They were still swathed in their robes, the long hoods pointing upwards like warlock hats.

'Well, hello again, princess,' said Gregor to Demelza, his guillotine tones slicing through the night air. 'How nice to see you!' He lunged forward, wrestling Demelza to the floor like she was a rag doll. He pinned her down by her shoulders. His ponytail had come loose and his long, ratty hair hung over her like a greasy curtain. 'What shall I do with 'er, boss?' he said, his stale breath hot on Demelza's face. 'Can I cut her fingers off now? Can I? Can I?'

Demelza began to struggle, kicking out with her legs and gnashing her teeth. 'No! Get off me!' she screamed. 'Get off!'

'Don't worry, Demelza, I'm going to get help!' she heard Percy shout. 'Whatever you do, don't do the Conjuring! I'll be back soon, I promise!'

Demelza looked up and watched as Percy took a deep breath before pushing himself upwards. He went higher and higher into the night sky, before zigzagging back towards the forest.

Boris cracked his knuckles and made to follow but Mr Grey held out a hand. 'Oh, leave him! There's nothing he can do to stop me now. There's no one who can help.' He stood over Demelza and crossed his arms. 'And besides, when Demelza here performs the Conjuring of Resurrection and he realizes how great it is to be alive again, he'll change his mind.'

Gregor nodded and hoisted Demelza over his gargantuan shoulders. As he lumbered forward, the graveyard flashed behind her in a grey blur, and feeling the hope drain from her body, she stopped struggling. Her satchel fell from her shoulder, and all that she could do was close her eyes and wait for the worst.

CHAPTER 33
The Crypt

Gregor came to a stop. Demelza felt him push against a heavy door and, as he walked over the threshold, the peals of thunder and coming storm above the graveyard were replaced by the echo of his heavy footsteps on stone. She couldn't make out where she was. It was pitch black and the pungent smell of damp hit the back of her throat. Some kind of cave or cellar or dungeon?

'OK, you can drop her now,' came Mr Grey's voice as he and Boris entered, and the door slammed shut. Following his boss's orders quite literally, Gregor loosened his grip, and Demelza came crashing down on to the cold, hard floor with a thump. She gasped as every bit of air was knocked from her chest like a balloon being popped.

'So, let's get started, shall we?' There was a strike of a match and Mr Grey lit a torch, filling the space with a low, murky light.

Demelza sat up slowly, letting her eyes adjust. Her chest was burning and she pulled her arms across it as she gazed around. The ceiling was low and arched, and the grey stone walls were dripping with condensation. Large, engraved sarcophagi were placed side by side along the walls. She wasn't in a cave or dungeon, Demelza realized. She was in a huge, dark crypt!

'Where's my grandma?' she demanded, getting to her feet. 'Let me speak to her!'

Gregor moved to restrain her, but Mr Grey stopped him. 'I suppose it might be motivational for you to say hello to her,' he mused. 'Although your grandma won't be able to say hello back, of course – she's a little bit *tied up* at present!' He laughed at his own joke. 'Boris, bring in the old woman.'

Demelza fell silent, watching Boris lumber to an adjoining chamber before returning with Grandma Maeve hoisted under one arm. Her limbs had been bound with rope and there was a gag pulled tight across her mouth. Under his other arm was Shiver, his paws tied together and his snout closed by a muzzle. Boris flung them both to the ground and they lay trembling. As Grandma Maeve's gaze landed on Demelza, she let out a muffled gasp.

'Grandma!' Demelza tore towards the old woman, dropping to her knees and flinging her arms around her neck. Her body felt as frail as the skeleton of a tiny sparrow, her skin as cold as marble.

Demelza turned to Mr Grey. 'Let her talk!' she demanded. 'Otherwise I *definitely* won't do as you ask.'

Mr Grey sighed. 'Oh, very well. You can have two minutes, but that's it.' He snapped his fingers, and Boris untied the gag and whipped it out of Grandma Maeve's mouth. She moaned in pain.

'Grandma!' Demelza cried. 'Are you all right?'

'Oh, my darlin' girl,' Grandma Maeve replied. 'You came to find me!'

'Of course I did!' said Demelza, kissing her grandma's face all over. She felt her heart brightening as if it were being lit up by an incandescent filament. 'Oh, it's so good to see you.'

Shiver let out a whimper. He looked weak and his fur was matted with dirt. 'It's so good to see you too, boy!' Demelza exclaimed. She threw her arms around the little dog and removed his muzzle. He gave her a lick on the nose, and even though his breath was stale, she beamed with joy.

Mr Grey looked at his wristwatch. 'One minute left.'

Tears began to roll down Grandma Maeve's pale, wrinkled cheeks and, as Demelza stared desperately into her eyes, she could feel the salty sting of tears welling in her own. 'Grandma, I'm so sorry,' she whispered. 'This has all been my fault. I told Percy about the Spectre Detectors when I thought that Ms Cardinal was the Snatcher. Mr Grey overheard and that's how he knew my powers had arrived and . . . and . . .' Her face dropped into her hands and she began to sob uncontrollably. 'I don't know what to do, Grandma. This is all such a mess.'

Grandma Maeve brought her voice down to a pressing whisper. 'You need to escape, Demelza. Save yourself.'

Demelza wiped her eyes on her sleeve. 'But if I do the Conjuring of Resurrection then you get to go home with Shiver. And Percy can have a chance at a proper, happy life.'

The old woman sighed heavily. 'Demelza, Percy's your friend. Do you think he'd ever be able to live a happy life knowing that you'd died to give it to him? And your old grandma has lived a long and full enough life as it is, don't you worry about me. Death ain't the end, remember? Please, my darlin', save yourself!'

'But—'

'Right, time's up!' interrupted Mr Grey. 'Get the old woman away from the girl! NOW!'

Gregor and Boris lumbered forward and as they wrenched Grandma Maeve to her feet, along with a whining Shiver, Demelza fixed the thugs with a ferocious stare.

'Love you more than teapots,' Grandma Maeve mouthed.

'Love you more than circuit boards,' Demelza mouthed back, but the anger inside her was blistering hot. No! There was no way that she would save herself and leave Grandma to die! She just *had* to figure out a way to bring down Mr Grey and his henchmen. She just needed to buy herself some more time to come up with a plan.

She got up and met Mr Grey's gaze with a disgusted sneer. 'OK,' she lied. 'I'll do as you wish.'

CHAPTER 34
Open Casket

Mr Grey grabbed Demelza by the neck and pushed her to the other end of the tomb, his fingers digging into her flesh. The stench of his cologne had begun to mingle with the heady reek of his stale sweat and it made her stomach turn.

'Now, your grandma has already told us what equipment you need for the Conjuring,' he said. 'She didn't want to at first, of course, but a little *gentle persuasion* seemed to get her to open up. I think you'll find everything you need here.'

He brought her to a makeshift workbench and revealed the collection of jars and bottles which had obviously been stolen from the summoning chamber. There was also a pestle and mortar, a Mask of Facelessness and a crucible hanging from a tripod. Mr Grey struck a match and soon enough a fire was crackling underneath it.

'Now get to it!' he said. 'And I'm warning you, girl, if there's any funny business, you know what will happen.' He turned to Gregor, who had a calloused hand over Grandma Maeve's mouth and was holding a knife blade dangerously close to her throat.

As the crucible began to bubble, Demelza looked through the Ingredients of Awakening on offer. As much as she was tempted to choose things she knew wouldn't work, she feared that would only result in more harm than good. Instead, she studied the various bottles and jars as slowly as possible, trying to come up with an escape plan. If she could think of a way out of all of this, then maybe Percy could come and live at Bladderwrack Cottage as a spectre? Eventually, he could get a job at the Quietus. But how was she going to get herself, Grandma Maeve and Shiver out? She didn't even have her satchel any more.

'Hurry up, girl!' said Mr Grey, coming to stand over her and looking down at his watch. 'We haven't got all night!'

Demelza felt her body tighten and she quickly took a flagon of spiced damson wine which had been bottled in the year Percy died. Then she reached for a phial of ink to reflect his love of comic books, and she picked up what must be his old school tie. Demelza pulled it close, thinking about the life her friend had led before she'd even been born.

But just as she was about to throw the ingredients into the crucible, something dawned on her. If she was going to perform the Conjuring of Resurrection correctly then she also needed a fragment of Percy's bone, the final ingredient required to bring a spectre back to life completely!

A glimmer of hope shot through her and she turned. 'Erm . . . excuse me, Mr Grey,' she said, attempting to feign naivety. 'I think we might have a bit of a problem. You see, in order for me to do the Conjuring correctly, I need a fragment of bone from the deceased.' She gestured to the workbench. 'You don't seem to have left that here for me. Maybe we'll have to postpone the procedure?'

Demelza crossed her fingers hard, hoping that Mr Grey's face would crumple with disappointment. But instead he let out a cold laugh. 'Oh, nice try, Demelza! But why do you think I chose to bring you here in the first place, hmm?'

He walked to the nearest sarcophagus, which Demelza realized had been draped with a heavy, black cloth. Mr Grey removed the material. Beneath it was a large stone casket, visibly cleaner and newer than all the others. 'Go take a look,' said Mr Grey. 'I think you'll find what you need.'

Demelza edged forward and let her fingers run across the brass plaque adorning the lid. It was engraved with the words:

HERE LIES THE BODY OF
PERCIVAL STERLING GREY
BELOVED SON
DEARLY MISSED
RIP

Demelza's stomach churned, bile rising up in her throat.

'This is our family burial chamber, you see,' said Mr Grey. 'My father is buried here, as are my grandparents and my great-grandparents. It was only right for Percival to be laid to rest here too.' Mr Grey smiled. 'But not for much longer! Boris, will you do the honours?'

Boris grunted, and with sinister delight, lumbered over to the casket and heaved at its lid. Stone ground against stone and Demelza's hand shot to her mouth in horror. She turned away.

Time had run out.

There was no time to figure out a way to escape.

No time to foil Mr Grey's plan.

She had no choice but to do as he asked: she'd die to save Grandma Maeve.

'That's it,' said Mr Grey as he pushed Demelza towards the casket. 'Just one fragment of bone is all you need—'

CRASH!

The chamber door flew open and Demelza spun around. She blinked, and for a second she thought that she must be dreaming. '*Melting meteorites!*' she gasped.

For there, standing in the threshold brandishing a fiery torch, was Mr Barnabas. And behind him were Percy and Miranda.

CHAPTER 35
The Army of the Dead

'Neville, stop what you're doing immediately!' shouted Mr Barnabas. He strode towards Mr Grey, flanked by Percy on one side and Miranda on the other. 'I know you've been through a lot, Neville, but this is not going to help anyone. Just come with us and we can talk it all through. You won't be much good to Percival if you're locked up in prison, eh? Now, order your men to stand down, and let the girl and her grandmother go.'

Demelza stood, stunned, her eyes flicking from the group at the door to her grandmother held captive by Gregor, then to Boris standing by the open casket. Where did Percy and Miranda find Mr Barnabas? Did he know the truth about Percy? And about the Spectre Detectors?

'Oh, come on, Emmanuel, old chap,' said Mr Grey,

beads of sweat now dripping from his forehead. 'I think there's been a bit of a misunderstanding here, eh? Why don't you just toddle back home, and I'll come and see you at your little sweet shop tomorrow. Maybe we can talk about some kind of *charitable donation* to go towards that new roof you wanted?'

Mr Barnabas's brow darkened. 'Don't take me for a fool, Neville. I will not be bribed. You're not going to get away with this.'

Mr Grey's mouth curled. 'And how do you intend to stop me exactly?'

'LIKE THIS!' shouted Mr Barnabas, and with two fingers to his lips he let out a whistle as piercing as a banshee's wail. 'ENTER, SPECTRES!' he bellowed, launching a fist into the air. 'ENTER NOW!'

For a second there was complete silence.

Demelza stood glued to the spot in confusion. Did Mr Barnabas just say what she thought he'd said? Was he a Spectre Detector too?

But Demelza daren't utter a word. Like the beginnings of a storm, a freezing wind burst through the chamber. The noise was unbearable, as if a thousand eagles were propelling forward, as if a cyclone was whipping its way through a desert. A battalion of spectres came careering inside, each one clasping a deadly-looking weapon.

Demelza recognized them at once – they were the spectres she'd seen at the Quietus! There was the Ancient Egyptian, the burly cowgirl, the Native American chief and a menagerie of spectral animals that growled and squawked as if ready to pounce. A pirate floated shoulder to shoulder with a bare-chested boxer and a rag-tag band of Victorian children brandished their chimney sweeps like swords. At their front Harry Le Quin, the jester who had sat at the Quietus reception, bounded forward on a spectral horse which galloped through the air like a breaking wave.

Gregor dropped the knife from Grandma's throat and Boris staggered back towards the wall, away from the grave and the approaching army of spectres. 'Arghhh! Keep away from us you zombie demons!' he shouted. 'Get away!'

But Mr Grey's face was set in determination, and the vein in his temple was pulsing like a worm trying to escape. He strode over to Grandma and, taking the knife from where Gregor had dropped it, locked his own arm around Grandma Maeve's throat. He angled the tip of the blade dangerously close to her face. She was trembling, but didn't move a muscle.

'Neville, put that down,' said Mr Barnabas sternly. 'We

can help you, just let Maeve go.'

Mr Grey laughed, spittle building in the corners of his mouth. 'I don't think so! Do you think I'm going to give up on what I've waited so long for? My son *will* be brought back to life! Demelza *will* do the Conjuring of Resurrection!'

'Father, please!' pleaded Percy. 'I've already told you, I'm happy as I am. I can go and live at the Quietus with all the other spectres. I'll be safe there, and we can still see each other. You can come and visit whenever you like . . .'

All heads turned to Mr Grey. Demelza swallowed. For a moment it looked as though he was considering his son's suggestion. His eyes were shining with tears, his hands trembling as he curled his fist tighter around the handle of the knife. Demelza knew that whatever this man said next would decide hers and her grandmother's fate.

'Well?' said Percy. 'What do you say? Let Grandma Maeve go and then we can talk.'

'No,' answered Mr Grey. 'We both know that if I give myself up, I'll go to prison – and then I'll never be able to bring you back to life. I won't give up on you, Percy. Some-day, somehow, I will succeed.' Still holding the knife to Grandma's throat, he backed towards the open door of the crypt. 'I'm leaving now, but if anyone tries to follow me, the old woman is chopped liver, you understand?'

And with that, Mr Grey disappeared into the darkness of the cemetery, taking Grandma Maeve with him.

CHAPTER 36
The Robotic Hand
for Homework Haters

Demelza ran her hands through her hair in despair. What was she going to do now? Unless she was able to somehow procure a shotgun or a cross-bow within the next few seconds, there was no way that she was going to be able to bring down Mr Grey without him hurting Grandma Maeve.

'Spectres, after him!' commanded Mr Barnabas from the doorway. 'NOW!'

'NO!' protested Demelza. 'Didn't you hear what he said? If anyone follows, Grandma Maeve's as good as dead!'

'She's right,' said Percy. 'My dad isn't thinking straight. Who knows what he'll do if we cross him again?'

THUD!

Demelza's satchel suddenly landed at her feet.

'You dropped it in the cemetery,' Miranda called from

across the crypt. 'Is there something inside that you could use? One of your inventions, maybe?'

Demelza grinned and, with adrenalin spurring her on, tore open the bag. She scrabbled through the pockets, searching frantically for something that might be of use. Out came a half-eaten bar of toffee, some marbles, a mouldy banana, her Magnificent Belly-Button Cleaning Machine, her Self-Playing Harmonica . . .

Then she spotted it.

Nestled right at the bottom was the Remarkable Robotic Hand for Homework Haters! Its clawed metal fingers were outstretched, as if waiting to grab hold of something, or maybe *someone*. Could she use it to seize Mr Grey? It hadn't had an official test run yet, but it was her only hope!

'Found anything?' shouted Miranda from the doorway. 'He's headed for the church!'

Demelza gave a big nod as she sprung to her feet. 'Wish me luck!' she said, and with her thinking cap pulled on tight, she tore out into the cemetery.

Outside, the night wind hacked at her skin like a sickle. It was still foggy, but up ahead Demelza could just about make out Grandma Maeve's slight silhouette being dragged into the steeple-topped church ahead. Mr Grey's laugh rang through the night, mingling with her grandmother's screams like a jarring, discordant concerto.

'Don't worry, Grandma,' whispered Demelza to herself as she slalomed through the tombstones to the church. 'I'm coming!'

She ran through the stone gateway of the church and slipped silently inside. It was dark, the only glimmers of light coming through the stained-glass windows throwing jewelled hues across the pews. Demelza tucked herself behind a pulpit and watched. At the altar, Mr Grey's back was turned, but it was clear that he was still holding the knife close to Grandma Maeve's throat. Her muffled cries echoed through the pews as she struggled to break free.

'Oh, be quiet, you stupid bag! I'm not letting you go until I know it's safe for me to escape,' he taunted, heading for a narrow door in the vestry. His jeers echoed through the church's stone pillars and Demelza breathed deeply, stopping herself from reacting too quickly. She only had one chance at this, one chance to save Grandma Maeve. She pulled the glimmering robotic hand over her own like a glove, adjusted the settings on the control pad at its wrist, and with the precision of an archer, pointed it in the direction of Mr Grey. She slammed the thumb of her other hand on to the control pad's red button and . . .

WHOOOOOOOOOOSH!

The hand was let loose from its metal wrist and flew through the air like a remote-controlled aeroplane. Using the device's control pad on the wrist piece, Demelza navigated the hand through the church's wide gothic arches: ducking and diving, zooming left and right, flying loop-de-loop.

But the buzz and hum of its motor were noisier than Demelza had expected, and as it hurtled towards Mr Grey, he spun around.

'What on earth—?' He jumped backwards, losing his grip on Grandma Maeve, who fell to the floor. As the robotic hand circled around him, Mr Grey began flailing his knife around, as if he were swatting an extremely large bumblebee. 'What's happening? Get away from me! Get off!'

'Oh, I don't think so, Mr Grey!' Demelza stepped out from her hiding place, and as soon as the contraption was close enough to its victim, she pressed the blue button on her wrist.

ZAAAAAAAAAAAAP!

The fingers of the robotic hand began to stretch outwards like tentacles, before closing around Mr Grey's neck. When they had clamped themselves tight, Demelza moved the lever on her control panel and Mr Grey was lifted into the air. The invention was working! It was just as strong as a real hand – perhaps even stronger!

'ARGGGHHHH! Let me go!' Mr Grey wailed as his feet left the ground and he was hoisted higher into the air. He thrashed about, wobbling all over the place like a moustachioed octopus. He tried to unhook the metal fingers, but the more he struggled, the tighter Demelza ordered them to squeeze around his throat.

'You're going nowhere!' Demelza shouted. Her forehead was dripping with sweat, her pulse racing. 'Apart from a prison cell, that is!'

Demelza glared up at Mr Grey, suspended on the end of the contraption. His face was green, his legs treading air like a duck's in water. 'N-n-now look here, Demelza,' he spluttered, 'put me down. I'll let your grandma go and we can just forget that all of this ever happened.'

'What? So you're free to find another apprentice to abduct?' Demelza shouted. 'I don't think so!'

Grandma Maeve looked up, clearly weak and woozy. 'Demelza, is that you?' she said. 'Oh, my darlin' girl . . .'

'Yes, it's me, Grandma! Just stay where you are, OK? Help will be here for you soon!'

And with the confidence of a pilot, Demelza began to guide the robotic hand back through the church and into the cemetery.

Through the night air it flew, Mr Grey dangling from its claws like a prize in a fairground machine. 'Help me! Boris! Gregor!' he croaked, looking around for his henchmen. 'The girl must be stopped at once! Get me down!'

But Boris and Gregor couldn't hear their boss's cries, as at that very moment, the spectre of Harry Le Quin was walloping them over their heads with his jester stick, while a murder of spectral crows pecked at their toes.

As Demelza navigated her flailing cargo back into the crypt she called to Miranda, 'Go and get Grandma Maeve from the church! Quick! I think she's hurt.'

Miranda nodded and was out of the tomb in a flash.

'Demelza, please let me down!' begged Mr Grey from the air. 'Please! I've been a fool, but I can't go to prison. Percival can't be left on his own!'

'It's too late for that now, Father!' shouted Percy. 'Demelza, do what you have to do!'

Demelza nodded and, taking a deep breath, pressed another button on her control pad. The robotic hand began to descend, bringing Mr Grey with it, and as his feet touched the ground, Mr Barnabas swooped in, binding Mr Grey's wrists and ankles with rope.

'NO! Let me go, you ruffian!' Mr Grey growled. 'You

won't get away with this, I can assure you! No one will believe you!'

'Oh, the police are already on their way, Neville,' said Mr Barnabas. 'And I think they'll find more than enough evidence here to convict you of kidnap, trespassing and grave robbing, without us needing to reveal *exactly* what has been going on here tonight.'

Demelza pulled off the robotic hand and let herself fall back against the crypt wall. Her face was burning, her ears ringing, but she'd done it! She'd stopped Mr Grey!

As she sat catching her breath, Shiver came toddling forth. His tail was waggling in what could have been applause, but more likely hunger, and Demelza patted his head. 'Don't worry, boy, we'll be home soon, and you're going to have the biggest, juiciest piece of steak I can find! Just you wait!' On hearing the word *steak*, the little dog lolled out his tongue and bared his teeth, as if smiling.

'Demelza! Oh, Demelza, you clever, clever girl!' Escorted by Miranda, Grandma Maeve came hobbling back into the crypt. 'You did it, you did it!'

Demelza tore towards them and she flung her arms around her grandmother. As she breathed in the comforting smell of her lavender perfume, she instantly felt her body soften. The smell of home.

'Are you all right, Grandma?' she asked, noticing the graze on her grandma's cheek. 'Did he hurt you?'

'Oh, it's just a little scratch,' replied Grandma Maeve with a wink. 'Nothin' compared to what that four-horned leopard did to me when I was trekking through the mountains of Tibet!'

Demelza smiled through her tears. 'Oh, Grandma, I'm so sorry. I've been so foolish! If it weren't for me and my big mouth then none of this would ever have happened.'

'Don't even give it another thought, my darlin',' said Grandma Maeve. 'It was y*our* quick thinking that saved the day. You were ever so brave back then in the church.'

'She's right, Demelza,' reassured Percy. 'It was *you* and your invention that put a stop to it all in the end.'

'Yeah, you're a hero!' said Miranda, putting a hand on Demelza's shoulder. 'I'm definitely going to write a poem about this! "The Ballad of the Robotic Hand".'

Demelza smiled and wiped her face. 'Thanks. But I couldn't have done any of it without you two by my side. How did you know to confide in Mr Barnabas?'

'He found us in the forest after I left you to get help,' said Percy. 'Apparently we aren't very convincing liars after all.'

Mr Barnabas came to join them. 'Yes, that tall tale you

told me about studying nocturnal animals didn't quite ring true,' he said with a wry smile. 'And after you left my sweet shop I had this niggling feeling that perhaps something wasn't quite right. So I followed the three of you at a distance. The path of bonbons that you'd left eventually led me to Miranda and Percy.'

'And you're a Spectre Detector too?' asked Demelza.

Mr Barnabas nodded.

'And not just any old Spectre Detector,' said Grandma Maeve, looking up at the dark-haired man. 'Mr Barnabas is one of our Spectral Sages!'

Demelza felt her eyes widen as thoughts began to come together like the teeth of a zipper: the realistic skulls in his shop window; the familiar chocolates she'd seen at the Dance with Death; his early-morning phone call to Grandma Maeve offering to post her letters; the bowl of sweets on the Quietus's reception desk . . .

It all made sense now!

'So you're one of the heads of the Quietus?' she asked.

Mr Barnabas nodded. 'I'm ever so sorry about what happened when you came to us yesterday looking for help, Demelza. I had no idea.' He leant in and said sotto voce, 'Mr Le Quin's a very efficient receptionist but can be a bit militant when it comes to checking paperwork. He was executed by the court of King Henry VIII, you see – apparently his juggling skills weren't up to much, and he wasn't able to fart on demand. Has been a bit of a jobsworth ever since.'

Demelza let out a snigger, but at the same time couldn't help feeling a little sorry for the poor jester. Imagine being killed for such a thing!

'Come on, let's go home,' she said, turning to Grandma Maeve. 'I don't know about you, but I could really do with a cup of tea. And a peanut butter and cheese sandwich, of course!'

CHAPTER 37
Home at Last

By Sunday morning, things were gradually getting back to normal at Bladderwrack Cottage. In the sitting room, Demelza and Percy were relaxing with Shiver in front of the roaring log fire. For the first time in a while it had been lit, and as it crackled, plumes of smoke unfurled from the grate, filling the room with its sweet, comforting incense. Grandma Maeve had agreed that Percy would stay with them for the time being, before moving to the Quietus when he felt ready.

'Ah, home sweet home!' said Demelza. She was in her dressing gown and thinking cap, tinkering with a screwdriver and circuit board, while simultaneously jotting down some new ideas in her notebook. She'd wasted no time in picking up the latest issue of *Young Inventor Weekly*, alongside a few new additions to her tool kit.

'Demelza, we're meant to be resting,' said Percy, who was reclining happily in mid-air, leisurely flicking through a comic book. 'Why don't you just slow down for a bit?'

'Percy, I've missed out on nearly two weeks of inventing,' she replied curtly. 'That's nearly 20,160 minutes of creating time lost. If I'm ever going to win the Nobel Prize for Physics, I have to keep my brain well oiled.'

Percy rolled his eyes and put down his book. 'Well, how about a game of chess instead? Will that help to *keep your brain well oiled*?'

Demelza looked up, her eyes glinting. 'Sure. But be prepared to be completely annihilated! Again!'

By the time the clock struck midday, Demelza had already won two games of chess and the friends were halfway through their third.

'I still can't believe you never guessed that you were a spectre, Percy,' said Demelza. 'Surely when you woke up after being summoned you felt – I don't know – different?'

'Well, I guess I did feel . . . lighter,' said Percy, staking out the chess board. 'But my dad said it was just down to me losing weight after being so ill. He'd taken all of the mirrors from the house, so I never realized that my face wasn't changing, or that I wasn't growing up. I was told that my skin was so pale because I couldn't go out in the sunshine because of my allergies. Dad had an answer to everything, so in the end I just stopped asking questions, I suppose.'

'But what about being able to float? You really never knew?'

'No! I thought I was just a regular human boy. You'd have to be completely crazy to think that you could actually defy gravity!'

Demelza blushed as she thought back to three years ago, when a test run of her Wondrous All-Weather Wings had resulted in her being rushed to hospital with a broken leg, three cracked ribs and two black eyes. 'Yeah . . . completely crazy,' she muttered.

'It's a pretty amazing perk of being dead, though,' said Percy. 'I feel like a golden eagle!' With that he shot up into the air, banging his head on the ceiling.

'A turkey, more like!' laughed Demelza. She looked intently at the chessboard, trying to work out her next move. 'Any word about your dad?'

'No, nothing yet,' replied Percy, floating back down to his spot. 'The police told Grandma Maeve they'd get in contact.'

'I wonder how long he'll be in prison for?' said Demelza, moving one of her pieces diagonally across the board and taking out another of Percy's. 'Do you think you'll go visit him?'

Percy looked up, his eyes watery. 'To be honest, I don't really want to think about it at the moment. Do you mind if we change the subject?'

Demelza smiled. 'Of course not. And you know you can stay here as long as you like, whatever happens.'

'Thanks.'

'We'd have to make you a bedroom in the shed, though,' added Demelza quickly, worried that she was starting to sound soppy. 'I can't have you cluttering up my inventing space with your comic books and fluffy toys for ever.'

The pair giggled, and Demelza felt a warm surge of happiness rush through her body. The feeling only improved when a few minutes later Grandma walked in carrying a plate of home-made biscuits and a steaming mug of hot chocolate. The doctor had told her to stay in bed for at least a fortnight, but she'd already donned her apron and had spent all morning in the kitchen.

'Here you go, my lovely,' she said, passing a mug to Demelza. 'A nice hot choccy. Thought you could do with somethin' to keep your strength up.' She turned to Percy and handed him a paper bag. 'And this, my darlin' boy, is for you. From Mr Barnabas.'

'Eh, what is it?' he asked, opening the packet. He pulled out a handful of purple triangular-shaped candies decorated with tiny skulls.

'Spectre Sweets!' said Grandma Maeve. 'I know you spectres can't eat proper food, but for the past few years he's been developing these for the young spectres to enjoy. Your system can digest them and they don't taste half bad, apparently!'

'Fascinating!' said Demelza. 'What a great invention!'

'Why don't you try one?' said Grandma Maeve to Percy. 'It's been a while since you've eaten something delicious, by the sound of it. I still can't believe your dad had been feeding you those empty pills for so long!'

Percy popped one of the sweets in his mouth. As he chewed, a huge smile spread across his face, his eyes sparkling. 'Mmmm, that's so yummy! Nearly as good as the real thing. A bit chocolatey . . . a bit nutty . . . with just a hint of strawberry!'

'Well, don't eat too many at once!' said Grandma Maeve, hobbling across the room. 'Now, lunch won't be ready for a couple of hours, so carry on relaxing until then. I've invited a few guests, so it's gonna be a real celebration!'

And a real celebration it was.

Percy and Demelza ran into the kitchen at two o'clock to find a table fit for a banquet. At its centre, a huge slab of roast beef sat on a platter, surrounded by a mountain of crisp roast potatoes and balls of stuffing. Little ceramic jugs were filled with gravy, bowls were heavy with horseradish and mustard, and Grandma Maeve had laid out her best silver cutlery. Lord Balthazar was waiting proudly atop the refrigerator, wearing a paper party hat.

'Someone's ready to celebrate,' said Demelza, looking up at the skull.

Lord Balthazar harrumphed. 'Well, it's a celebration after all. Even the upper echelons of the English gentry are allowed to let their hair down once in a while, are they not?'

'Of course,' said Demelza, before muttering under her breathe, 'if you *had* any hair.'

'What was that?' said the skull.

'Nothing, Lord Balthazar! You look . . . erm . . . very distinguished!'

Before long, the guests had arrived and everyone was nestled around the long oak table, filling their plates and talking loudly. Everyone sat on mismatched chairs, with even a couple of upturned garden crates doubling up as places to perch. Grandma Maeve had invited Miranda, as well as Mr Barnabas and his wife, Zelda.

'I think it's time for a toast!' Grandma Maeve said halfway through the meal. She clapped her hands together and stood at the head of the table holding a glass of ginger wine, her cheeks already ruddy from one too many.

Mr Barnabas reached into his bag. 'In which case, I think the children deserve a glass of my home-made dandelion and burdock,' he said. He pulled out a tall bottle filled with a fizzy, amethyst-coloured liquid and poured glasses for Demelza and Miranda. 'I haven't quite figured out how to make the recipe spectre-friendly yet, I'm afraid, Percy, but I promise I'll have it done for next time.'

'To my very wonderful granddaughter and her very brave friends,' said Grandma Maeve, 'without whom, I might not be here today. They've shown fearlessness, loyalty and a whole lot of courage. I think you'll all agree that they're three very special children indeed. To Demelza, Percy and Miranda!'

'Demelza, Percy and Miranda!' chorused everyone, and they clinked their glasses to the centre of the table, sloshing their drinks with careless abandon.

The doorbell rang.

'Eh? Who could that be?' said Grandma Maeve, getting up from her seat. 'I wasn't expectin' no more guests.'

'Don't worry, I'll get it, Grandma!' said Demelza,

stuffing a huge roast potato in her mouth before pushing back her chair. 'I think I know who it might be.'

She flitted out of the kitchen and was back within a minute, a mischievous grin painted across her face. 'Now, don't be angry with me, Grandma,' she said. 'But I didn't think it would be much of a celebration without one of the most important people of all.'

She stepped aside to reveal a rather nervous-looking Ms Cardinal. She was wearing her usual floor-length skirt and crinoline blouse, but instead of her hair being tied up in a bun, it fell to her waist in long grey waves.

As she shuffled into the kitchen, the two sisters studied each other intently, their arms crossed over their chests, their shoulders back. A deafening silence filled the room, and both Percy and Miranda shot Demelza a worried look.

'Margaret,' said Grandma Maeve, without a hint of a smile.

'Maeve,' replied Ms Cardinal, with the same grave glare.

'It seems my little sister has turned into an old woman. Is that grey hair I see, Margaret?'

Ms Cardinal huffed. 'Ha! You're not looking too youthful yourself, Maeve. At least I have all of my own teeth!'

Everyone in the room gulped and Demelza shuffled from foot to foot. Maybe this wasn't the right moment for a big family reunion after all.

But just as Demelza was about to suggest that Ms Cardinal go through to the lounge, Grandma Maeve threw her cane to one side. She hobbled across the room with her arms outstretched, and a huge smile broke across her face. 'Oh, Maggie, you silly old bat!' she gushed. 'I've missed you so much! Come on, give your big sis a squidge. I can't believe it's been so long.'

'Oh, Maeve!' gushed Ms Cardinal, tears beginning to run down her cheeks. 'All these years wasted, and just because of my stupid, stupid prank. I'm so, so sorry.'

'Hush, hush, it's all right.' Grandma Maeve stepped back and put a finger to her sister's lips. 'We're both to blame anyway. I shouldn't have been such a stubborn old mule when you tried to make peace. But it's all in the past. Time for us to move on.'

'Indeed it is,' said Ms Cardinal, with a sniff. 'And it's all thanks to one person, of course. If it wasn't for your extremely wild and unruly granddaughter then we wouldn't be here together now. Thank you, Demelza. You are a truly remarkable girl.' She grabbed her great-niece's cheeks and planted a big, wet kiss in the middle of her forehead.

'*YUUUCK!*' said Demelza, pulling away and wiping her facc. 'It's great that you're both here together again, but enough of the slushy stuff! Isn't it time for some pudding, Grandma?'

Grandma Maeve chuckled. 'Well, I know your Aunty Margaret probably don't approve of sugary things, but I'm sure she won't mind just this once.'

'Oh no, she does approve!' Miranda cut in. 'She likes doughnuts and pastries and chocolate eclairs. Demelza says she has a huge secret stash of them hidden in the kitchen at Stricton and—'

'Thank you, Miss Choudhury,' said a red-cheeked Ms Cardinal. 'That's quite enough.' She threw Miranda her trademark iron glare and, just as if they were back in the classroom, she was silenced immediately.

'Ha! Well, I never,' said Grandma Maeve. 'Goody-two-shoes Margaret has her own secret stash of sweets. Strawberry mousse it is, then!'

The party atmosphere continued late into the evening. After lunch, everyone retired into the sitting room, where constellations of candles illuminated every corner. Harry Le Quin and the other spectres that'd helped at Eternal Sorrow Cemetery had been invited to join the celebrations, and as Mr Barnabas struck up a jaunty tune on his banjolele, humans and spectres alike danced.

Percy was in his element, repeating the story of how

they'd escaped Crookescroft Castle, with the dangers and perils getting bigger and bigger with each retelling. Miranda sat listening to the historical spectres recounting their tales of yesteryear, and noting down any romantic happenings that could inspire a new sonnet or haiku.

And on the sofa, cocooned between Grandma Maeve and Ms Cardinal (who'd newly been named Aunty M), Demelza cuddled up with her animals, enjoying the warmth of the fire and the deliciousness of finally being home.

'Wow! That was a *great* day, Mrs Catchpole,' said Percy, as he and Demelza helped Grandma Maeve dry the dishes later that night. Everyone had finally left, and Bladderwrack Cottage was a bomb site of party poppers, glasses and copious empty bottles of ginger wine. 'Thank you so much.'

Grandma Maeve swung her tea towel over her shoulder and smiled. 'Aw, it was an absolute pleasure, young man. You deserved it. Now why don't you head on up to bed, hmm? I don't want to sound like your father, but I think you could do with a few early nights. You too, Demelza.'

'But Grandma,' she whined, 'I wanted to finish dismantling that clock mechanism I started earlier. Just half an hour longer . . .'

Grandma Maeve shook her head. 'Not a chance. Your

Spectre Detector apprenticeship starts again first thing in the mornin', and I've already got a summoning booked in for you to do tomorrow night.'

'So soon?' drawled Demelza . 'Don't I at least get a few more days off? Compassionate leave or something?'

'Days off?' said Grandma Maeve. 'Death don't stop just because you fancy a few days lazin' around in bed, my darlin'. And the mourners don't stop mournin'.'

Demelza nodded. Grandma was right. If she was going to become the world's first Spectre-Detecting Inventor, then she had to put in the work.

The children made their way up the rickety stairs. When she was nearly at the top, Demelza poked her head through the bannister. 'Love you more than circuit boards!' she shouted down to Grandma Maeve with a smile.

'Love you more than teapots,' came the reply. 'More than all the teapots in the world!'

Up in the attic, Percy fell sound asleep in minutes, snoozing gently in his makeshift bed with his bunny slippers by his side.

Even though she was tired too, Demelza pulled her patchwork quilt over her shoulders and sat down at her desk. She looked up to the shelves and couldn't help but grin. Her soldering iron now shared a space with her ghoul-

322

box, and her microscope sat next to her crucible.

And stacked atop her notebook marked *Demelza Clock: Inventor* was a new notebook embossed with a skull bearing the words, *Demelza Clock: Spectre Detector*.

ACKNOWLEDGEMENTS

I'd like to thank the following people for helping me lure Demelza out of her attic room and on to the page . . .

To everyone at Chicken House – you were always my dream publishers, and I'm so honoured that you took a chance on me and my manuscript. I had no idea how much of a team effort publishing a book would actually be, and I'm humbled by the huge amount of time and work you've all put into making this story the best it can be. A huge salute also to my cover illustrator Alex T. Smith for rendering Demelza so beautifully – ginger plaits, deerstalker, freckles and all!

Massive gratitude to my agent Kate Shaw for guiding this debut author through her first years in the industry with passion, patience and a cracking sense of humour. I'm so glad to have you by my side.

I'd also like to say thanks to Chloe Seager for championing Demelza from the get-go. Your wonderful feedback early on really gave me the confidence to put my writing out into the world.

To everyone at the Golden Egg Academy, especially my wonderful mentor and friend Charlotte Maslen. Your wholehearted belief in my writing means so much, and I wouldn't be in print without your guidance, ideas and chats. Also, to my fellow Foundation Course writers for allowing me into your magnificent fictional universes.

I'm so lucky to have such a supportive family. Mum, thanks for giving me a childhood full of stories, art and roast dinners, and an adulthood full of love and support. Dad and Mary – I couldn't ask for better cheerleaders. Your enthusiasm for this book has been unyielding and I'm forever grateful for your warmth and encouragement (the supply of Picon and French cheeses never goes amiss either!). And of course, my dear siblings: Jack, Poppy, Lottie and Jude.

Manda and Mr Glen – thank you for always having an open door, a spare bed and Tupperware full of cakes. You are very, very special people.

To all my family, friends and colleagues in Cardiff, West Wales, London, Brighton and beyond – I tip my (thinking) hat to each and every one of you. Thanks for making my world a very lovely place to be.

Most of this book was written in various libraries across London, so a big shout-out to all of the brilliant librarians and staff members (especially the inimitable Magnolia at Stroud Green and Harringay Library) who make these places such magical and much-needed environments.

I've been lucky enough to teach and hang out with so many wonderful children over the years, but a special mention must be given to: Úna Kieran-O'Brien, Edward Bowyer, Autumn Ackroyd, Iris Burton, Felicity and Violet Nicholls, Alice Marzocchi, Juno Wilson, Hazel Eston, Isla Fransman-Powell, Isabel Comer, Samuel Sharpe, Finn and Greta Lawrence, Hazel and Gwilym Kaye, and Rocco Ercolanoni. There's no doubt that fragments of your inventive (and sometimes mischievous) personalities found their way into Demelza, Percy and Miranda, and made their characters all the richer.

Finally, *grazie mille* to my darling Fred for always being by my side. I love you, and I owe you a very big pizza.

MIDNIGHT HOUR by BENJAMIN READ & LAURA TRINDER

Emily's parents have vanished into the secret world of the Midnight Hour – a Victorian London frozen in time – home to magic and monsters. Emily must find them in the city of the Night Folk, armed only with a packed lunch, a stowaway hedgehog and her infamously big mouth. With bloodthirsty creatures on her tail, Emily has to discover the truth to rescue her parents. What family secret connects her to the Midnight Hour? And can she save both worlds before she runs out of sandwiches?

> *Anarchic humour, rich imagination and poetic writing, interspersed with elegant line drawings, add up to pure delight — with a stowaway hedgehog as a bonus.*
>
> GUARDIAN

Paperback, ISBN 978-1-911490-90-6, £6.99 • ebook, ISBN 978-1-911490-91-3, £6.99